CRUEL SUMMER

THE JAKE SAWYER SERIES (BOOK 7)

ANDREW LOWE

GET A FREE JAKE SAWYER NOVELLA

Sign up for the no-spam newsletter and get a FREE copy of the Sawyer prequel novella **THE LONG DARK**.

Check the details at the end of this book.

Email: andrew@andrewlowewriter.com
Web: andrewlowewriter.com
Twitter: @andylowe99

First published in 2022 by Redpoint Books
This edition April 2024
Cover photographs © Shutterstock
Cover by So-So Design

ISBN: 978-1-9997290-7-3

For Tom and Josh

It is what one takes into solitude that grows there, the beast within included.

— NIETZSCHE

PROLOGUE

'Mum! Dora's hair is *green*.'

Ruth Carter caught her daughter's gaze in her dressing table mirror. 'It is not green, darling. It's electric blue.'

Dora Carter hurried past the door to the master bedroom. Her sister Shannon turned and lunged for her, but Dora was gone; too quick.

Shannon chased her, anyway. Up the final flight of stairs to the fourth floor, framing Dora in her phone screen: long-limbed, coltish, ponytail swinging.

She turned and glared at Shannon, pushed a spread palm towards the phone. 'If this gets posted, we are talking instant execution, okay? No arrest, no trial.'

In the bedroom, Ruth Carter laughed. 'No mercy?'

'Yes,' said Dora. 'No fucking mercy.'

'Dora,' Warren Carter called from his office, opposite the bedroom. 'Is that a good example?'

Dora faced Shannon at the top of the stairs, dipping

1

and weaving her head away from the phone. 'She knows all the swear words, anyway. She swears more than I do.'

'Bullshit!'

Dora gaped, in mock shock. 'See?' She swatted at the phone, almost knocking it from Shannon's hand, then scrambled away. Shannon followed, re-aiming the phone; capturing her sister's escape into their bathroom at the top of the stairs.

Dora tried to slam the door behind her, but Shannon made it in time, jamming her foot into the gap and trying to shoulder her way in.

'*Girls!*' Warren from downstairs again.

Dora called out from the gap. 'Dad. Tell her.'

Ruth burst out of the bedroom and stood at the bottom of the stairs. 'For goodness' sake. We have literally just walked in the door. Can we have five minutes without a fight? *Shannon*. Leave your sister in peace.'

Dora held the door firm and poked her face into the gap, close to Shannon's. 'Let go now, or I'll tell Mum and Dad about your little stash.'

Shannon lowered the phone. 'What stash?'

Dora smiled, sweet and evil. 'Starbars. Double Deckers. Aeros.' She whispered. '*Shoebox in your wardrobe.*'

'You look like someone sneezed in your hair.'

Ruth appeared behind Shannon and yanked away her phone. '*Enough.* Shannon, homework. Dora, homework, and then you can help me with dinner.'

Shannon sneered at Dora, who slammed and locked the door.

Tap, tap.

Warren Carter sat back from his Mac screen and sighed. The clock in the corner ticked forward a minute as he flicked his eyes up to check.

11:32pm.

Tap, tap. This time, the door eased open.

'Sorry, sorry. I know I said eleven. I'm still unravelling this. Twenty more minutes.'

'Dad...'

Warren swivelled his Herman Miller chair to face the door. 'What is it?' He smoothed out his thinning blond hair and reached out to Shannon, barefoot in the doorway in purple pyjamas, cradling a plush polar bear. 'Angel. I'm sorry. I thought you were Mum.' He smiled. 'Look at you. Bit different from the hellcat terrorising her sister a few hours ago.'

Shannon closed the door behind her. She padded over and slumped into Warren's arms. 'There are funny noises, Dad.'

'Uhuh. From where?'

'Upstairs. I was thirsty and when I got a drink, there were these noises.'

Warren pulled her close. Citrus face cream, avocado and coconut shampoo. He flicked her hair out of her face and over her shoulders.

'It wasn't a dream, Dad.'

'I never said it was, sweetheart. What kind of noises? Was it Dora?'

She shrugged. 'Breathing. Loud breathing.'

'Panting? Like a dog?'

Shannon raised her eyes. 'Yes. No. It was slower. I don't know. It was really weird.'

Warren kissed his daughter's forehead. 'Maybe your sister was watching something on her tablet.' He stood up, escorted her to the door. 'Or sometimes, when we've been sleepy, the dreams take a while to fade away. We imagine things.'

She sighed, dropped her shoulders. Theatrical. 'Mr Beatty says I've got a good imagination.'

He opened the door. 'Is Mr Beatty your English teacher?'

'Drama.'

'Well, he's right. Dora is good with numbers. So maybe you're good with... creative thoughts.' Warren ushered Shannon outside, stroking her hair. 'Don't worry, angel. Everything's fine. I have to finish some work now. Go back to bed and give that brilliant brain a recharge. I'll be doing the same soon.'

———

Warren sent the computer to sleep and clicked off his desk lamp.

Just gone midnight. He sat in the dark and mapped out the day ahead.

Six hours horizontal. Into the Maserati by half-six. Office at seven. Early finish. Gym. Drink, ideally singular, with Peter Craig at five.

4

Friday. He would have his PA order fresh Italian from the new place by Hammersmith Tube. Gnocchi with truffle and parmesan sauce. Ravioli for the girls. A tub of tiramisu. Ruth would make her Italian salad. Red onions, cherry tomatoes. The ideal primer for their fortnight in Umbria.

He crept out of his office, easing the door shut behind him, and walked into the master bedroom: vast and immaculate, with a partitioned walk-in wardrobe and an en-suite wet-room installed at cost by contractors from a recent hotel rebuild.

Moisturiser, teeth, Aesop mouthwash.

Warren set his phone down on the corner armchair, slid off his belt and hopped out of his trousers, aided only by the screen light.

The weighty belt buckle clunked against the wooden floor; he winced and turned to check on Ruth.

No movement.

Warren squinted into the gloom, confused. Ruth always slept on the left side, but the blankets were gathered on the right.

He held up the phone to cast more light on the bed.

Ruth wasn't in it.

The office was close to the bedroom; he would have heard her if she'd gone upstairs to check on the girls, or downstairs to get a drink.

Warren swung the phone over to the bathroom door.

Ajar. No light inside.

He startled, as something small and sharp dug into his neck.

He raised his fingers to the pain, brushed against softness. Fluffy, like a dandelion seed head.

An insect? Had he been stung?

He swiped at his neck, dislodging something. Bee? Wasp?

Movement, in the shadows on the far side of the room.

'Ruth?'

No whisper. Alarm in his voice; alien and urgent in the almost-dark.

Warren moved forward but stumbled as his knee gave way. He crouched at the foot of the bed, holding his phone high to expand the light.

Ruth's yellow blanket cover, crumpled in the corner.

Her bare foot.

Jagged panic now, and an abysmal fatigue.

He reached down, tried to grip the blanket cover, missed.

His hand flopped onto skin. Bone.

Ruth's ankle. Warm.

A ripple of nausea.

The wooden floor, like rubber.

Melting.

He slapped a palm onto the bedpost, hauled himself upright.

And the movement in the shadows came for him.

A muscular hand, gripping his chin, covering his mouth, forcing him backwards onto the chair.

Warren willed himself to resist, but could not transfer the struggle from mind to limb. He tried to force something out of his lungs: a roar of outrage. Only whimpers came, appalling in their authenticity. The sound of a child's fear from the mouth of an adult.

He fought his assailant with ragdoll arms, matchstick legs. The room was a kaleidoscope in monochrome, churning and swelling, blackening.

A glitch of time, and the world had tilted.

His cheek squashed against the cold floor, thick tape tight around his mouth.

The shadow leaving the room.

Warren squinting and blinking, but no focus.

Ears ringing. Smothering agony, seeping down from his head, through his arms and legs. Shutting him down.

Tears now, staining his vision.

The shadow, passing out onto the landing, climbing the stairs.

PART ONE

SALVA MEA

1

An orange-and-black Mini Convertible slid into a space opposite the security booth. The guard looked up from his phone, sighed and gunned the intercom.

'Those are reserved for overnight. Plenty of parking on Level Two.'

The car engine fell silent and the lights dimmed.

The driver climbed out and walked along the verge, approaching the booth. The guard set down his phone and Cookies & Cream protein bar, and gave the situation his full attention. The guy was tall, slim but muscled up top. Light jacket, trainers. Didn't look like he was carrying anything. Flashes of neck-length black hair as he passed through the grimy puddles shimmering beneath the feeble strip lights.

Head high. Steady gait. A slight sway, bordering on a swagger.

The guard brushed aside a graphic novel, revealing his panic button.

The driver stopped at the booth window.

'Like I say, bro. Only twenty-four hours in those spots. How long y'gonna be here?'

The driver raised his head, surveyed the inside of the booth with emerald-green eyes. 'How did you stop?'

Not a Londoner. Flatter northern vowels. The voice rang deep and rich, even through the oval gap at the base of the window.

The guard frowned. 'Stop what?'

'*The Killing Joke*. I had to read it in one burst. I might be wrong, but by the way it's lying there open, face down, I'd say you haven't finished it yet.'

'No shit, Sherlock.'

The man shook his head. 'Not quite. I am a lawman, though.'

The guard smiled and sat back in his cheap swivel chair; it gave an unhealthy squeal. 'A *lawman*? So, what, you're Judge Dredd?'

The man reached into his inside pocket with his left hand, raised his right in submission. 'It's okay. I left my lawgiver at home.' He took out a police warrant card and held it up to the glass.

The guard wheeled himself closer and studied it. '*Sawyer*. So, what do I call you? DI or gaffer or boss?'

'Jake, Detective, *bro*, your highness. It's all good. So, what are you hoping to do with your psychology degree?'

'How do you know I'm doing a psychology degree?'

Sawyer nodded to the book poking out of a backpack behind the guard's chair. 'I can't imagine anyone would read *Foundations of Physiological Psychology* for pleasure.'

'Too right.'

'Pain, maybe.'

'Studying to be a counsellor. Therapist, yeah?'

'OU?'

'Yeah.'

'You should study, then. Perfect environment. No distractions. Tedious job.'

The guard chewed his tongue, hissed. 'You my dad now?'

'You should study, instead of playing *Bullet Symphony*.'

The guard looked down at his phone, turned over but playing low-level music. Portentous strings, operatic. 'That game is *sick*. It's like crack.'

'Cheaper, though. What's your highest on Level One?'

'Two hundred thousand something.'

Sawyer whistled. 'That's good going. I got into the global top one hundred. Two hundred and thirty thousand. I'd say the max is somewhere around two hundred and seventy. But you'd have to be a fucking fighter pilot or something. PS4 version is definitive.'

The guard took a breath. 'Yeah, so—'

'Hopefully not long. Few weeks. I should be on your system for temporary residents. Staying upstairs. Waterfront House, is it?'

The guard checked his screen. 'Yeah.'

'Nice place?' Sawyer checked his phone.

'Never been in. Flats, innit. You on a case, then, lawman?'

Sawyer smoothed out his hair. 'No. Off duty. I thought I'd take some downtime in Putney. Nightlife. Bit of rowing.'

Tongue chew again, and the hiss. 'Getting a bit of sarcasm there.'

'You're taking the right course. Sharp judgement, Milan.'

The guard did a comedy double take. 'The fuck you know my name?'

'Lucky guess.'

Milan scowled.

Sawyer held his phone screen up to the glass. 'Bluetooth. Local devices. *Milan's Galaxy*. Maybe tweak those privacy settings. And, yeah. On a case.'

'Any details? Or is that... what do you call it? Need to know basis?'

Sawyer pocketed his phone. 'More like you don't want to know.'

———

He wheeled his case out of the lift and trundled it along a narrow corridor with an ungenerous carpet, patterned with geometric tiling in clashing colours. As the connecting door closed behind him, an overhead light clicked on, too bright. He winced at the off-white panelled walls, the insipid abstracts. His nose wrinkled at the fug: perfumed wood polish, stewing steak, foot odour. Muffled music pulsed from one apartment; a television chattered in another.

His door sat at the far end, beside an oblong window that looked out on the alley between Waterfront House and the mottled brickwork of an office block, windows open to the oppressive evening.

Sawyer parked the case by the door and pushed his face close to the window, cupping his hands around his eyes. One or two desk lights on. Aircon vents embedded in the window panels of the upper floors. A faulty bulb fluttering behind the drawn blind of the office directly opposite. He craned his neck and squinted along the alley to the wharf, and the twinkling Thames.

The apartment was showhouse chic: second-least expensive wooden flooring; circular glass dining table directly beneath a functional, wall-mounted TV; IKEA-type coffee table on a Lidl-type rug. Something woody and vanilla in the air; probably the bowl of potpourri placed dead centre on the glass table.

He took the tour: box-room bath and sink; corner kitchen with beige fittings to complement the fawn sitting room walls; bedroom with low bed and condemned-cell mattress; small, high window above a forlorn desk with white plastic fan, box of tissues, more damned potpourri.

Sawyer prised open the sitting room window to little effect, and put the kettle on. A shoebox-sized package wrapped in glossy orange paper sat on the unit by the microwave. Inside, he found a tightly packed selection of mini brownies courtesy of artisanal bakery Cutter & Squidge: salted caramel, Nutella, peanut butter fudge.

The card bore the C&S logo with a printed message, off centre.

Maggie would know the quotation would irritate him; they had previously bickered about its provenance. But that was the point; she would also know he would think that. And the connection buoyed him, summoned her into the room.

Sawyer picked up a brownie and wheeled his case into the bedroom. He threw it open on the bed and removed a spherical white smart speaker with a flat base, and a notebook with a dark orange cover and handwritten label.

Jessica Mary Sawyer
My life and thoughts

He slipped the notebook into the bedside table drawer and pulled out a coin from his pocket, flipping it over the tops of his fingers. It was around an inch in diameter. One side bore an illustration of a skull in the centre, flanked by an hourglass and tulip. The image hovered between the words *MEMENTO* and *MORI*. On the other side, six words in block capitals were stacked in groups of two.

YOU COULD LEAVE LIFE RIGHT NOW

He set his father's coin down in the drawer beside his mother's journal and lowered his head, studying the knot patterns in the wood flooring. The overhead light caught a small albino patch at the crown of his skull.

Sawyer closed the drawer and set up the speaker on the bedside table, eager to imprint something of himself onto this generic limbo.

He scrolled through his music app and cued up 'Strange Weather' by Anna Calvi and David Byrne. Brooding, bleak, but open-hearted.

His screen blacked out, replaced with an incoming call.

He gulped in a breath and tapped the *ACCEPT* button.

The caller spoke first. 'Who's been a busy boy, then?'

Sawyer sat down on the bed. 'Sir.'

'Many things, eh, Detective Sawyer? But never boring.'

'I'm working on it, sir.'

DCI Colin Hatfield gave a doubtful laugh. 'Oh, you're in the foothills, son. The worst is yet to come.

Your body starts falling apart once you get north of sixty.'

'And how's yours at the moment, sir?'

'You're going to regret asking that.'

Sawyer picked a corner off the brownie. 'Bullet points?'

'Okay. I've got some kind of stomach bacteria that causes chronic reflux. Hitting the antibiotics for that at the moment. So, no booze. The pills make me feel wretched, the lack of alcohol makes me snappy. Loads of little domestics over nothing. My missus is considering a Travelodge until I'm back on the Guinness.'

'Lot of detail for a bullet point.'

Hatfield scoffed. 'Not lost your cheek, have you? The rest is standard. Tinnitus is clanging away like Big bloody Ben, and I'm going gluten-free for the night sweats.'

Sawyer popped the brownie chunk in his mouth. 'I'm sure the physical struggle hasn't blunted your deductive edge, sir.'

'Blowing smoke up arses might work in the sticks, Sawyer, but it butters no parsnips in the big city. I trust the accommodation is to your satisfaction?'

'I can cope. I assume The Savoy was full?'

A belly laugh, from Hatfield's considerable belly. 'C'mon, Sawyer. I read the piece in *The Derbyshire Times*. You lived in some tumbledown cottage in the bloody Lake District for six months. I think you can handle the hard water in South London. You have the option to stay for three months. An agency cleaner will clear up the pizza boxes on Saturday mornings at ten.'

Sawyer set the phone on speaker and walked back into the kitchen. 'Sub-letting? Parties? Guests?'

'No, and no. But it's your lookout who you invite into your bed. Just make sure the pillow talk doesn't touch on the case.'

Sawyer checked the fridge. Milk, butter, eggs, miniature pot of jam.

Silence from Hatfield.

'Sir? You still there?'

'Yes, Detective. I'm about to get gushy. Takes me time to get in character. Listen, Sawyer. You're not here to make up the numbers. I've had half an eye on your... activities since you left us. You've achieved almost as much as I expected you to, son. But as far as I know, you're still human.'

'I'm good. There's wear and tear, but I'm fully functioning.'

'If I know you, Sawyer, and I do, you're just as interested in why I wanted you here as you are in the case itself.'

Another beat of silence. Hatfield had probably forgotten he'd taught this trick to Sawyer. Leave space, make it uncomfortable. How the other guy fills silence is often more illuminating than his answer to a direct question.

Sawyer left him hanging, busying himself with teabags and sugar.

'I was sorry to hear about your father,' said Hatfield, dampening his tone.

'Thanks. You do have quite a catchment area of

talent here, sir. Surely you're not going to pull out the speech about how you need the best man for the job.'

Hatfield stifled a sigh. 'Actually, you're not far off. I know it's been colourful for you up there, but this is about me, not DSI Keating. I asked, Sawyer. I didn't get. You're not a problem child referral.'

Sawyer poured the water, took another chunk of brownie. 'Why, then?'

More silence. Hatfield cleared his throat. 'I've been working in major crime for thirty years. I've seen all kinds of bad. Ugly bad, tragic bad, gory bad, sickening bad. But I have seen nothing at this level, with this degree of—'

'Cruelty?' said Sawyer.

'Yes.'

'But isn't that a projection? First week I joined the Met, you said, "You solve cases with your head, not your heart".'

'This is why I'm asking after the wear and tear, son. I really do need you specifically, but fully you. Present. Correct.'

Sawyer squeezed the bag against the mug, clinking the spoon.

'Are you making tea?' said Hatfield.

'Multitasking. See? I'm on it. I can knock up a brew while discussing a family annihilator.'

'Two families.'

'Since when?'

'Looks like a couple of days ago.'

Sawyer held up the teabag, let it drip into the mug. 'Same method and signature?'

'Mirrored. No details released from the first family, so no chance of a copycat.'

'Scene open?'

'Indeed.'

'Are we still meeting tomorrow morning?'

'No. We're meeting now. At Putney MIT. Get your arse down here. Hold the refreshments. And welcome to London.'

2

DC Ross Moran scowled at the scruffy rooster strutting along the edge of the brook. The bird pecked at the water edge, ruffled its feathers, hurried away from a chasing child.

'Is this your local?'

Moran turned, blinked out of his reverie. 'No. Used to come as a kid. My dad hosted antique fairs here.'

DCI Robin Farrell placed a hand on the wooden picnic bench and lifted himself onto the seat opposite Moran, straddling it for a moment before settling in with his half-pint. 'Did it give you the bug? For stale old furniture? Grandfather clocks? Vintage pisspots?'

Moran hitched up his wire-frame glasses. 'Like fuck. Some of it went in, I suppose. Wouldn't mind flushing it out again.' He sipped from a glass of cloudy ale, already halfway depleted. The pub's kitchen door opened, sending a flare of light across the beer garden tables perched above the brook. Moran turned away, wincing, his scrawny features rendered skeletal by the contrast.

'If I had to guess,' said Farrell, taking off his suit jacket, 'I'd say you're a man who doesn't get on with his father. Not really the follow-in-footsteps type, eh?'

Moran took another drink, buying time for a response. He wiped his mouth. 'So what's your status? Do I have to call you sir?'

Farrell tidied his hair, suspiciously thick and dark. 'If it makes you feel better, yes. But I won't take it personally if you don't. I'm on a... leave of absence. Out of the way, pending the IOPC farce. Keating and the GMP Chief Constable felt it was too embarrassing for me to serve an official suspension over the Terry Barker business. He was hardly an upstanding character. He won't be missed.'

'But you would be.'

Farrell nodded, squeezed out a thin smile.

'Will anything stick?' said Moran.

Farrell shuffled in his seat, looked around. 'What's this place called?'

'The Little Mill.'

'And where are we?'

'Rowarth. Obscure village. Not really on the tourist map. And I thought you'd appreciate the closeness to Manchester.'

'Proximity.'

Moran took out a slim black folder. 'Whatever. See the wooded valley at the back of the brook? They call it Little Switzerland.' He smirked. 'Isn't that quaint?'

Farrell craned his neck and peered through the dusk, surveying their backdrop with studied indifference. 'I suppose. If you're an *American*, and you like this sort of thing. And no, it won't stick. I had nothing to do with the Barker killing, and they know that. I might get a stiff letter over my conduct with the Sawyer situation. But, again, at the time there was an urgency to find him. I just cut a few corners. I doubt there will be any appetite for further action. Not enough benefit, too much potential legal pushback.'

Moran opened the folder. 'They're not going to throw a senior detective under the bus for something so trivial.'

Farrell slurped his lager, keeping his eyes on Moran. 'Okay. Put me out of my misery. What exactly are we doing, skulking around this rural idyll?'

Moran sat forward; Farrell stayed back, but obliged with a wry glance over his shoulder.

The beer garden was busy, but their table was comfortably out of earshot of the nearest drinkers. Even so, Moran kept his voice low.

'Late last year, when Sawyer was serving his suspension for the Bowman death in custody, he did some work for a guy called Lewis Vaughn, the boyfriend of a student, Virginia Mendez, who had been missing for a couple of weeks. Mendez was found and spent some time recovering in Cavendish Hospital. I ran into Sawyer and Vaughn there. A few days later, we got a tip-off that led us to an abandoned abattoir near Ashbourne. An ex-worker, Scott Walton, had been given keyholder status for the buildings, as demolition wasn't workable. According to Mendez, Walton kidnapped her when she came snooping for a missing teenager, Darren Coleman, as part of a podcast she was producing. Walton eventually let her go.'

Farrell took a deep glug of lager. 'Why?'

'We're not sure. We excavated the grounds and surrounding woodland, and discovered the bodies of the boy and a missing professor, Milton Pope.'

'Who took the tip-off?'

'One of the Buxton MIT crew. DS Matt Walker.'

Farrell nodded, looked up at the blackening sky. 'Sawyer's little bitch.'

'The very same. So, the search teams didn't find Walton, but they did find a filleting knife in one of the outbuildings, with his DNA all over it. And there's another profile, not in the database. Whatever happened there, it had been cleaned up, but they forgot the knife. Wedged into a gap in the lower wall.'

'A struggle.'

'I'd say so.'

Farrell leaned forward, too close to Moran in the centre of the table.

Moran sat back. 'So I was thinking, maybe Sawyer was the tip-off source and Walker followed up. Was Sawyer present during this struggle? Does he know the whereabouts of Walton?'

'And who does the other DNA profile belong to?'

Moran smiled. 'I looked into surrounding CCTV to see if there was any sign of Walton leaving the scene himself. No luck.' He took a few sheets from the folder. 'But I did pick up a car on the main road that connects to the approach track leading up to the woods near the abattoir.'

Farrell browsed the sheets: enlarged, grainy freeze-frames, time-stamped. His eyes lifted to Moran, who was grinning. 'This is Sawyer's Mini.'

'It is.'

'And these images are from the night your team discovered the bodies, and the knife?'

'Oh, yes. A few hours before the tip-off.' Moran laid out two of the sheets. 'There's no CCTV on the approach track, but from the timestamps you can see that the Mini isn't picked up further down the main road here, and here. So it must have turned off towards the abattoir.'

Farrell took in a long breath, held it, exhaled. 'So, from the DNA on the knife, Scott Walton was at the abattoir that evening, then Sawyer arrived, and Walton mysteriously disappeared.'

Moran's grin grew broader. He slid another sheet out of the folder. 'And Sawyer's car pops up again on the CCTV much later, about half an hour before the tip-off came in.' He held up a finger. 'Now, here's the really good bit. I looked into the background paperwork. The professor, Milton Pope, went missing back in 2011, and the case was investigated by a DI Martin Pittman. Died of cancer a couple of years ago. According to Pittman's old report, he visited the abattoir outbuildings in April

2011, but found nothing. Although he did have a companion that day.'

'Sawyer.'

'At the time, he was a humble DC.'

Farrell finished his drink, shook his head. 'Has Sawyer ever been humble?'

Moran jabbed his finger onto the sheets. 'Sawyer knew the location. He'd been there before. It seems to me—'

'He might have encountered Walton, took his knife off him using gloves, killed him, disposed of the body, rang in the tip-off. Any CCTV of Sawyer's car later on?'

Moran dropped his head. 'A camera at the crossroads near his house shows the Mini arriving shortly after his car popped up on the main road that second time.'

Farrell dug his little finger into a nostril, rotated it. 'Not long enough to dispose of Walton, if he was with him.'

Moran leaned forward again. 'No. But there's another car that appears on the main road soon after the first Mini sighting. A dark-coloured Fiesta. And it also turns up just before Sawyer's second appearance, but then goes off the radar. Can't get a reg reading on the Fiesta. But, sir. It's the middle of the night. There are no other cars around. I think Sawyer met the Fiesta driver at the abattoir. If we can track its movements in more detail, it might lead us to Walton's body.'

Farrell pinched his nose, tugging it from side to side. 'And that might put Sawyer at the scene of a murder.'

3

'Ladies and gentlemen.' Hatfield strode out to the front of the vast open-plan office. He held up a hand, and the detectives' chatter fell away.

Sawyer had found a seat close to the case whiteboard, mounted to the wall behind Hatfield. A floor-to-ceiling corner window looked out on the evening traffic juddering across Putney Bridge, four storeys below. Close to nine now, but no sign of winding down; the concept of London rush hour was distant history. Sawyer had lived it all before, but it would take time to recalibrate, to tune himself back into the perpetual motion.

Hatfield draped his royal-blue suit jacket over a chair and rolled up his shirt sleeves. He was short and spherical, with a combed forward widow's peak, which only drew attention to the dwindling fluff across the rest of his head. Half-frame glasses, trousers slightly too long, with a sag above his sensible shoes. This was one of the Met's most respected senior officers, but he looked more like a kindly financial adviser, or the sort of character who might run a fishing tackle shop.

'First. We have a new recruit. Temporary. Ideally.'

Sawyer turned to the room of twenty men and women and smiled, activating a dimple in his right cheek.

'I've signed Detective Inspector Jake Sawyer on loan from Buxton MIT to help us with this case, which has just gone from awful to fucking awful. The other Met squads are pushed to the limit. Even the elites up at Hendon.'

Murmured laughter and grumbles. Sawyer's eyes lifted to the centrepiece of the case board: a detailed map of the Greater London Urban Area with the thirty-two boroughs colour-coded for population. Close to ten million souls sardined into six hundred square miles, with the City in the centre.

Hatfield continued. 'Sawyer is here at MIT Seven partly because he has history with the Met. I taught him all he knows. He's recently been involved in some high-profile cases up north. You might have read about them. If not, do some Googling. Due diligence.' Hatfield coughed, so hard he staggered and had to steady himself on a desk. He styled it out by slapping the map with an open palm. 'He's an experienced and talented detective, and, like I say, we need every swinging dick in the field. Seek his counsel, put him to work, buy him a pint.'

'Don't drink, sir,' said Sawyer.

'Right. He's an experienced and talented detective, and his body is a temple. Luckily, he's with us because of his mind.' Hatfield turned to the board. 'To business, folks. As I hope you've all seen on HOLMES, the bodies of four people, members of the Carter family, were discovered by their cleaner at 9am yesterday morning. Warren and Ruth, the parents, and Dora and Shannon, nine and twelve.'

Sawyer looked around. Most of the detectives had taken out tablets and were accessing digital versions of the materials fixed to the case board. He took a laptop from his bag and accessed the HOLMES database system.

Hatfield gestured to a group of photos stacked along the left side of the map, connected to one of the central boroughs by a line of thin red thread. 'There are many similarities with the Prior scene from two weeks ago, and I'm going to say it now. We're still waiting on forensics, but for me, this is the work of the same killer or killers.'

Sawyer pulled up the case hub and scrolled through the reports and imagery.

'Specifically,' continued Hatfield, 'victims murdered in their own home. Affluent. Big houses in the same area. First family, Barnes. Second family, Hammersmith. Hands and feet bound with heavy-duty gaffer tape. The fathers and kids suffocated. The same tape wrapped repeatedly around nose and mouth. The mothers had gaffer tape only around the mouth, and their throats were cut. Puncture marks on all the necks. Graffiti on the walls. In the Priors' case, they all had a heavy dose of sedative in their system. Neil?'

An older man on the far side of the room sat up. He

wore a blue-and-white polka-dot bow tie, underscoring a neat grey goatee.

'Neil Shah,' said Hatfield to Sawyer. 'Head of Forensics. In quieter times, we share him with MIT Four and Six.'

'They all had heavy traces of the same combo,' said Shah. 'Tiletamine and zolazepam, with some flumazenil. The first two are benzodiazepines, the third is a benzo reversal. The benzos would take a minute or two to shut down a healthy human system.'

Sawyer looked up. 'He lays them out individually, one by one. Then brings them back round together.'

'That's a reasonable analysis,' said Shah. 'Although, as I say, loss of consciousness wouldn't be immediate.'

'He's strong,' said Sawyer, scrolling through scene photos from the new scene. 'And confident.'

A beat of silence. Hatfield nodded at Shah. 'The first scene, the Prior place, is still available for you to look around, Detective Sawyer.'

Sawyer looked up from the laptop. 'I might pick that up later, if that's okay. I'd like to see the latest scene first. Fresh. You say the Carters' cleaner discovered the bodies?'

'Yes. In the master bedroom.'

A male voice in Sawyer's ear. 'Bet this makes a change from dog walkers, eh?' A hand on his shoulder, squeezing.

Sawyer didn't turn. 'What about the Priors?'

'They'd organised a dinner party for the following evening,' said Hatfield. 'The two other couples were worried when they didn't get in touch, and so the plod went round and found them. TOD three days earlier.'

'No cleaner?'

'Sorry?'

'Did the first family have a cleaner?'

'Yes,' said another detective, near to Shah. 'But she was away that week.'

'Interesting.' Sawyer studied the crime scene photos, side by side. The bodies all sat slumped in chairs pushed up against the wall, facing out. The killer had taped the feet to the chair legs, keeping the wrists in place by taping them to the underside of the thighs. In both scenes, the killer had daubed a pentagram in a circle above each victim's head and a series of symbols across the top of the wall.

ᛁᚾᛁᚠᛗ

'What's interesting?' said Hatfield. 'The markings?'

'The short time between the murders. This is complex work. Takes a lot of planning, devising contingencies. You said on the phone that the details were non-public?'

'That's right.'

Sawyer closed the laptop. 'He's organised, meticulous, intelligent. The markings, the runes... It doesn't fit. He's a psychopath, not a psychotic.'

'Psychopathy is a personality trait,' said a female detective sitting in front of Hatfield. 'Psychosis is usually a symptom of another condition. The mind losing its grip on reality.'

'Yes,' said Sawyer, 'and our friend has a good grip on reality. It's just that his reality is a long way from ours. He, and it will be a he, simply doesn't live in a world we would recognise.'

Hatfield leaned back on a table. 'Don't you want to know what the symbols mean?'

Sawyer caught his eye. 'Yes, but it won't be as important as the detail in the work itself. What represents him? What expresses his urges? How are his urges reflected in his methods?' He stood up and walked to the board, taking a moment to study the imagery. 'There's dissonance here. All the boxes are ticked. Manipulation, domination, control. He's bold, not reckless. But the symbols seem outside of that. Cosmetic.'

'You think he's trying to lead us up the garden path?' said Hatfield.

Sawyer turned to Shah. 'Is there any evidence of more than one individual?'

'There's no evidence of *any* individual. Apart from forced entry to the houses, in both cases. No trace or DNA at the Prior place. My team are still working at the Carters', but so far it's the same story.'

Hatfield sighed. 'Sawyer, I don't understand why you're so quick to dismiss the symbols and the posing.'

'Because I don't think it's posing. It's not for his benefit. It's for the camera. Much more like staging.

Misdirection.' He sat down again. 'Are the symbols written in the mother's blood?'

Shah raised an eyebrow. 'In the case of the Priors, yes. I expect it'll be the same with the Carters.'

Male voice from the back. 'So why spare the mother from suffocation?'

'He gets in,' said Sawyer, 'and he stalks the family members one by one, for minimum fuss and lowest risk of counterattack or injury. He overpowers them, gets the drug in their system, subdues them silently until the effects kick in. Then, he tapes over the mouth at least, and onto the next one. If I were him, I'd try to take out the two adults in the room where they'll die. Then I would carry in the children and secure everyone before reviving them. If the motive is sexual sadism, and I'd say it is, then he needs to feed on the suffering during suffocation. He probably kills the children first, one at a time. Triple the pleasure, as he can simultaneously enjoy the child's dying distress and the horror of the parents, who I imagine are forced to watch. The mother comes last. The blood would be messy and he'd want to make the markings and leave straight after. But the mother would be forced to watch the whole thing. I'd hardly say that's sparing her.'

'Jesus,' said Hatfield. He pushed up his glasses and pinched the bridge of his nose. 'HOLMES, people. Feed the machine. Everything indexed for the decision logs. Trace, interview, eliminate. Anyone with access to the houses. Sitters, family friends, domestic help. Anyone with a connection to both families.

Victimology. Dig out any family feuds or tensions. Any beefs with work colleagues. Any secrets, indication of affairs, discarded lovers. Focus on the most likely outcome. It's someone who knows them, or knows of them, rather than a London night stalker. Back here first thing for updates.'

'Sir.' The male voice from behind Sawyer, from the detective who had squeezed his shoulder. 'It's great to have DI Sawyer here. Don't get me wrong. But it feels like he's assuming a lot. As we always say, believe nothing and check everyone. These crimes are horrible, but there's a puzzle to solve slowly and carefully.'

'Not only is that idea a cliché,' said Sawyer, still not turning round, 'but it's inaccurate. This isn't a puzzle. It's more of a drama. A story. The deaths are the end point.' He turned his chair to face the detective: heavy black beard, crumpled suit, chewing his biro. 'We need to establish the events up to now. We're more like storytellers than puzzle solvers. What's the story of this family? How did they get from their inception to their appalling deaths? And what's the story of the person who did this? He wasn't born with it as his destiny. What in his development, his past, compelled him to act this way? We have to filter and focus on outlying details, decide what's important, and examine it from every angle, with our minds wide open. This isn't a crossword, DS...'

'DI. Rowan McHugh.'

'We don't have to "solve" the whole thing to catch the perpetrator. We're not cryptographers, DI McHugh.

We're civil servants. Collecting and testing evidence, building a case for the other civil servants at the CPS.'

McHugh gave a good-natured shrug.

'Sorry if that sounds like a lecture. It's just good to keep the emphasis on the graft.' Sawyer turned back to Hatfield. 'I would also look at recently released murderers with similar methods or obsessions. An interest in strangulation, asphyxiation. Similar unsolved cases. Look for parallels.'

Hatfield grinned. 'You heard the man. DI Sawyer, DI Conway.' He pointed to a large corner office with an open door. The female detective who had spoken about psychosis got up and walked with Sawyer, following Hatfield into the office. The DCI closed the door behind them all.

'DI Sawyer, this is DI Brianna Conway. She's worked on major crime teams in Cardiff and London.'

Conway smiled. She stepped forward and shook Sawyer's hand. 'I've been with Putney for a year or so. Good to meet you.'

Conway's fingers were long and slender, but her grip was fierce. She was a lot shorter than Sawyer, but the heels and pinned back shoulders bought her a few extra inches. As she pumped Sawyer's hand, she kept her head level, raising her eyes to meet his.

'I work alone, Guv,' said Sawyer. 'Partners slow me down.'

Conway glanced at Hatfield.

'I mean, good to meet you, Detective.'

Hatfield dropped into his overlarge desk chair.

'Strategy comes from the SIO. This guy.' He pointed at himself. 'Brianna is one of the two DIs here, above four DS's and fourteen DCs. The DS's fine-tune everything and dish it out to the DCs. The culture's good, diligent. Particularly on cases like this. I don't expect anything sticky for you personally, because you won't be giving orders. You have full access, but you're a shadow, and I want you to focus on the Prior and Carter murders, with DI Conway as your contact. DI McHugh is covering other cases, but DI Conway is exclusive.'

Conway brushed a hand over the undone cuffs of her blouse. 'We're lucky to have you here, DI Sawyer. I've read a lot about you.'

'Sorry to lumber you with homework.'

She smiled. 'Oh, it wasn't an obligation.' Conway stepped to the side of Hatfield's desk and glanced out of the window, her straight blonde hair bleaching white in the overhead light. 'I read for pleasure. Unlike my young son.'

'TikTok and Netflix?' said Sawyer.

Conway smiled and turned to face the room. 'I was wondering, sir. Could there be something in the affluence of both families? Nothing was stolen.'

'This is personal,' said Sawyer. 'Not political.'

'Open minds, Detective,' said Hatfield.

'So, why do you think he cut the women's throats, DI Sawyer?' said Conway. 'Why were they not suffocated like the others? Has he got a soft spot for women?'

Sawyer lowered his head. 'Maybe. I need to see the work for myself. Like I said in the briefing, he might require the greater depth of suffering drawn from the parents' reactions to their children suffering. Once the children are dead, he can enjoy the mother's distress at the father's demise. But when he's alone with the mother, one on one, the dynamic doesn't do it for him. We need to look into how his life brought him to that place. Why he's wired that way.'

'You keep saying "he",' said Conway.

'You're right. I'm assuming. But do either of you seriously believe this is the work of a woman? I also think it's a single individual.'

Conway took a seat by the window. 'Why?'

'Logistics. The way he isolates them, knocks them out, brings them together later. That's focused work with fine timings. Better to keep the potential for error to a minimum.'

Hatfield drummed on his desk. 'Both of you get down there. Have a look at the "work" for yourself.'

Sawyer took a green boiled sweet out of its wrapper and slid it into his mouth.

'You still on those?' said Hatfield. 'Honestly, Sawyer. I don't know where you stick it all. Look at you.'

Conway smiled, tilted her head. 'Yes. What's your secret?'

'You'll have to be more specific,' said Sawyer.

'Scouser steals something. Why is this news?'

'It's not what he did.' Leon Stokes got to his feet. He was forty-odd, short but sturdy, with hard-earned biceps on show beneath a designer T-shirt with a sequined skull design. He walked over to the window where Mickey Doyle—taller, younger—stood. Two gigantic men in tailored suits behind Doyle braced, but he raised his hand, and they relaxed. Stokes bent forward and fussed the American pit bull at Doyle's feet. 'It's what he said.'

Doyle took a sip from his chunky crystal glass and narrowed his piggy eyes. 'Sticks and stones, Leon.'

Stokes raised himself upright. 'Don't get me wrong. I could do without the three hundred grand hole in my accounts. But this boy was a bold one, and he spilled a name before giving me this.' He pointed to the bandage fixed to the top of his closely shaven head.

'Suits you,' said a smiling man hovering by the sitting room double doors. Undersized black wifebeater vest, bald and spray-tanned with a neat salt-and-pepper beard. He raised an eyebrow. 'Sir.'

'Deon Kinsella,' said Doyle. 'Have you met?'

Stokes headed back to his sofa. 'No. I'm guessing, *consigliere*?'

Doyle snorted a laugh and glanced at Kinsella. 'Oh, he'll love that. He's a culture vulture, this one. Gay as a window, but not soft, mind.'

'You've softened your accent, Mickey.' Stokes retook his seat on the deep purple sofa, beside a heavyset man with a manicured black beard and thick-rimmed glasses, typing into a laptop.

Doyle sat down in a matching armchair opposite Stokes. His goons parked themselves behind, flanking him. He held his moment, then gave an exaggerated shrug. 'I'm a man of the world. Scouse equals thick. Equals not to be taken seriously. Not as bad as the Brummies.'

'Or the yam-yams,' said the bearded man, glancing up from the laptop.

Doyle laughed. 'Oh. Fuck's sake. Can't understand a word them lads say. So, this fool who robbed you. He told you his name?'

Stokes shook his head. 'He said I didn't want to fuck with his boss. *Jake Sawyer.*'

Doyle gazed up at the ceiling for a moment. 'Ringin' no bells. And your man. Deffo Scouse?'

'He didn't even bother to try and hide it.'

'He's got a death wish.' A pasty-faced man in a sky-blue Manchester City baseball cap spoke up. He sprawled forward in his seat at the vast dining table and double-tapped what looked like a hand grenade on the surface. 'That's the thing with you bin-dippers. You spawned a few pots when football was shit and you think you're invincible.'

Doyle, smiling, glanced back at Kinsella, grim-faced. 'And who's Billy Big Bollocks over here?'

'Peyton,' said the man, sitting upright. 'That ringin' any bells?'

The pit bull sidled over to Doyle; he petted it, keeping his eyes on Peyton. 'You Eddie's lad?'

'Younger brother,' said Stokes. 'Wesley.'

Peyton bristled. 'Brother.'

'Not sure you've inherited his brains,' said Doyle. 'Unless that's a fake.'

Peyton looked down at the grenade. 'Course it's a fuckin' fake.'

Kinsella leaned forward, smiling. '*My First Explosive.*'

'Is it a pencil sharpener or something?' said Doyle, squinting.

Kinsella sniggered. 'Or a butt plug?'

'You'd know, eh?' said Peyton.

Kinsella raised his eyebrows and pointed at Peyton with both index fingers. 'So, what's the score with big bro, Wes?'

'He's a killer,' said Doyle, scratching the dog between its ears. 'One of his crew was popped in some Salford shithole, what, ten years back?'

Peyton nodded.

'So he sniffed out the bloke who did it. Waited for

him outside his local. The fella gets in his car, and Eddie rolls a grenade underneath. The explosion didn't kill him. He crawled out, burned to death. In front of his missus, I think. That showed 'em, eh?'

'He's a fuckin' *king* inside,' said Peyton.

'*Anyway*.' Doyle patted the dog and nudged it to the side. 'Leon. Who the fuck's this Jake Sawyer? And what's he doing hiring Scousers to rob upstanding Manchester businessmen like yourself?'

Stokes took out his phone and handed it to Doyle. 'The boy was careful, but we got him on camera when he left. Round the back. Wearing a bally, but...'

Doyle studied the image on-screen: a dark and fuzzy shot of a heavily muscled man in a black balaclava, carrying a holdall over one shoulder. The security lighting had picked out a detailed tattoo of a fire-breathing wolf on his forearm.

Doyle passed the phone to Kinsella. 'He's a brother, then.'

Stokes nodded. 'Hard bastard. Took me a week to shake the fucking headache. So... I thought you might recognise him? Or at least his tats?'

Doyle scowled at Stokes. 'This is bad form, Leon. Invite a man into your home and accuse him of robbery.'

'We're not doing that,' said the bearded man, closing the laptop. 'It wouldn't add up, anyway. We just wondered if you'd seen him around your fine city. Or if the tattoo might connect to any of the Mersey crews.'

'This is Boyd Cannon,' said Stokes.

Doyle nodded. '*Consigliere*?'

'I'll take that,' said Cannon, unsmiling.

'This looks like Murray's work,' said Kinsella, studying the screen. He handed the phone back to Doyle who passed it to the taller of the two goons. 'Murray Walsh. Place in Walton called Tattisfaction. Does some pretty mad designs. Biotechs, body suits, insane freehand work. This is American Trad, which isn't quite his thing, but he'll probably recognise the artist.'

'I'll send a screenshot,' said Stokes.

Doyle held up a hand. 'Just remind me. Why am I suddenly your best buddy, Leon? This looks like a YFP-type situation.'

'It's my fucking problem now,' said Stokes, 'but if we let it go, it'll soon be yours. Three of my top boys have had similar visits in the past couple of months. Clayton, Droylsden, Tameside. One of them, this fucker ran an iron across his bollocks.'

Doyle whistled. 'Someone's on a suicide mission.'

'And you don't even know the twist yet.'

'Sawyer is filth,' said Peyton. 'CID.'

Stokes sat forward. 'So, I'm wondering what possessed a toerag like Mr Wolf Tattoo to give up a copper's name like that.'

Doyle took a drink. 'Some undercover black ops bullshit? Bizzies targeting ill-gotten gains, hoping to scare us off.'

'Sawyer is major crime.' Another man, seated at the far end of the dining table rose a wagging finger as he spoke. 'But he's a rock star. Quite a history.'

'Is this fella a Russian?' said Doyle.

'*Polski,*' said the man, pivoting his head to Doyle.

'Mickey, this is Jakub Malecki. He's working with Wes and his brother, hopefully to get us clarity on Sawyer and our tattooed friend. Sawyer has links with Derbyshire, as does Wes's brother.'

'What's your diary looking like, Jakub?' said Kinsella. 'I could do with getting the bathroom retiled.'

Malecki ignored him and lowered his head, like an android powering down.

'That's racist,' said Peyton, eyeballing Kinsella.

Kinsella waved a hand. 'I'm only messin'.'

'I'm just suggesting we... share intelligence,' said Stokes. 'Mutual interest. We each have our patches. No issues. But this is fucking hardcore, and it will be coming along the M62 for your boys soon.'

'So, we're fucking with coppers now?' said Doyle.

'They're fucking with us. They're costing us money.'

Peyton spun his grenade around on the table. 'If there's coppers to be fucked with, I'm there.'

'That went well for your brother,' said Kinsella.

'I know this fella.' The shorter of Doyle's goons held up Stokes's phone. 'I recognise the tat from time I did in Strangeways last year. Something *Mavers*. Hard bastard. One of the top dogs wanted him to hide some brown in his room, but he wouldn't touch it. Took a beating, went after the four lads who did it, one by one. Hung around with this posh cunt, Wilmot. Proper psycho.' He handed the phone back to Stokes. 'I'll do some digging.'

'So, he's not a fan of drugs,' said Cannon. 'Let's find out why.'

Stokes glanced at Malecki. 'I'd be keen to ask him in person. I also want to know why an ex-con is spraying a detective's name around. I'd rather not fuck with coppers if we can get all we need from Mavers. But we might require Jake Sawyer to help us with our enquiries.'

5

Sawyer climbed the second flight of stairs, ahead of Conway. 'Only four people lived here? There's room for forty.'

'We're just over the line into Fulham,' said Conway. 'That's another million on top, at least. Four storeys.'

'A million a floor?'

Conway spluttered. 'I can tell you're not from round here. Add three mil to that and you're close. Gothic Revival. The rich do love their retro.'

On the third-floor landing, Sawyer sidestepped through a group of Tyvek-suited forensic officers and looked into a large office room opposite the two officers posted at the door of the master bedroom.

One of the forensics emerged from the crowd and lowered his face mask. A corner of Neil Shah's blue-and-white bow tie poked up from inside his suit. 'Warren Carter's study. Architect. Ruth was a doctor.'

Top-range Mac Pro, designer desk chair, hardwood floor, Linn turntable on a custom-built cabinet.

'So, this is the house his salary built,' said Sawyer.

Shah surveyed the distant ceiling. 'I should say so. My father was a doctor, DI Sawyer. Our home looked nothing like this.'

Sawyer poked through a rack of vinyl on a shelf above the turntable. Roxy Music, Jean-Michel Jarre.

'Just had a new technician lose his breakfast,' said Shah.

Tago Mago, Bitches Brew.

'Did he make it outside?'

'If he'd spewed on my crime scene, we'd have five dead bodies on our hands.'

Sawyer glanced at Conway; she raised an eyebrow. He left the office and walked across to the master bedroom. Conway followed, and they flashed their warrant cards at the sentries. Shah followed them in.

The Carters remained in place, lined up against the far wall, on the right side of the enormous bed. They were all dressed in pyjamas, apart from Warren Carter, who wore boxer shorts and a T-shirt. Ruth Carter's nightwear was crimson, and her chair sat above an oceanic bloodstain that had spread across the right side of the room and dried into the wooden floor. The forensics had also marked out splashes of blood on the edge of the bed, lower parts of the adjacent wall and dressing table mirror.

All the family members' feet had been bound and

gaffer-taped to the chair legs, with wrists fixed to the underside of their thighs. The two girls sat side by side, slumped towards each other in futile solidarity.

Sawyer hitched up his face mask and pulled on a pair of latex gloves. He approached the body of Warren Carter, taking care to step around the blood. He crouched and leaned in close to the tape around the face and nose.

He glanced back at Conway. 'Not the eyes.'

'No. It's the same with the Priors. Mouths and noses sealed but the eyes untouched.'

Sawyer turned back to the bodies. 'Apart from the women, the mothers.' He moved over to Ruth Carter's body, the only one with the nostrils untaped. She had a deep slash wound across her throat. 'Ruth's chair isn't quite flush with the wall.'

'Struggle?' said Conway.

Sawyer took in a deep breath. Copper from the blood, something bleachy from the mask. 'He watched Dora and Shannon die. Then Warren. Then he stood behind Ruth and cut her throat, avoiding the blood spray.'

'The markings were made with a standard grade paintbrush,' said Shah. He moved in. 'No sign of defensive wounds. He had them secure before starting his—'

'Work,' said Sawyer.

Shah gave a sigh of disgust.

'We can't project our own outrage onto this. They're human beings to us, but to him, this is all just a means to an end. His gratification. We need to understand his story. Not through the who, but the why.' Sawyer looked up at the blood markings on the wall behind the bodies.

'It's Ruth's,' said Shah.

Sawyer closed his eyes for a moment. 'None of the family would have seen the markings.'

'All for his benefit,' said Conway. 'They're Anglo-Saxon runes. Translates as, *I LIVE*. Crypto guys think it might be some occult crap. Demons.'

Sawyer walked back across the room to the door. 'Like plenty of other alienated undergraduates, he probably read a bit of Crowley, maybe some LaVey. But like I said, there's so much theatre, it feels more like staging than posing. He's a sadist, not a Satanist. So, what's that story? How did he get to this point? It's our job to find out who he is, but we'll do that by seeking who he was.'

'Do you really feel confident about profiling, DI Sawyer?' said Conway.

Sawyer shrugged. 'I'm reacting to the work. What's the root of his gratification? It will lie somewhere in his past, his early experiences. The disconnect is strong, between what he needs to do for himself and how he presents it.'

Conway stared at Warren Carter's bound hands. 'Is there shame?'

'Could be. Or he might need to occupy some kind of role or persona to complete the work, and the markings are part of that. Any fibres or fluids, Neil?'

'Nothing we can work with. Probably wearing

protective gear, generic clothing. We do have a small trace of compound taken from the bed. It looks similar to something we found at the Prior house, but I'm waiting on results. Nothing yet that doesn't come from the victims.'

'No semen?' said Sawyer.

Shah shook his head.

'How did he get in? Windows? Doors? You mentioned forced entry.'

'At both scenes. Back doors forced. Locks broken. Looks like a screwdriver.'

'Both houses have security systems,' said Conway. 'They're deactivated by the residents on entry. Key codes. There's a grace period for deactivation before they signal the company that relays to the police. Doesn't look like they activated them when they went to bed. Probably just when they were out of the house.'

Sawyer walked out of the bedroom and climbed the stairs to the top floor. Shah and Conway followed.

Sawyer nudged open the door to a small bathroom. Towels on a heated rack: pink and purple. Two toothbrushes: red and yellow. Square bath. Shelf overloaded with toiletries and female hygiene products.

'This was the girls' bathroom,' said Conway. 'No parents allowed, according to the cleaner. Two bedrooms on this floor, too. And a spare that used to be their playroom.'

Sawyer moved from room to room in silence. The bedrooms were adult-sized, with fitted wardrobes. The spare was more modest, but still had a double bed, TV, storage closet, expensive-looking chest of drawers.

They paused for a moment at the top of the stairs, watching the forensics on the landing below.

Sawyer moved to run both hands through his hair, stopped when he remembered the gloves. 'I need a shower.'

'Go on, then, DI Sawyer,' said Shah. 'Who do you think he was? Where the hell does the root for this lie?'

'Who did you used to be?'

'Sorry?'

'How did you get here from there?'

Shah looked at Conway. No help. He squinted at Sawyer and took off his glasses, held them up to the dim landing light. 'I suppose I followed the things I was interested in. Mathematics. Science. Measurables. Provables.'

Sawyer nodded. 'You weren't born that way, though. That's your doctor father. As children, we look to adults for how to behave. We mimic. We copy. For most of us, our behaviours and impulses develop organically around those models. But for some there's a corruption, and the development is stifled, sometimes toxified.'

'So, this corruption is our goal,' said Conway.

'Exactly. We'll find our killer through their story, through the early chapters. How they were corrupted. When we know who he was, we'll be on the way to discovering who he is.' He held Shah's eye. 'You understand how crucial those early years are, Neil. How they form our nature, our psyche, our reality. I'm sure you encountered a lot of racism in Coventry in the seventies and eighties.'

Shah replaced his glasses. 'Very good. Most people assume Birmingham, from the accent.'

'We also need to find out as much as possible about both families. Look for reasons they might have crossed paths with the sort of individual who could be responsible for what's down in that bedroom. Who they were, what they did for fun. Parallels, crossovers. Did they know each other? Are there mutual connections who might benefit from their deaths? You don't need a rube from the shires to tell you this, but most murderers are known to their victims. So, let's start there, alongside all the victims' stories. What brought *them* to this point?'

'I'll be here with my teams for most of the night,' said Shah. 'I apologise in advance for the smell of my egg and bacon sandwich at tomorrow morning's briefing.'

Conway leaned against the wall and folded her arms. 'So, apart from whatever screwed up the killer in the past, how's he getting his kicks in the present? If he's a sexual sadist, then why no evidence of sexual activity? No semen. I know it's unlikely, but the killer could be a woman.'

'Could be,' said Sawyer. 'Won't be.'

'So, is he just watching them die and leaving?'

Sawyer read the sign on one of the girls' doors.

DO NOT DISTURB
I'M DISTURBED ENOUGH ALREADY

'The killings are fuel for his fantasies,' said Sawyer. 'He may be photographing the deaths to enjoy later. Or filming them. I've seen that before.'

6

THREE YEARS EARLIER

'So. I talk, you listen. Right?'

Carl Bancroft—jowly, flushed—held his pen up in the air. 'That's what it says on the shirt. But it's only one part of this. We're about support. Prison life can be harrowing. The officers are decent people, but their time is tight, and the job is stressful. They're jailers, not therapists. We're not going anywhere, and one thing we do have a lot of is time. So some volunteer to do this.'

The second man sat upright, keeping his crystal-blue eyes on a point behind Bancroft, as if he were talking to someone standing at his shoulder. 'Out of the goodness of your hearts.' His speech was slow and precise, and his deep, dark voice bounced off the walls of the box room.

Bancroft gave an indulgent smile. 'Some prisoners

volunteer for the wrong reasons, yes. To help with their record, reduce sentencing. But the Samaritans recruiters tour the prisons and there's a rigorous screening process before applicants get to become Listeners.'

'So, none of this gets back to the governor?' He raised a hand and tapped his hefty fingers on the edge of the table.

'These meetings are completely confidential, Dennis. But should you confess something that implies another inmate may be in danger, then I'm obliged to report it.' A weak smile.

Dennis pushed himself to his feet and tilted his head back, rolling his head around, cracking the muscles in his thick neck. 'Mind if I stretch my legs?'

'As long as you stay in this room.'

Dennis walked to the back wall and leaned his hulking frame over a cracked sink. He took a sliver of soap and lathered his hands under the cold tap as the water filled the basin. 'What are you in for, Carl?'

Bancroft sighed. 'You see. This is the issue. There are certain... guidelines inside. Things you do, things you don't do. Enquiring about an index offence—'

'*Grassing,*' said Dennis, with contempt, rinsing his hands.

'Yes. You've been here a short time, but already you're getting something of a reputation. It's not a great idea to get a reputation.'

Dennis splashed water onto his face. 'Better to keep your head down. See out your time.'

Bancroft opened a document on his laptop. 'Well...'

Dennis ran his hands over his wet face, burrowing his fingers through a scruffy beard. 'I don't have time for that.'

'I realise that your... sentence is—'

'Long. Yes. Relatively.' He stood at the sink with his back to Bancroft. 'This is our biggest problem.'

Bancroft turned in his seat. 'How do you mean?'

'Time. Our perception of it. Humanity, that is. How quickly we lose sight of the past, and have such a limited interest in the future. We would do well to stop taking our lessons from economics and focus on geology.'

'Ah. Yes. You're interested in—'

'Our planet has its own time, measured in rocks. Geologists are the true timekeepers of the earth. The pompous proclamation of some high court judge is so insignificant it barely warrants contempt.'

Bancroft swiped at his screen. 'Yes... You've been in an institution before. When you were a teenager, following your mother's death. Did you struggle with the culture there, too?'

Dennis stood upright at the sink. 'Flowers, plants, trees. They come, they go. A tedious cycle. But rocks remain. Implacable. Forever old.'

'Your mother died quite young, didn't she? And you were only thirteen at the time.'

'Are you religious, Carl?'

Bancroft turned his chair to face the man. 'I suppose I am. Childhood habits, mostly.'

'Religion is an aberration. A dumbing down. An extreme oversimplification. A petty fairy story, compared with the geological truth of creation. I despise the way we litter our ancient history with such trivia as dinosaurs. They're just attention-hogging celebrities who get too much media coverage when we should be following the important stories told by the rocks.'

'Could we perhaps try to focus on—'

'The future?' Dennis lunged at Bancroft and gripped his head between his huge hands. He dragged him over to the full sink and pushed his face into the water, holding him there, untroubled by his flailing arms. 'You should always respect the past, Carl.'

The door crashed open and three guards stumbled in.

Dennis pulled Bancroft's face out of the water, leaned down, and hissed in his ear. '*We are what we were.*'

7

PRESENT DAY

Hatfield exited his office and plodded over to the whiteboard, cradling a lidded cup of coffee. 'Morning, all. Tell me things. Make them positive, if you can. I'm not great with bad news when I'm low on caffeine.' He leaned on a desk. 'I know it's early and we had a late one, but I want to get moving before the press get on it.'

The team settled and took their seats, facing the front. Neil Shah, in his usual spot at the far side of the room, sat forward in his chair. 'We have confirmation on the compound found at both scenes. Rubber-based. Could be a raincoat or jacket.'

'In this weather?' said DI McHugh.

'Might be from his gloves,' said Sawyer, standing outside one of the side offices.

Shah nodded. 'We found a little of it at the first scene on one of the chairs. Not from the vics. It's unusual, so finding it at both scenes...'

'It's a lead,' said DI Conway, glancing up at Sawyer. 'Can you get any more on it, Neil?'

'Not without a comparable item. So it's not much use until we have a suspect.'

'The markings?' said Hatfield.

'Same as the Priors. The mother's blood. No other trace.'

Hatfield set down his coffee and opened a top section of the corner window, to little effect. A squall of commuter traffic noise drifted up from the bridge. 'DI Sawyer. Thoughts on the scene?'

Heads lifted in anticipation.

Sawyer walked out onto the floor. 'The markings are staging. Ritual killings usually show a degree of frenzy, but there's self-control here. Calculation. If it's misdirection, we have to explore why.'

'Why he would bother?' said McHugh.

'Exactly.'

'Maybe he doesn't want to be caught,' said Hatfield, to a few titters.

'Maybe he actively wants to waste our time,' said Sawyer. 'The short space between the killings is a major worry. This isn't a killer who strikes, then lies low, then strikes again when the coast is clear. He's calm. His method is organised, meticulous. He has a plan and he might want to keep us busy to reduce the chance of us stopping him before it's complete. Maybe he's on a tight schedule.'

'Early PM indications as expected,' said Shah. 'Same drug combo in all their systems, including the reversal.'

Sawyer shifted position, momentarily blinded by the line of sunlight from the window.

A prickle of nausea at the light patterns.

A distant dog barked. Was it reality, or memory seeping through a crack opened by lack of sleep?

Deep, slow breaths.

He stood beneath the window opened by Hatfield, looking out at the clamour below.

'What about this *I LIVE* thing?' said Conway.

A detective sitting close to Shah cleared his throat. 'The runes do have connotations with the occult, ritual magic.'

'DI Sawyer?' said Hatfield.

Scurrying commuters.

Gridlock behind a lorry, halfway between lanes, forced to stop at the light before the bridge.

Angry horns.

'DI Sawyer.'

'The pentagram seems corny.' He turned from the window, glanced at Hatfield. 'He wants to send us down rabbit holes. Investigating obscure websites and wacko churches. We should stick to the hard realities. The earthly science instead of the astral plane.'

Hatfield sipped his coffee. 'Neil?'

'The gaffer tape is the same type. Strong. So, I suppose he's not trying too hard to hide the connections. Signs of forced entry at both scenes, and in both cases, the children and father died of asphyxiation, the mother of exsanguination.'

'DC Rodgers?' said Hatfield. 'Anything from device data? Socials?'

A young detective with a cropped Afro sitting near Shah almost got to her feet but then settled back down. 'Shannon Carter posted on TikTok on the night of the murder. Just film of her messing around with her sister, who had recently dyed her hair.'

'Any family friction?' said Conway.

'Nothing unusual. Just standard sisterly stuff.'

'TikTok?' said Hatfield. 'At nine?'

'Faked her birthdate,' said Conway. 'They don't exactly enforce the thirteen limit.'

'CCTV?' said Sawyer. 'Both houses in decent areas. Any home security? Doorbell cams? Any Neighbourhood Watch schemes? Anyone spotted staking out?'

'I'm directing house-to-house in the Carter area,' said McHugh. 'We took security cam footage from a couple of places near to the Priors, but there's nothing on them.'

'We're following up on numbers that pinged the local masts on the evenings of the murders,' said Rodgers.

'Cross-ref with nominals?' said Sawyer, taking a seat at a desk and opening his laptop.

'We have a team of juniors working the drone work,' said Hatfield. 'Feeding everything into HOLMES, bouncing things off the NPD, liaising with NCA. We won't miss any red flags.'

'What about the drug?' said Sawyer. 'Seems exotic. Where could he have got the ingredients from?'

'There's this thing in the big city,' said McHugh, grinning. 'It's called the internet.'

Sawyer ignored him. 'Professions that might have easy access to the drugs? Anaesthetists, general health care, vets.'

Rodgers wrote something on a notepad, nodding. 'Sir.'

'There's no need to call me—'

'On the nominals,' said Hatfield, pushing up from the desk. 'We're not pinging on anyone recently released for similar offences. But there is something I'd like you to follow up, Detective Sawyer.' He slurped his coffee, gulped it down with a wince. 'I'm thinking about the method. Mostly asphyxiation. Denial of air. There's a guy I arrested back in the 2000s when I only had two letters in front of my name. I can't see you getting in to Broadmoor to talk to him directly, but pop into town for me. Have a chat with the forensic psych who's assessing him ahead of a parole hearing later this year.'

'Taylor Maxwell?' said Sawyer.

Hatfield nodded. 'Oh, yes. Plenty of parallels with our friendly neighbourhood family annihilator. Maxwell mostly killed sex workers, but he was also a home invader. The psychiatrist, Cabrera, is the top boy in the paraphilia field. He will have peerless access. Go see him. Dig around in Maxwell's psychopathology. Maybe we'll get some insight on our new boy. How did Maxwell select his victims? What did he get out of it? What kind of minor offences might he have committed along the way? And what's his state of mind at the moment? Is he producing any art in his room? I assume he'll be aware of the murders, so has he referred to them?'

'And this is the perk of London policing, Sawyer,' said McHugh. 'All the best experts live just down the road.'

Sawyer looked up from the laptop. 'We have a thing up north. It's called the telephone.'

'I'm redirecting resource into mostly victimology,' said Hatfield. 'Victim associations. Friends of friends of friends. Now, I thought I asked politely yesterday, but I'm still seeing nothing, so this is me being less polite. Find me those fucking connections. Who has access to the houses? Who used to live there? Who knew the victims? Where did they go frequently? Who did they see there? Why are these people dead? Why now? If there *is* no why, I want to know that.'

'It's not the same, sir,' said Sawyer.

'What isn't?'

'Maxwell strangled most of his victims. He only suffocated one, with a plastic bag over the head. He raped them all. He tortured one. This is hands-off, detached. Strangulation is intimate. And, given the lack of DNA, I'm sure he's filming or taking photographs. He wants to enjoy the suffering later. Watch them die repeatedly. Maxwell didn't have that. He didn't need that.'

'He was into the Satanist rubbish, though,' said Rodgers. 'They found books and equipment at his house. Tried to claim some sort of possession.'

Sawyer glanced at Hatfield. 'Being in a high-security hospital at the time of the murders is a good alibi.'

Hatfield took out a crumpled handkerchief and blew his nose. 'Sorry. Hay fever. Look, we're not profiling, Sawyer. We're gathering insight. This is why you're here. My focus now is twofold. Catching the bastard doing this and stopping him doing it again. The team can focus on the cure, while you work on prevention. We can't help the families he's already targeted, but if we can get an idea on the family who might be next—'

'Families,' said Sawyer.

'Sorry?'

'More than one family to come. And soon. He's smart, organised, meticulous, conscientious. These crimes are complex and high risk with high reward. Two in two weeks. Not only is he organised, he's a planner. He has a list of targets. He doesn't want to be forced to suppress his urges while he messes around with the tiresome business of finding and arranging his next victim. He's hungry. Insatiable. And he's bingeing.'

Hatfield tilted back his head, studying Sawyer. 'And this is why I want you in his head, Jake. What might he be getting out of this? How is he choosing the victims? If he's bingeing, what's his capacity? If he's a planner, what's the endgame? Look deeper into his work. Understand the artist. We'll tackle the how, you focus on the why. Pardon the tabloid speak, but you've built a reputation as an expert in sickos and psychos.'

Sawyer held his eye. 'You taught me all I know, sir.'

8

Dale Strickland poked his head around the door of his partitioned office. 'Oliver. No calls. Fifteen minutes.'

The young biracial receptionist looked up from his standing desk and lifted the ear of his remote headset. 'Roger that.'

Strickland closed the door and drew down the blinds. He ambled over to the giant glass desk by the window, draped his suit jacket across the back of the chair, sat down. He rolled up the sleeves of his tailored white shirt, checked his watch, then opened his personal laptop and plugged in a dongle, which connected him to a private Wi-Fi signal. He splashed a finger of Glenfiddich into a heavy glass, knocked it back, then topped up.

He activated his IP-masking app and opened the video conference software. The call came through, on time almost to the second.

Strickland took a small sip of his whisky, set down

the glass. He slid off his heavy-framed glasses and connected the call.

A face appeared in the half-screen viewing window from the side. Too close, too bright. The caller adjusted the light and leaned back in a cheap-looking chair. He folded his meaty arms, revealing a tattoo of a wolf with crazed eyes, breathing fire from its open jaws. White walls behind him, smoke wafting.

The man gave a slow nod. 'Dale.' He leaned forward slightly, squinting into the screen. 'You been on the bleach?'

Strickland smiled, took another drink. 'White beats grey. It looks more like a style choice.'

The man whistled. 'I bet your lackies told you... Roy Batty? I'd go Aryan Brotherhood.'

'And I'd go Travelodge, New Brighton.'

The man glanced around his room. 'Cold.'

'I'm not looking for you, Curtis. But I know someone who will be. Are you *smoking*?'

'Incense. Bit musty in here.' Curtis Mavers took a slug from a bottle of Red Stripe. 'I know the bizzies will be up for a chat.'

Strickland shook his head and ran his fingertips across his close-cropped hair. 'Much worse than that. You've kicked a hornet's nest, Curtis.'

'Posh watch. Behoves a man of your stature.'

Strickland held his wrist up to the screen. 'Audemars Piguet. Eighteen carat gold.'

'10k?'

'Double it.'

Another sip of Red Stripe. 'For that price, they could have put proper numerals on it. You're getting flash, Dale. You've conned your way to the top floor of Broadhurst House. You should mind you don't make it an ivory tower. Bright white hair, shiny watch. You know the score. Stand out, you get shot down.'

'You win first. Then you go to war.'

Mavers laughed. 'Still with the Sun Tzu shit. So, what's that all about? Come and have a go, eh? Are you the big boss now, then? The King in the North?'

'Effectively.'

Mavers beamed into the screen. 'G'wed, then. Tell me about this hornet's nest.'

Strickland leaned back in his chair. 'I'm hearing about a meeting, yesterday, at the house of the main man from the biggest Manchester crew. A target I acquired from our minty-breathed friend in GMP.' He leaned forward again. 'And which I passed on to you, Curtis.'

Mavers nodded. 'Leon the Lion. He's flash, too. Gold taps.'

'Also present at this meeting was Michael Doyle.'

'They call him Mickey. Not quite so catchy.'

Strickland forced a smile. 'No. But he's pretty much top of the tree in your forest.'

'He's a fucking woollyback.'

'St Helens. But in terms of the Merseyside drug trade, he's an oligarch. So, riddle me this. Why is the biggest bad in Greater Manchester inviting his Liverpool counterpart over for drinks and nibbles?'

More Red Stripe. 'I know what you're thinking.'

'So, what's the answer?'

'Yes. I did speak to him. When I paid him a visit. I kind of had to. Needed the combo to his safe.'

'And did he note your accent?'

Mavers grinned. 'Deffo.'

'I'm assuming you kept my name out of it?'

'Don't be soft. Come on, Dale. We're not falling out, are we?'

Strickland glared at the screen. 'Could you blame me for assuming you've swiped me left? Given that you've taken sole custody of Leon's safe contents.'

'I'm a wanted man. I need resources.' Mavers took his time to finish the bottle of beer. He clunked it down on the table. 'Look. We just had a chat about art and Polish torturers. No mention of yourself. I did drop one name, though.'

Dale raised his eyebrows.

'Jake Sawyer.'

'And why would you do that?'

'Hoping to put a stick in his spokes. He almost collared me. And he sent my friend to prison. Y'see, Dale. You're the one feeling ghosted. But trust is a big thing in relationships. And I hear you're not done with teenagers' veins.'

Strickland nodded, composed. 'You hear wrong, Curtis. My whole Deputy Mayor ticket was all about changing the approach to drugs. More prevention instead of cure. Treat the addicts as victims, not criminals. I've been spearheading new rehab clinics, working with recovery charities. Helping people who are sliding into the same world as your sister to change direction before it's too late. And alongside that, I've been getting a foot on the supply pipe. Making it harder for the likes of Stokes and Doyle to conduct the kind of business that led to Jayne's death. The work you and Wilmot were doing was a key part of that.'

'The off-the-books part?'

'More of a necessary back-channel. But... things change.'

Mavers beamed, showing his teeth. 'Ah. Now I get it. You really do want to be a legitimate businessman.'

Strickland dropped his gaze. 'We need to power down.'

Mavers angled his head. 'Smooth the trail.'

'Despite your unilateral actions with Stokes's money, I still feel our partnership has a future, Curtis. We're committed to each other's welfare, but our mutual friend, currently residing at Her Majesty's pleasure in the old Strangeways, might not be.'

'Wilmot won't spill anything.'

Strickland raised his head. 'Maybe not to the police.'

Mavers sat back and rolled his head around, crunching the muscles. He took a deep, slow sigh. 'I need to get out of the UK.'

'Where?'

He waggled the bottle. 'Jamaica.' He paused. 'Seriously, though. The Med will do me. Old school. But I can't just stroll out to John Lennon Airport and jump on a plane.'

Strickland finished his drink. 'I can fix that. If we can

kiss and make up, then you'll be sipping limoncello in Sorrento before the month is out. Stokes heard you were from Liverpool, and he's called on Doyle to help ID you. You might have wasted a bit of time making them snoop on Sawyer, but when they hit that dead end, they'll come after you. And when they can't find you, they'll look for Wilmot's help. And they know where he is. And they have ways of making him talk.' He leaned forward. 'You need to unfriend him.'

'With extreme prejudice?'

'And you need to do it quickly. Before Stokes gets in first with the thumbscrews.'

Mavers tapped the lip of the bottle on his front teeth. 'Soon come.'

9

Sawyer jinked through the bustle of disembarkers on East Putney Tube platform, shielding his coffee. Conway overtook him and hopped onto the train first, diving for a double seat before the flow of new passengers had a chance to block the doors. She angled her legs to reserve the seat beside her, and Sawyer fought his way through and flopped down.

'Jesus. And this is the District.' He opened his Pret A Manger bag and peeled a ring off the flaky cinnamon swirl.

Conway sipped through the spout in her cup. 'You've been away too long if you think there's such a thing as a quiet Tube line.' She watched him crunch into the pastry. 'Is this breakfast?'

He shrugged. 'Quick fuel-up.'

'It's basically a fistful of sugar. You'll crash before lunch.'

'Let's not snack-shame.'

The Tube moved off; Sawyer just about compensated for the jerk by tilting his coffee cup. He took a slurp and eyed her. 'Have you met this guy before?'

'Cabrera? Yes. Seventy-odd. Came over from Spain in the eighties, I think. He does a lot of psych profiling for us. A tiny bit... idiosyncratic. He helped McHugh with an utterly dismal case last year. Couple of sadists who got off on beating and imprisoning their foster children. One was put into an induced coma after a nasty beating from the man. She died a few days later. The bloke's brief tried to push for abnormality of mental function, substantial impairment. He was hospitalised himself by his father as a kid. Usual story. Cabrera tore it apart and he got a full life term, twenty years for the woman.'

'So, not the touchy-feely type?'

'He has a few unreconstructed views on offender psychology and rehab.'

The train squealed to a halt at Fulham Broadway. Sawyer and Conway's carriage emptied, then took on a fresh load of stern faces. The first wave lunged for the seats, while those behind shuffled into the corners or simply parked themselves in a space, shoulders hunched, heads down.

Sawyer devoured the pastry while Conway freshened her lipstick. He caught her eye in the compact mirror.

An elderly gent opposite sent over a judgy glance. Sawyer scooped up the pastry flakes by his feet and scrunched them into a ball with the bag. He looked up with a sheepish smile, but the man had already buried himself in his *Metro*.

'They made a TV thing with Cabrera,' said Conway. 'A couple of years ago. *The Psychopath Whisperer*. Just a one-off. ITV, I think. You can have a little celebrity-off.'

'I'm not seeing many autograph hunters round here.'

Conway smiled. 'Maybe your profile is restricted to police circles.'

'Or criminal.'

'So, do you think it might be a double bluff? The markings? Maybe our man *is* some kind of Satanist.'

Sawyer looked up at the station map above the seats. 'It's too systematic for a ritual murder. He's not getting what he needs that way. Sacrifice wackos aren't home invaders. And they use designer daggers. He's enjoying the pain, the fear. There's no sense of higher power. The means is the end.'

'So he finds the asphyxiation itself erotic?'

'We should consider it, since he's used the same method across both killings.'

'But only for the men and children.'

The train rocked and rattled through the Brompton interchange; Sawyer and Conway fell silent, unable to compete.

'Do you know any sex workers?' said Sawyer, as the noise settled.

The elderly man opposite glanced up over his *Metro*. 'Not personally. Why?'

'The method is unusual. An outlier. Could be

something fulfilling a deeper sexual fantasy. Asphyxiation fetish. They call it breath play.'

Conway grimaced. 'The key word there is "play". It's consenting. Power exchange. Not about causing harm.'

'Maybe he started consensual and then refined. Getting permission wasn't doing it for him.'

Conway sipped her coffee. 'No semen on scene. You think he might have been filming? Taking pics? Getting himself off later?'

Metro Man shuffled in his seat.

'No sexual assault. Asphyxiation, not strangulation. He's not a fan of intimacy, direct contact. He might have discovered that through specialist fetish sex workers. One of them might remember the weird guy who asked to watch as they restricted their own air.'

'You should talk to SCD9. Clubs and Vice.'

'The rebranded Vice Squad?'

She nodded. 'Their gaffer's been consulting with Hatfield and a few of the other MITs.'

The train slowed on the approach to Earl's Court.

'I know someone there. Max Reeves. DI.'

'I've seen him at Putney once or twice. Didn't you work with him? Before you moved back up to Derbyshire?'

Sawyer smiled and held her eye. 'Gold star.'

———

'Hello, hello! Do take a seat, Brianna.'

Dr Guillermo Cabrera sprang up from his panelled

74

corner desk and scurried over to Conway. He was tall and twiggy; bald, with a fulsome white beard and moustache, accentuating his golden skin.

He shook Conway's hand and turned to Sawyer, delighted. 'Detective Jake Sawyer. I was just reading about you. *Derbyshire Times* online.'

Sawyer pumped his hand, suppressing a wince at Cabrera's potent cologne: soapy, woody, a hint of rum. 'I wouldn't believe everything you read.'

Cabrera peered at Sawyer with furrowed brow, then broke out a broad smile. 'Even if you wrote it? Well, ghost-wrote, I suppose.' He walked back to his desk and switched on an electric fan mounted on the windowsill. 'It was an article I found online. An interview you gave. I apologise for the lack of view down here.'

'It's okay if you're into pavements,' said Sawyer.

Cabrera nodded, studying Sawyer. 'I prefer the tidal marshes of Andalucía. Basement flats attract rodents, too.' He screwed up his face and leaned across the desk. 'I'm with Winston Smith, aren't you?'

'You should get a cat,' said Conway, taking a seat next to Sawyer on a two-seater Chesterfield beneath a tall, overstocked bookcase.

Cabrera waved a hand. 'Cats would be in my Room 101. They put me on the top floor at the Cromwell. I can see here from there, but not there from here.'

She smiled. 'You're looking well, Dr Cabrera. I love what you're wearing.'

He reeled, mock shocked. 'You *love* it? My partner here, Dr Grosz, takes a different view.'

'White Stripes,' said Sawyer, nodding at Cabrera's tomato-red jacket and trousers over a black polo neck.

Cabrera looked down at himself, confused.

'He means the band,' said Conway.

'Ah. I'm afraid if it isn't jazz, we're speaking different languages.' He nodded to a custom corner unit with a stacked hi-fi, turntable and upright stack of vinyl records. 'I'm a fan of your orange tie, Detective Sawyer. We're kindred for primaries. There's too much grey in the world, I feel.' He settled into his seat. 'You also have an orange Mini, yes? I saw it in the article.' Cabrera took a thick file from a drawer and opened it. 'The colour predilection. I assume that's one of the few things you remember about your mother?'

Sawyer glanced at Conway.

Cabrera looked up. 'I saw a photograph of her, in another article. A beautiful woman. An appalling tragedy.'

'She was murdered,' said Sawyer. 'The Aberfan disaster was a tragedy.'

'Of course. And her beauty was undeniable, but irrelevant.' He patted the file. 'You do have quite a situation here. Two families. Home invasions.' He looked up. 'He's a bold one.'

'We were wondering about parallels,' said Conway, 'with the Taylor Maxwell case.'

'The psychopathology feels distinct to me. Do you have evidence of a specific connection?'

'What does Maxwell read?' said Sawyer. 'Does he

write? Draw? Any artistic expression? Is he still into the occult? Demons? Church of Satan? Crowley?'

'I'm not aware of his current reading habits, but I have seen all the materials he's dredged up since his incarceration. Spidery drawings, horrendous poetry, etchings on his skin. I see nothing meaningful there. And his interest in the occult at the time of the murders was instilled many years earlier, by abusive parents.' Cabrera took out another file. 'The scale of Mr Maxwell's childhood abuse is truly nauseating. His father held... gatherings at the family home. There's some debate about his mother's complicity, but he would certainly have been routinely exposed to adult sexuality in his most formative childhood years.' He opened the file and browsed. 'It's a wonder he survived at all.'

'Is Maxwell aware of the Carter and Prior murders?'

'If he is, then he hasn't mentioned it to me.'

'Are his parents still alive?' said Conway.

'No. His mother died a few years after his imprisonment and his father soon after.' Cabrera knitted his fingers and rested his hands on top of his head, remaining upright in his chair. 'Around the time of his crimes, Maxwell visited his father in his care home and attempted to sneak broken glass into his food.' He held Sawyer's eye. 'Mr Maxwell is as much of a victim as the people he murdered, Mr Sawyer. But I will not be recommending him for release.'

'Do you have any insight into his victim selection?' said Conway. 'Motivation? Escalation?'

Cabrera laughed. 'Oh, he's pure central casting.

Animal cruelty, bedwetting, pyromania. Given the violence and chaos of his early life, it would be a wonder if he *didn't* cover at least two of the classic markers. As far as I understand, though, his adult victims were easy pickings. Sex workers, homeless. From the interviews, he's revealed little about his psychopathology, but his early offences escalated from petty violence to serious violence, then rape.' He pushed the files aside. 'I'm intrigued, DI Conway. Does DCI Hatfield feel you're incapable of arresting this character without the help of DI Sawyer?'

Conway glared at him. 'No. It's just that... DI Sawyer has had a lot of experience with some quite extreme cases, and—'

'He seemed like such a normal man,' said Cabrera. *'Kept himself to himself. You would never think, to look at him...* Our inner terrors rarely manifest externally. Wouldn't you agree, Detective Sawyer?'

'Yes. And there's no bad seed. Just rotten soil.'

Cabrera startled, delighted. 'I couldn't agree more. I have a colleague who has written about her theory of the five-number combination lock of psychology. The stressors align, and the lock springs. The first two numbers are socio-political, a reflection of attitudes to masculinity, vulnerability, poverty.'

'Most violence is committed by poor young males,' said Sawyer.

'Indeed. And the second two numbers are specific to the individual. Childhood adversity, substance misuse, abuse. The final number invokes an act of harm or cruelty. There's something in the victim's action which has meaning only to the perpetrator. A gesture, a phrase, a smile. How does it speak to the person's life and experiences, their story, their self-narrative? So, with your killer here, whom we assume can only meet his needs through observing the suffering of others, you need to find this context in his self-narrative.' He slapped a palm down on the desk, making both Sawyer and Conway jump. 'What was it in his life and experience that warped his responses to such a catastrophic degree that a stranger's pain becomes the source of his pleasure? Given your role and history, Detective Sawyer, I wonder if your own lock has ever been sprung? Have you experienced a degree of pleasure in the administration of suffering to a perpetrator because something in their actions speaks to your own pain? And this is not necessarily a criticism. The urge for destruction is a creative impulse.'

Sawyer thought for a moment. 'I'm not a destroyer, Dr Cabrera. I'm a displacer.'

'You channel your turmoil, yes? Into sport? Sex? Hedonism?'

'I have a wooden workout dummy. I make it suffer for my art.'

Cabrera ran his fingertips across both eyes. 'You have extraordinary defences. It's clear you've cast yourself as survivor, not victim. I concur.' He leaned forward, scrutinising Sawyer like a child with a captured bug. 'Many of us experience the deaths of both parents, but few witness it.'

Conway shuffled in her seat. 'Doctor—'

'Taylor Maxwell is a sexual sadist. Other people's suffering is his motivation. Just another link in a long chain of abuse. Another banal monster hiding in plain sight. He could do that because of the way we have tabloidised his breed as sick, evil. But of course, this is just distancing. It helps us feel better about what we know is the truth. That they aren't so far from ourselves. One bad decision too many, a setback too far, a difficult start in life.'

'They hide in the darkness created by society,' said Sawyer.

'And it's up to people like us to bring them out into the light. But...' Cabrera glanced up and out of his window at a shadow from a passer-by on the street above. 'But we see too much, don't we, Detective Sawyer? It makes us blind. So we have to study by a dark lamp.' He leapt to his feet and poured a glass of water from a jug on a side table. He waggled the glass at Sawyer and Conway; both shook their head. 'But, you know, for me, there's nothing remarkable about these people. Nothing to study and learn from. They are aberrations. Invaders in the body of humanity. And the police should function more like doctors. Rooting out the disease, excising it.' He sat down, drank the whole glass in two large gulps. 'I don't treat patients any more. I prefer to help the police find these people, make the world a better place.'

'But surely the process can be reversed?' said Conway. 'If bad people are made, not born, then they can be unmade. Address the factors that opened the locks.'

Cabrera drummed his fingers against each other. 'Do you believe in rehabilitation? In change?'

She nodded.

'It depends,' said Sawyer.

'For some, perhaps. But I believe there are people for whom the disease runs too deep. Whatever infected them in their formative years is endemic for life. Trauma, no love or affection... And cruelty. Especially cruelty. Some find a way to... *channel* this into legitimate outlets. But there are others for whom this flaw is too strong, and they have to feed it, regardless of the threat to their sanity. And, with crime, their liberty. Perhaps the people who are good at catching these diseased individuals do so because they are examples of the former. Flawed individuals who recognise elements of the disease in themselves and so can identify it in others.' He leaned forward, propped his elbows on the desk, and rested his chin on the backs of his fingers. 'My father fought in the Spanish Civil War, where many terrible atrocities were carried out by the local populations. Everyday people, not hardliners or zealots. He said that it made him realise how thin the line is between a socialised individual and the animal within. Some learn that to keep functioning they must access a dreadful emptiness, a numbness. A void.'

'An abyss,' said Sawyer.

'Yes. And this is not the abyss staring back at them. They *are* the abyss. They become it. Some accept it, learn to live with it as a background texture. Others indulge the void. They feed it, telling themselves that it's the only way to survive.' Cabrera tapped one of the files. 'Your suffocator friend has become a master of this process. He will have worked on it all his life, Detectives. He has rebuilt himself. There's no trace of the person who existed before his locks were sprung. He's a feeder, and he's worked up quite an appetite.'

'So why kill the women, the mothers, differently?' said Sawyer.

Cabrera opened the file and sifted through the crime scene photos. 'If the victims are proxies for his own suffering, then perhaps he's visiting a unique punishment on the women. He relates to their distress differently. As you know all too well, Detective Sawyer. Boys and their mothers. It's complicated.'

10

Farrell trudged up through the Little Mill beer garden—shoulders rounded, unhurried—and set down his half-pint on the table near the brook.

'I'm fine, thanks,' said Moran, turning to face him.

Farrell sat opposite, made a dismissive sound with his wet lips. 'I'm sorry, but am I wearing a waiter's uniform? You're on duty, anyway.'

An attempt at a smile from Moran. 'It's okay. I don't like to drink in the daytime. I spend the afternoon in and out of the toilet.'

Farrell winced. 'A delightful image.' He took a long drink of lager, not troubled by the silence.

Moran swiped at his forehead. 'Hotter than Satan's arsehole today.'

'You're a poet, Ross.' Farrell looked over his shoulder at the lunchtime crowd, the tables overloaded with rowdy office cliques. 'Did you get here early? If we were a romantic couple, this would be *our* table now.'

Moran took off his glasses and ran a rolled-up shirt sleeve across his face. 'I did bring a girl here once. Woman, I suppose. Probably a decent ride, but I don't remember a moment when she didn't have a Benson & Hedges in her mouth.'

Farrell shook his head. 'Women who smoke are almost as bad as women who swear. So, where are we? Give me a *sit-rep*, if you'd be so kind.'

Moran replaced his glasses. He laid his phone on the table, opened Google Maps, and pinch-zoomed to a patch of green. 'Woodland near Mayfield. About ten minutes' drive from the old abattoir. I had our IT guy trawling CCTV within a ten-mile radius. It's a small patch, but isolated and overgrown enough. The dark Fiesta pops up at a junction nearby, then appears driving in the opposite direction two hours later. I did think about comparing the suspension depth, but the images weren't good enough.'

Farrell leaned in to the screen, sloshed his drink around. 'I'm feeling a bit like Dr Watson here.'

'But I did get a reg, and a name.' Moran opened up his photo app and enlarged an image of a fierce-looking man in his mid-forties. His blond hair was slicked back into a short ponytail that poked around the side of his muscular neck. He scowled into the camera, pinhole eyes blazing beneath an overhanging brow. 'Meet Austin Fletcher. This is not a guy who's gone for a night drive because he's having trouble sleeping. Dutch father, English mother. Ex-Marine. Kicked out of the SAS for laying one on his CO. Sexual assault allegations. Has... associations with your boss up in Manchester.'

Farrell sat up. 'What?'

'Part-time Deputy Mayor. Full-time toerag.'

Farrell's eyes flared. 'Dale Strickland is not my boss, Ross.'

'Maybe not your line manager, but—'

'So, Sawyer meets Fletcher at the abattoir. There's some kind of struggle with Walton, whose DNA is all over the knife that was found. Walton dies. Sawyer leaves. Fletcher drives the body off to the woods, disposes of it...'

'Then drives right back.'

'What's Fletcher's association with Strickland?'

'They went to the same college. And he's been seen with him on a couple of occasions.' Moran leaned forward, lowered his voice. 'If we can find Walton's body, we might be able to prove Sawyer's involvement.'

Farrell nodded. 'He would have to park the car somewhere near to a good disposal spot. It shouldn't be difficult to narrow down the search.'

'Still a lot for two people. If I could sell Buxton on it, we could put together some resources. We need Keating in the loop.'

'No, we don't. I'm in exile, but I can cash in a couple of favours. Independent contractors. GPR.'

Moran slipped his phone in his pocket and shuffled over in his seat, ducking away from the direct sunlight. 'GPR won't find us the body.'

'No. But it can detect changes in shallow soil. We can

narrow the search to sections that have been disturbed in that way. Then bring in the dogs.'

'But even if we do find Walton's body, it'll be tough to pin it on Fletcher. Even tougher to bring Sawyer into the mix. And I don't imagine Fletcher is an easy man to track down.'

Farrell jabbed his little finger into his nose and indulged in a lengthy rummage while Moran watched in horror. 'Maybe there's another way.'

11

Sawyer angled the dressing table mirror to capture his shirtless reflection. He slowed his breathing and eased into the first Wing Chun Kung Fu form, *Sil Lum Tao* ('Little Idea'). A series of prescribed movements to condition his arms, and reinforce the system principles: economy of movement, directness, efficiency.

He executed the moves with precision and rigour, arms arcing through the air, chopping and slicing. He worked at double intensity to compensate for the lack of his wooden man training dummy. The process embedded the form, but was also meditative, greying out the impersonal surroundings, clearing the waters of his mind.

I LIVE.

Did the killer see himself as a survivor? Was he celebrating that? Did he feel he'd been dormant as a non-killer but was now alive as a killer?

Sweat ran down Sawyer's back, tracing the contours of his muscles, running through his tattoo: a Greek inscription meaning *true to his own spirit*.

He found the centreline, directed his movements along it, pivoting, punching.

Cabrera's words came through. *Boys and their mothers.*

Why did the killer want the women to witness the horror?

A shaft of afternoon sun slipped in through the open window and found the corner of the mirror. Sawyer checked his movement, paused. He tried to swallow, but it was difficult, as if something had blocked his throat.

Keep moving.

But the movement wouldn't come. He saw the action in his mind's eye, but the message would not travel from brain to limb.

The sunlight, smothered by cloud.

A shirtless man, in front of a mirror, willing his arms to rise and move.

Move.

The man sinks to one knee, breathing too fast.

Run.

And now his legs won't raise him upright.

Don't look back.

A woman's voice. A barking dog.

A dark movement in the corner of the bedroom. Too big to be a spider. And yet, it crawls up, across the ceiling.

Just a shadow.

The man lies on the floor, breathing slowing, listening to his phone ringtone: a looping arpeggio. Nineties-style synthesiser.

Just fatigue.

Sawyer willed his arm to push him upright and, at last, it obeyed.

He slumped forward onto the bed, sweating, gulping at breaths.

He raised his head to the ceiling: white, spiderless.

I LIVE.

Sawyer wiped his brow, accepted the video call.

'Well, hello there.'

The woman on-screen wore large sunglasses. As Sawyer composed himself, she nudged them down her nose and peered over the top, revealing owlish, hazel eyes.

Sawyer coughed, caught his breath. 'Mags.'

'Jake, you could at least remember to dress for our calls. Have you just got out of the shower?'

'No. Just working out. It's hot here.'

Maggie Spark ruffled her rust-red hair, cut shorter than usual. 'That's not a fight you want to start. I'm in Greece, remember?'

Sawyer took a glass of water from his bedside table. 'How are the Greeks?'

'No gifts. Although I think one of the waiters had his eye on Mia. Freddy was keen to point this out, of course.'

'She can't help it. The hormones are taking charge.'

'She actually said, "Eww". Like an American teenager.'

He pulled on a faded grey *Clockwork Orange* T-shirt. 'Canadian.'

'What?'

'That's from *Schitt's Creek*. Canadian show. One of the DVDs I watched up in the Lakes.'

Sawyer took a drink of water; it was still a struggle to swallow.

The face of a blonde teenage girl loomed into Maggie's screen from the side. She lifted her sunglasses and waved. 'Hello, Uncle Jake! Freddy can't come because he's eating, *as usual*. Bye, Uncle Jake!'

He laughed. 'Hello, Mia. Goodbye, Mia.'

Maggie paused, then leaned close to the screen. 'Wish you were here.'

'So do I.'

'I even think you could cope with the food. Simple, but amazing. You get grapes after meals, though. They're not big on dessert.'

'Haven't eaten much since I got here.'

Maggie tipped back her head, admonishing. 'That's right. Not a lot of options in *London*.'

'The case isn't exactly appetising. Family annihilator.'

She held up a hand. 'Spare me the details, Jake. I don't want it in my head. We're washing all of that off for a week.'

'In the azure Aegean?'

'Mia and Freddy go into the sea while I watch, but I stick to the villa pool. I know what's in the water and I don't have to pay to lie down and read my book.'

Sawyer lay back on the bed, his body aching from the workout. He held the phone at arm's length in front of his face. 'How are the dogs?'

'With Justin. He's house-sitting. He's taken some time off, after the... thing.'

Sawyer nodded. His eyelids drooped. 'He's lucky.'

'He was stupid. How is the cat?'

'Walker is popping in every day. I offered to pay him, but he wouldn't have it.'

A siren wailed outside. Soon after: shouts, as a heavy vehicle clattered past.

'Can you hear that?' said Sawyer.

'Big city. Everyone wants to be there. Until they're there. Then they want a nice place in the country.'

The pillow, cool and yielding.

'You know what I miss the most?'

Maggie raised her eyebrows.

Sawyer smiled. 'Second most.'

'The Bakewell tart at The Nut Tree?'

'The silence. The stillness. London is all motion, action. Sound and fury. It's like it's afraid to stand still in case someone takes a shot at it.'

Maggie opened a jar and rubbed something into her cheeks. 'You're tired. Are you sleeping?'

'Sort of. Different quality of sleep, though. More functional than nourishing. Last couple of weeks, it was like my mind had settled down, slowed down. And now, here, it's up and *moving* again. I feel like an overstimulated child.'

'Afraid to stand still? Keep yourself in balance, Jake. It's just a case. Just a job.'

'Yeah, yeah. Stay out of the misery.'

Maggie leaned closer to the screen until only her eye was visible. 'This is helping, though?'

'Keeping an eye on me...' Sawyer's head sunk deeper, the pillow muffling the noise outside. 'Yeah...' His eyes flickered shut. 'Always helps...' The arm holding the phone wilted.

Maggie waited a moment, then replaced the lid on her jar. She sent a sleeping face emoji with an orange heart and a single *X,* and disconnected the call.

———

And he was a child, reaching up to the dining table from his chair, to his toast and jam.

A chubby young boy sat opposite, scraping his spoon around the edge of his cornflakes, churning the milk.

A tall, broad-shouldered man stood by the door, wriggling into a tight police uniform. He pointed at the bowl. 'Breakfast, Mikey. School in five.' He scowled down at his other son. 'Is that all he's having?'

A slender young woman turned from the sink with a swish of long inky-black hair. 'That's all he'll eat. He wouldn't have an egg.'

He pouted, crunched into his toast. 'But it isn't right. It's *stealing*. From the chickens.'

A Jack Russell dog burrowed at something by the table leg.

'Jake, you'll get scurvy.' The man smoothed down his uniform and reached for the woman. She submitted to a chaste kiss. 'And the chickens don't mind us taking their eggs. I'm a policeman, remember. I know what's right and what's wrong.'

The woman turned away.

He knew the next part.

She turned back, and there was no Harold and no Michael and no Henry. Just the fear in her luminous eyes, as she gazed over his shoulder, as if alert to some threat behind him.

As usual, he resisted the turn, but knew it would come, and there would be nothing there, and he would return to a version of the world his mother had no part in.

A melody cut through; a synthesiser line, rising and falling in arpeggio.

And he was back.

The thrumming traffic. The evening air, lukewarm.

The room had darkened. Light glowed from somewhere off to the left; his phone, still in his hand, slumped close to the edge of the bed.

Sawyer raised himself out of the sunken pillow and answered the call.

'Are you nearly there?' Male voice, estuary accent.

He leapt up. 'No, I'm here. Are you there?'

'This is a bit fucking existential, Sawyer. I've had a long day chasing paedos.'

'Sorry, Max. I'll get the Tube. Half an hour?'

'No, you won't. District is down. Just drive. Over the

bridge. Stick your car on Fulham Park Road, round the corner from the bar.'

He gathered his keys, wallet. 'You make "over the bridge" sound so simple. A few hundred other people might have the same idea.'

'Yeah. Well. You're not in Kansas any more.'

12

Max Reeves split open a packet of Walkers cheese and onion crisps and laid it on the centre of the table. 'They had Kettle Chips but I assume you still have your proley tastes?'

Sawyer dug out a handful and picked them out of his open palm. 'You've got London ways, Max.'

Reeves balked on his beer. 'I fucking hope so. I am a Londoner, after all.' He took out a packet of Marlboro Lights and a burnished gold Zippo lighter.

Sawyer raised an eyebrow.

'I'll nip out for one while you talk to Poppy.'

Reeves was burly, borderline heavy, but he dressed like a man who had made peace with his metabolism: a well-cut grey suit, good shirt but no tie, thick grey-black hair with matching full beard. He had a prominent nose, whisky-blushed and crooked from an old break.

Sawyer looked around The Little Blue Door cocktail bar. Reeves had bagged a carpeted mini snug, with three curve-backed armchairs surrounding a low wooden table and red leather footstool. Midnight-blue walls with wooden panelling, framed Walter Kupfer prints, arcane knick-knacks. A tall glass-framed cabinet sat in the corner, displaying classic model cars on the lower shelf and a silver ram's head above. Reed diffusers fragranced the room with a smoky leather essence.

Reeves smiled. 'A far cry from Ye Olde Man And A Dog tavern, eh? Shall I shut us in?'

The snug door at Reeves's shoulder lay open to a rowdy west London dinner crowd: corporate types nursing bottles of craft beer. Most wore perma-grins, heads tilted back, nobody too far north of thirty. They crowed and bellowed at each other, competing with a thunderous retro soundtrack. Billy Idol, Flock of Seagulls, Frankie, Bananarama.

Sawyer nodded. 'Yes, please. Is it eighties night?'

'You don't miss much, do you?' said Reeves, swinging the door shut. 'Modern pop music is shit, ain't it, though? They put that fucking Auto-Tune all over it 'cos nobody can sing. It's like covering bad food with salt and calling it good.'

'Streaming generation, I suppose,' said Sawyer, jiggling the ice cubes in his Coke. 'They're used to having the history of music in their pockets. No need to distinguish between old and new. Everything, all the time.' He sipped his drink. 'So, how do you know Poppy? Do I want to know?'

Reeves shrugged. 'Few years back. After that Radlett thing. I knew her from the parties. She helped with the fallout. Steady with her, Sawyer. She's a fierce one. Doesn't suffer fools.'

'I hate that expression.'

He grinned. 'I know. Hey. How did things go with that Fletcher geezer? Since you're still breathing, I assume he lost interest?'

'We came to an arrangement.'

Reeves eyed him. 'That's a hell of a euphemism.'

'No. We really did. It was a robust negotiation, but we got there in the end. So, you're working Vice? That sounds like a punishment.'

'Nah. It's the good fight. They split things up into units. Terrorism, trafficking. I do the paedos. Online grooming. Preventative, ideally. Proactive policing. You know the score. Follow the red flags. Head off the harm before it arrives. But I do tweak the truth a bit when people ask me what I do.'

Sawyer looked up at the wall-mounted TV behind him. *Some Like It Hot* with the sound turned down, subtitles on. 'I suppose, "Hello. I work in the Paedophile and Child Pornography Unit" doesn't dazzle the ladies.'

'I'm surprised they've dragged you down here to work on the Carter and Prior murders. Is it a stunt posting, after that Bowman business? Lob the big fish back in the wild waters? A dose of urban reality.'

'Maybe Keating has got pictures of Hatfield.'

Reeves attempted another sip of his beer, balked again. 'Fuck's sake. Thank you very much for *that* internal movie.'

'Hatfield wants me to do the head work. Focus on

the why, while his DCs work on the how and who. Have you had anyone in for roughing-up sex workers? Strangulation, suffocation, restricting air?'

'Like I say, I'm mainly about the kids, these days. We get a lot of nightmare parental abuse in that area, but that's for the power and domination, mainly. No direct sex stuff.' Reeves drained his glass and clunked it down on the table. He leaned forward, elbows on knees. 'Nice and neat, though, don't you think? All the mess you caused, then shipped off on a glorified consult job, over the hills and far away.'

'By "mess", you mean—'

'I know, I know. You got the collars. Feels like more, though.'

'Keating said Hatfield's resource was stretched. He's my old gaffer.'

Reeves leaned in. 'You planning to look up your ex? The blonde CSO.'

'Sheena?'

'That's the one. I remember you saying she liked her eighties music.' He leered. 'She'd like it in here. Old time's sake, eh?'

'Revisiting the past isn't a good look for me.'

The snug door opened and a young woman entered, followed by the Pet Shop Boys' 'Being Boring'. She closed the door behind her, pushed her long auburn hair over one shoulder and strode across to Reeves, who sprang to his feet and embraced her.

'Look at you, Max, in your secret little boys' room.'

She hitched her sunglasses onto her forehead and air-kissed him on both cheeks.

'You already know all my secrets.'

The woman shook her head and looked up to the TV. 'You wouldn't say that if I did. Oh! I love this film.'

Reeves grinned and scooped up his cigarettes and lighter. 'Jake, this is Poppy Fuller. Poppy, Detective Inspector Jake Sawyer.'

Fuller switched her attention to Sawyer, shrugging off a cropped denim jacket to reveal a fitted black dress. 'Max has told me all about you, Jake.' She embraced him, too, but held the kisses. 'Apparently, I need to keep a close eye on my belongings.' She tossed a black leather clutch onto the footstool.

'I told her about your pocket-picking thing,' said Reeves, heading for the door.

Fuller took Reeves's seat. 'I take it that isn't your most celebrated talent, Jake?'

Sawyer sat. 'I'm in the top five per cent on the global high score table of *Tiny Wings*.'

She regarded him for a moment, then glanced at Reeves. 'He doesn't look like a geek.'

'Geeks look normal, these days,' said Reeves, exiting. 'Sorry, but I'm gasping. I'll leave you to get acquainted.'

'Are you drinking?' said Sawyer.

Fuller waved at his glass. 'Since you're not, I'll pass. Are you teetotal or on duty?'

'Never liked the taste.'

'I know what you mean. Warm summer night, though. Nothing like an ice-cold beer.'

'Or a Strawberry Mivvi.'

She nodded, eyes wide. 'I haven't had an ice lolly for ages. What's the one with the hundreds and thousands?'

'Fab.'

'Yes!' She leaned back, crossed her legs. 'You're quite the expert. I'm sensing a misspent youth.'

'Just the stealing and videogaming.'

'And sugar worship.'

He took a drink. 'Are you working tonight?'

Fuller laughed. 'No. This is me dressed down. Office heels. I bring out the stiletto calf boots when I'm on nights. Depends on the clients. How are you with sex work? Twitchy moral compass? Leering liberal?'

Sawyer shrugged. 'Depends on how you acquire the clients.'

'I run my own affairs. No brothels or pimps. No street stuff. But you're not interested in vanilla, I hear.'

'I'm more of a Neapolitan man.'

She laughed. 'You're not the typical copper type.'

'In what way?'

'Sense of humour, for one. How are you getting on with the big city?'

'I couldn't eat a whole one.'

'Don't give me the farm boy thing. You're from Manchester, right?'

'Derbyshire.'

Fuller winced. 'It's all The North to me. Is it really as grim as they say?'

'Some parts of Stockport could give Peckham a run for its money.'

She took a phone out her bag and laid it on the table. 'Sorry to be rude, but I have to keep an eye on my messages. I've got a new client. Text only. We used to do live cuckold play with his wife, but then she left him for another woman.'

'Is that worse than leaving him for another man?'

'Oh, I think so. Don't you?'

Sawyer pondered for a second. 'Yes. You've turned them away from the whole idea of men.'

Fuller laughed, fiddled with her phone. 'Max said you were interested in restraint play.'

'Not personally. Just a hunch about a case I'm working.'

She tapped out a message, raising her eyes to him. 'It can get pretty serious. Not just paddles and gimp masks.'

'Where would you go if you were... restraint-curious? To try it out. Test your limits.'

Fuller put down the phone, closed her eyes in thought. 'Plenty of clubs to try. Not the mainstream places. More private. Heavily vetted, invite only. You know the deal. They haven't changed much. Big houses on the fringes. Middle-aged husband and wife owners. Business in the week, pleasure at weekends.' She opened her eyes. 'Didn't you work with Max on the Radlett murder? Few years back.'

'Sort of. Do you know any places around west London? Hammersmith? Barnes?'

'A couple.'

'Have you heard about any recent unusual incidents?

A punter pushing it too far with restraint, breath play? Getting a warning or thrown out, maybe.'

She shook her head. 'You wouldn't really get that at a party. It's a closed scene. Everyone involved would go in with eyes open. It's not something you just spring on someone. There's a place up near Heathrow which runs a night called Kinks & Queens. That's a bit more mix and match.'

'Queens?' said Sawyer.

'It's fluid. Not exclusively straight, but by no means gay. I suppose they came up with the title first and it was too good to change for clarity. They assign various rooms to different tastes. It's a good way to meet potential new partners who are into the same thing. The woman who runs it, Mistress Zhia, is a pro dominatrix, and much bigger on the kink scene. She might have heard something or be able to help with the standard gateways, give you a bit more on specialist services.' Fuller reached over and took a sip from Sawyer's glass. 'If I asked about the case you're working on, could you tell me?'

'No. If I asked you about the party, could you tell me where it is?'

She pursed her lips. 'I could do better than that. I could take you there. Guest night on Saturday.'

'Blindfolded?'

'That's extra.' She leaned in, whispered. 'You'd need to be *undercover*, though. They are suspicious of police.'

'I'll be on my best behaviour.'

'You'd have to be.' Fuller's phone tinkled. She picked it up, typed something. 'I have a reputation to uphold.'

'I assume nobody wears enough to have their pockets picked, anyway.'

Fuller smiled, continued typing. 'It's formal to start with, but later on, it can get wild. C'mon, *Detective*. Loosen up a little. You don't have to take part. You can just watch.' Her eyes lifted from the screen. 'You might learn something.'

13

Sawyer threaded the Mini back into a spot by the security booth and killed the engine. He opened the passenger window a couple of inches and tuned in to the chatter of drinkers and diners on Putney Wharf.

He took out his phone, navigated to his secure cloud folder exported from HOLMES, and opened a video file. Dora Carter, scrambling up the stairs. Ponytail. Greenish-blue hair.

'If this gets posted, we are talking instant execution, okay? No arrest, no trial.'

The frame skipped; a ragged edit.

'No fucking mercy.'

Freeze-frame on Dora's face, crumpled in anger.

An animated arrow prodded at Dora from the side.

Caption: *MY SISTER.*

More arrows around her head.

Caption: *MY SISTER'S GREEN HAIR.*

The video resumed, jumped again.

Dora disappearing into the girls' private bathroom.

Frame skip.

The image shook as Dora tried to close the door, Shannon pushing it into the gap.

Brief shot of Dora inside the bathroom.

Toilet, bath. Pink and purple towels. Yellow walls. Deep shelf of toiletries.

'You look like someone sneezed in your hair.'

The video ended. Blank screen.

Both families' devices and social media had been plundered and scrutinised, hardware and software. No hits on potentially harmful contacts or websites. Dora had an illicit Instagram account where she followed a few seedy profiles, but nothing troubling. Shannon's TikTok was mostly Taylor Swift, viral challenges, duets. A few shaky pans of the ocean from a beach in France. She'd recently searched for information on laxatives and diuretics: red flags for bulimia ideation.

Sawyer pocketed the phone, closed the window, risked a peek in the rear-view mirror. No ghosts.

As he walked to the lift, Milan opened the security booth side door and called out. 'Hey, lawman. Caught any bad guys yet?'

Sawyer held up a hand. 'Got them on the run.'

14

Leon Stokes steadied himself, glanced up, and swung into the ball, scooping it into the chipping net.

'Short game's gone up a gear,' said Boyd Cannon, taking a seat in a spectator chair at the side of the bay.

Stokes snorted. 'Couldn't get much worse. Why can I make these shots here but when I get on the course it all turns to shit?'

Cannon scrubbed at his beard. 'Maybe your practice is too holistic. Take ten balls to work on balance, ten on accuracy, ten on power. Don't do it all here. Put it together on the course.'

Wes Peyton and Jakub Malecki walked out from the driving range club house and hovered behind Stokes. He nodded, then replaced his sand wedge with a driver and set a new ball onto the tee.

'Fancy a round, Wes?' said Cannon. 'They've got crazy golf here, too.'

'Not into it. Old man's game.'

Stokes took a couple of practise swings. 'It's the hardest game. Any idiot can hoof a football into a twenty-four-foot space.'

'They often do,' said Peyton, 'while wearing a sky-blue shirt.'

Stokes launched the ball from the tee with a solid contact. It soared, travelling straight and true to the driving green, coming to rest at the far edge. 'What are you, Jakub? Warsaw Academicals?'

'Chelsea.'

Cannon turned his head. 'You were all-in for West Ham last week.'

Malecki shrugged. 'I like winners.'

'Glory hunting,' said Peyton.

Stokes balked. 'This from a City fan? Where were you when you were shit?'

'On the Kippax Stand with my dad and Eddie. One of my uncles played golf for a few years. I used to watch him when I was a kid. I was so bored I used to chuck rocks at the pigeons in the car park. He did his back in and went on to bowls. Another old man's game.'

Stokes set up another ball. 'It might have escaped you, Wes, but I'm not ready to retire yet.' He hit the shot, slicing it. '*Bollocks.*'

'Doyle's been in touch,' said Cannon. 'Your visitor. Full name is Curtis Mavers.'

Stokes rolled another ball into play with the face of his club. 'Doyle's goon mentioned a Wilmot.'

'Adds up,' said Cannon. 'Wilmot's on the register. He's in Strangeways at the moment. VPU.'

Stokes nodded, stared down at his ball, tapping it back and forth. He turned his gaze to Malecki.

'Beast Wing,' said Malecki. 'It's easier. We have friends there.'

'So, this is the death wish double act helping themselves to our money.' Stokes set himself up for the shot.

'Mavers is a bad, bad boy,' said Cannon. 'GBH, assault, burglary, weapons possession, theft. His younger sister Jayne got turned on to smack by a boyfriend when she was training as a nurse. Dropped out a couple of years ago, OD'd. Mavers kneecapped the boyfriend with a cricket bat. He was about to throw him off the fifth floor balcony of his flat block when the coppers turned up.'

Stokes turned his back on them and stared out across the sunlit driving range. 'It's my birthday next week. I've got my little heart set on a private party at my place, with Curtis Mavers as the guest of honour. I'm *really* curious about where Detective Jake Sawyer fits into this, and why Mavers felt the need to mention his name.' He turned and took a seat next to Cannon. 'Hold the cake. Talk to your doctor friend, Jakub. Find out Mavers's blood group and bring a transfusion. Let's make it a special occasion.'

'I spoke to Eddie,' said Peyton. 'He says he's heard of this Sawyer. Quite a while back, at a pub in Matlock. Some of his boys were knocking a stray dog about. A vet saw it and took them on, telling them to stop. So they fucked him up...' He sniggered. 'He only goes and gets his old man on them. So, this guy comes in, and Eddie's about to shut him up, too, when this copper turns up and drags him outside. He tells Eddie he knows the pub is a base and if he sees any of them again... yada, yada, yada. Eddie was already a face. Sawyer would have known, and he didn't have back-up, no tools.'

'So, he's a psycho,' said Cannon.

Stokes played a drum pattern on his knees. 'I like him already.'

15

Sawyer hustled through the platform crush and coiled his hand through the standing strap opposite a pale middle-aged man in a crumpled suit, head lolling. As the carriage filled up, the man startled and leapt to his feet, just about making it out of the doors as they closed. Sawyer looked around, then sat down, catching a whiff of stale sweat.

A student type with sunglasses wedged up into his unruly blond hair moved into the space Sawyer had vacated and smiled down at him. 'That's your day off to a good start, mate.'

'*Ladies and gentlemen!*'

A tall young man barged into the centre of the standing commuters and held on to the overhead rail with both hands.

'Ladies and gentlemen, I hope you're having a good morning. I love you all and we have to return to living morally.' The train moved off, and he raised his voice to compensate, aiming his words into the air above the passengers. 'Our children are growing up with no sense of right and wrong.'

Sighs, exasperated looks, passive-aggressive newspaper flaps. The blond man slipped in a pair of AirPods and focused on his phone.

'We will all have to stand before God.'

A woman jammed into the carriage divider waved her hand in the air. 'Give it a rest.'

The man pointed at her. 'No! I will not give it a rest. *I love you all*. I am here to warn you. We will all face His judgement, one day.'

'Nobody wants to hear this,' said Sawyer, standing. 'You should be quiet and let everyone get to work.'

The man laughed. 'Oh! Sorry to disturb your peace, my friend, but these words need to be spoken. We are free to speak our minds in this country.'

'What about our freedom to not have to listen?'

'Quite right,' said the woman.

'Well, if you refuse to hear my message, you can always wear headphones like this gentleman.'

Sawyer nodded, looked around. Many eyes were on him now, raised from phones and tablets. 'And what if I don't have headphones? I have to stick my fingers in my ears until you shut up?'

'My friend. Please consider this. We care more about saving whales than we care about saving unborn children.'

'You say that like it's a bad thing.'

The man reeled. 'Are you serious?'

Sawyer took a breath. 'Just look around this train and

see if you can tell me one of the top two problems facing humanity today?'

A beat. Someone behind Sawyer shouted, 'Overpopulation!'

He pointed over his shoulder. 'Nailed it. The other is environmental degradation. Climate change, fossil fuels. Look, I'm not going to replace your sermon with one of my own. I've asked you nicely to be quiet so we can enjoy our smelly and crowded journey in peace. So now I'm going to ask less nicely.' He smiled. 'Pretty please. With sugar on top. Shut the fuck up.'

'Whales play a vital role in the marine ecosystem.' An elderly man sitting opposite Sawyer lowered his newspaper and took off his glasses. 'They provide around fifty per cent of our oxygen, sustain fish stocks. And they help combat climate change by the sheer amount of carbon they absorb.'

'They fertilise the ocean,' said a woman next to the preacher. 'Their excrement produces plankton, which sucks up the CO_2.'

The elderly man nodded.

Sawyer stepped forward and spoke to the preacher. 'Yeah. You have every right to choose to express your opinions. I'm just asking you to do it in a place where people also have a choice. To either stop and listen or move along. On the street. Here, there's no choice. Your expression is our oppression.'

Laughs. Scattered applause.

The train slowed for Putney Bridge.

Sawyer continued. 'And you say our children are

growing up with no sense of right or wrong? I'd argue that if we want them to grow up at all, we should be easing the strain on the planet's resources by making fewer of them. So, yeah. Team Whale.'

———

Sawyer took a standing spot at the back of the briefing room, near to Conway, seated and typing into her laptop.

She glanced up at him. 'I spoke to Reeves. Says you're off to some sex party.'

'Business, not pleasure. Lateral enquiries. Exploring the suffocation angle.'

'You really think there's something there?'

Sawyer slurped through the spout of his coffee cup. 'Don't ask, don't get. I have a date with a dominatrix.'

She laughed. 'Be careful not to enjoy it too much.'

'You're annoyed that I haven't invited you.'

Conway stopped typing and looked up at him. 'Not really. Like you said, you work alone. I'm happy to play plausible sidekick if you need, though. I assume you'll be a dentist for the night or something.'

'Do I look like a dentist?'

'Good morning, good morning!'

Hatfield strode out of his office and perched on a desk by the whiteboard. 'Please don't mistake my sunny demeanour for contentment. It's more mild hysteria.'

The detectives stared at him; a few side-eyes.

'At 3:07 this morning, my first granddaughter was born. Nine pounds on the nose. Caesarean.'

A female detective at the front whistled.

Hatfield patted his belly. 'Runs in the family.'

'Congratulations, boss,' said DI McHugh.

The others followed his lead.

'Thank you. Now I have to stay healthy enough to see little Olivia graduate. So, before we start, all best wishes gratefully accepted. But any comedy grandad cards and I'll have you filing ANPR logs for a week. Okay. Talk.'

McHugh spoke up. 'We're confident that there's no connection between the families. No cross-ref hits from HOLMES or any of the aggregators, no lines from FLOs. They were strangers.'

Hatfield pinched his nose, screwed his eyes shut. 'So, how did he select them?'

'Posing as a tradesman?' said a female DC near Conway. 'Stakes them out?'

'That might explain the short time between murders,' said Sawyer. 'He does his legwork, makes a list, plans it all to the second. No margin for error. Maybe he's watched his targets, worked out their routines.'

'Maybe he just knows the area,' said Conway.

Sawyer gazed out at the commuters hurrying across Putney Bridge below. 'And we're happy with the forced entry at both scenes?'

'I'm not happy with it,' said Neil Shah, 'but I'd confirm it as method of entry, yes. Back door locks broken. Marks consistent with a flat-head screwdriver.'

'He stakes out,' said McHugh, 'clocks the routines. Gives it an hour or so after lights out...'

Sawyer nodded, unblinking. 'And both houses had alarm systems?'

'Yeah,' said McHugh. 'Both were deactivated. They're the type where occupants set them live when they leave the house, then shut them down with the code when they come home.'

'A lot of modern systems use electronic key fobs,' said DC Rodgers. 'But the Prior and Carter alarms are a few years old. Still effective, though. They're rigged to the doors so that a quiet alarm sounds for a minute or so. Then, when someone enters the code, they shut down.'

'What if they don't enter the code?' said Hatfield.

'The alarm goes loud, and the monitoring company gets an alert.'

Sawyer took out a packet of Fruit-tella chews, unwrapped one. 'So, the killer must have known the alarms would be deactivated before he broke in.' He flipped the sweet into his mouth. 'Otherwise, the alarm would have gone loud straight away, right?'

Rodgers nodded. 'Right.'

'So,' said Conway, 'as Rowan says, he waits for them to come home and switch off the alarm.'

Hatfield took out a handkerchief and blew his nose. 'And they only activate the alarm when they're not in the house. They don't bother at bedtime.'

'But how does he know that?' said Sawyer, walking out to the front. 'How can he be confident that the alarm isn't active and won't trip when he gets in? Could he have some kind of device that could confirm?'

Eyes turned to Rodgers.

'I haven't heard of that, but I suppose it's possible. The circuit sensors will be magnetic, so he might be able to detect whether the alarm is activated or not.'

'Or disrupt it,' said Sawyer, chewing.

'You going to share those with the class, DI Sawyer?' said McHugh.

'Rodgers,' said Hatfield. 'Look into the alarm systems. Talk to the companies if you have to. How could our man deactivate or disrupt the alarms if he's nerdy enough? And find out who else might have access to the codes. Extended family? Domestics?'

Rodgers dropped her head to a notepad and scribbled.

'A bit more on the compound we found at both scenes,' said Shah. 'It's waterproof. So, a coating of some kind. Black. Popular with rainwear.' He shrugged. 'Seems even more likely it's from his gloves.'

'Or from the camera he's using?' said Sawyer. 'If he's filming.'

Shah shook his head. 'Either way and like I said, it's no good until we have a comparable item.'

'Where are we with the drug?' said Hatfield.

A male DC sitting near Shah cleared his throat. 'There's telazol in there, too. In the incapacitating dose. That's a ketamine derivative, used as an animal anaesthetic by vets and zoos.'

Hatfield clapped his hands together. 'Love that, DC Bryant. DI McHugh, co-ordinate that one with Neil and DC Bryant. Look into vets and zoos. How do they store the drug? Control conditions. Who has access? DI

Conway, cross-ref with abuse incidents, hospital admissions, thefts.'

Sawyer took a seat near the whiteboard. 'I know someone who could help with that.'

Hatfield narrowed his eyes. 'I bet you do. Anything in the Carter TikTok video?'

'Just the girls winding each other up. We saw Dr Cabrera. Some interesting views on criminal justice, and he's clearly in no mood to help Maxwell's pitch for parole. He thinks of him and our new friend as expendable anomalies. Why waste energy on fixing their bad parts when it's cheaper to eliminate the cause of, as he put it, the "disease"?'

'When you look at what the killer did to these people,' said Shah, 'it's hard to argue against that.'

'The courts judge,' said Hatfield. 'We build the cases, gather the evidence. Right. Get busy. DI McHugh, set up a media brief. No gory details, though. Not until we've got him. DI Sawyer...' He nodded to his office and walked away.

Sawyer glanced at Conway, then followed Hatfield inside, closing the door behind him.

Hatfield spun round his chair and crashed down into it. 'I'm cream-crackered, Sawyer. We were all set to go at ten last night, but the kid was too cosy in there. Had to induce, in the end.' He held up his phone, showing a picture of himself clutching a flushed newborn, screaming, face distorted.

Sawyer smiled. 'Hello, cruel world.'

Hatfield sat back in his chair, rolled up his shirt

sleeves and propped both hands on the top of his head, elbows wide. He grinned at Sawyer.

'You're waiting for me to speak first,' said Sawyer.

'I'm waiting for the question. I can't believe it's taking you so long.'

Sawyer smiled, flashing the dimple. He took a seat. 'Okay. Why am I here? And I'm not being philosophical. Supplementary question. What's Cabrera's assessment?'

'Of the case?'

'Of me.'

Hatfield took out a folder. 'I didn't send you to Cabrera for a therapy session.'

'You wanted to know what he knew. About Maxwell.'

Hatfield smiled and slid a few papers out of the folder. 'Still got it, Sawyer. Cabrera's a cantankerous fucker, but completely brilliant. And he's got a dirty great ego.' He whispered. '*Hell of a shagger, too.* Given your reputation, and the presence of a young blonde woman to show off to, I thought he wouldn't be able to resist a strut around.'

'I know something you don't know.'

'Yeah. So, the fact that you *didn't* get that...' Hatfield pushed the papers across to Sawyer. 'It means that I know something *he* doesn't know.' He flopped back in his chair, rubbed at his eyes. 'Also, I've been working on a nice trip for you. It's taken a few days to get clearance.'

'Where and when?'

'To the wilds of Berkshire. This afternoon.'

Sawyer looked up from the papers. 'I'd always hoped I'd stay this side of the Broadmoor gates.'

'I made the Maxwell arrest back in 2003 when I had more up here and less down there.' He pointed to his head and belly. 'I did a placement in Broadmoor when I was a DS. Got pally with one of the psych orderlies. Fella called Everett Asher. He's now the senior on Maxwell's manor. I've kept an eye on Maxwell through Asher for years now. He's been no trouble, worked himself down to medium security. Outgoing mail and packages are all checked, but nobody can screen his incoming. Everett called me a few days after the Prior murders.' He nodded to the papers. 'Those are copies of pictures he took of Maxwell's sketchbook.'

'Is that legal?'

'It's a grey area. Depends on suspicion. So, he made two drawings four days after the Prior murders and another a couple of days after the Carters'. Sawyer. Nobody outside this team knows this detail about the case, and nobody outside this room, apart from Everett, knows about these drawings. *This* is why you're here.'

Sawyer spread the three sheets out across Hatfield's desk. Each showed a series of symbols, rendered in heavy pencil.

ᛁ ᚾᛁᚠᛗ

16

Luka Strickland chested the ball down to his feet. The dumpy boy standing crouched between the goalposts— two orange backpacks—scurried towards him and dived at the ball. But Luka sidefooted it through his legs and turned in celebration, hitching his Liverpool shirt up over his head and raising both index fingers into the air.

'We said you can't shoot that close!' said the dumpy boy, collecting the ball from a bush near the path that ran through the centre of Bakewell Recreation Ground.

'It's called shithousing,' said Luka. 'It's what the Premier League players do. They're all so good that they have to do little things to get a tiny advantage.'

'Yeah,' said one of the other boys. 'Like diving or holding shirts so you can't jump at corners.'

'It's not fair,' said the goalkeeper, underarming the ball out to one of his players.

Luka pushed his floppy blond hair off his forehead and wiped away the sweat with his sleeve. 'No. It's just winning. If you can't win by being fair, do it by being clever.'

The boy ran with the ball along the sideline of the marked football pitch. 'It's not called shithousing. It's called cheating.'

He hoofed the ball infield to one of his two teammates. The game was three versus four, with rush goalie for the three. They all wore shorts and football kit tops. The nine-a-side pitch was a heavy prospect for seven twelve-year-olds in the midday June heat.

Luka chased back; he was the quickest of the group, but he surely couldn't catch the boy with the ball as he sidestepped a defender and closed in on the goal. Luka planted a hand on his shoulder and the boy stumbled, but got a shot away. It sailed high over the head of the goalkeeper and he peeled off to the side, pumping his fists.

'That's over,' said the keeper, heading off to get the ball.

'No way!'

Three older boys rode their e-scooters to the edge of the path and dropped them in a pile in the shade of a gigantic copper beech tree.

The largest—worked out, eyes shaded beneath a flat-peaked baseball cap—headed over to the backpacks, flanked by his two friends.

He called to Luka. 'Room for a few more players, yeah?'

'No. Friends only.'

The boy turned to the other two and hissed a laugh

through his clenched jaw. 'We ain't your *enemy*, fam. C'mon.' He pointed both hands at himself. 'I'm Anton. I'll go midfield. Conner is goalie for his school.' He hitched an arm around the shoulder of his friend with frizzy red hair and matching chin beard. 'He's like, *none shall pass*. Get me? Like fuckin' Dumbledore. And Sameer...' He held up his thumb and forefinger, aimed at a glowering boy in a red bucket hat. 'He's, like, Mo Salah.'

'It's Gandalf,' said Luka.

Anton slowed. 'What is?' Sameer and Conner kept moving, heading for the backpacks. Anton smiled at Luka. Sweet and evil.

'Gandalf says, "You shall not pass!" in the *Lord of the Rings* film. Dumbledore is from *Harry Potter*.'

Anton scowled, dropped his head. He held up a hand. 'My bad. Who's you, then, blondie?'

'My name's Luka. We don't want you to play.'

'Yeah,' said the dumpy boy. 'Leave us alone.'

Conner picked up one of the backpacks and unzipped it.

'Hey!' The midfield boy ran over. 'Leave my stuff alone.'

Sameer held up a stubby folding knife, blade out. 'Y'wanna get *cut*, bro?'

The boy stopped, backed away.

'You're not allowed to have that,' said Luka. 'You can go to prison.'

Anton hissed again. 'Fuck me. You an expert in the law, little man?'

'My dad has been to prison.'

Conner looked up from the backpack, glanced at Anton.

'What for?' said Sameer.

'He beat someone up.'

Anton grinned. 'Yeah? What is he? Fucking cage fighter?'

The dumpy boy turned and ran, off down the path, followed by two of the others.

Conner took a wallet and phone out of the backpack and shoved them into the pockets of his shorts. The midfield boy backed off a few more paces, then turned and followed the others, sprinting hard.

Sameer opened the second backpack, took out a phone and a thin green wallet, and handed them both to Anton, who slid them into his pockets.

'That's mine!' One of the two remaining younger boys ran forward, but stopped when Sameer held up his knife again.

'Back the *fuck* up, bro.'

An adult man and woman walked in through the park gates and headed for the path alongside the football pitch.

'Need to leave,' said Conner.

Anton nodded. 'You go. I'm good.' Conner and Sameer jogged back to the e-scooters. Anton walked over to Luka. 'What you got, blondie?'

'My stuff is at home. Apart from the ball.'

'Check him,' said Conner over his shoulder.

Luka turned the pockets of his shorts inside-out. 'I've

got nothing, but Jude's got ten quid in his pocket.'

The boy who had stopped in his tracks gaped at Luka. 'I haven't!'

Anton squinted at Luka, then Jude. He laughed. 'You've got a friend for life there, bruv.' He laid a hand on Jude's left shoulder and checked his right pocket.

Luka stepped in. 'No. The other one.'

Anton dug his hand into Jude's left pocket. He took out a thin green wallet. Jude snatched it away.

Anton spun round, facing Luka. He checked his own pockets.

'Here's your phone, Jude.' Luka handed the phone over. In the confusion, Jude bolted, running towards the man and woman, shouting something.

'The blond kid took them off you!' called Conner, raising his scooter.

'I got this, too,' said Luka, holding up a knife similar to Sameer's. He backed away, opening the blade.

Anton lunged at Luka.

Luka stumbled but swung the knife around, plunging the blade into the side of Anton's leg.

Anton howled in pain and fury, grabbing the knife and twisting it free, splashing Luka with blood.

'*Hey*!'

The man and woman ran over, onto the pitch.

Conner and Sameer rode away at speed.

Anton dropped to his knee, cursing, pressing bloodied hands onto the wound.

Luka grabbed his ball and ran, laughing and whooping.

17

Farrell glowered at the two men who'd taken the table near the brook. Matching beards, lime-green Lycra, high-end helmets side by side at the end of the table. Two slender, expensive-looking hybrid bikes stood on kickstands behind the bench.

They laughed at something, loud. Farrell winced and took a comb out of his inside pocket.

'Sir.'

Farrell smoothed out his hair, not looking up at Moran as he sat down.

'This place must be raking it in.' Moran sat opposite and settled a cup and saucer on the table. He looked around. 'Not the best perch. Under a tree, near the bins.'

Farrell took out a breath mint. He wetted his thin lips and sucked it in. 'Sorry it's not to your liking. If you could have got here earlier...'

'I was up late at the Mayfield woodland, working with your radar boys.'

'Good to know we got our money's worth. They're sub-contracted to GMP. Retainer.'

Moran blew on his drink. 'You said you'd cover—'

'Of course. But I want my name kept out of it. The location is in Derbyshire, so, depending on what we find, it'll end up on Keating's spreadsheet. I'll take care of it for now. But I'll need to repay the favour when they lift this ridiculous ostracisation.'

'Sir. We need to go official now, with Keating. He'll have my bollocks.'

Farrell narrowed his eyes. 'Who do they think is going to steal those bikes?'

'Sorry?'

For the first time, Farrell glanced at Moran, then back at the two men. 'They're sitting right next to them. Why lock the things together like that?'

Moran shrugged. 'Keeps them upright? Kickstands are basic. And they look like the types who're pretty... close. Maybe they get weepy if their bikes are too far apart.'

Farrell sneered. 'Who do you think goes on top?'

'They take turns, on a strict rota system.' Moran sipped from his cup.

'You seem to know a lot about how it works.'

'You seem to be very interested in how it works.'

Farrell turned his back on the couple and shot a poisonous smile at Moran. He nodded at the cup and saucer. 'Herbal tea?'

'Black coffee. Like I said, I was up late.'

Farrell eyed him, rolling the mint around his mouth.

'And like *I* said, we don't go official with Keating. Not yet. This is off duty. A private investigation. It has to be, for obvious reasons. He'll understand that once we move to the next phase.' He stared at Moran, who set down his cup and took out his phone.

'Recently excavated areas,' said Moran, navigating to an image with a series of layered grey lines, kinked and curved at several points. 'All sub-surface disturbance. The team leader called it "inconsistent geomorphology".'

Farrell leaned in to the image. 'How many?'

'Three significant.'

'Three?'

'If Fletcher did dump Walton there, maybe he split up the pieces and buried them separately. Then he wouldn't have to go too deep with each.'

Farrell screwed up his face. 'And there's no record of official excavation at this site?'

'No. These are rough, not back-filled. Consistent with shallow graves. We surveyed a decent-sized patch of the woods, and it's only a small area. Overgrown and out of the way, though. There's only one dirt track road near the woodland. So he'd need to get close to reduce the distance he'd have to carry the body. Or bodies.'

'We need to get Keating involved. Bring in dogs, dig, ID remains.'

Moran sat back, smiled. 'I'm glad you've had that idea, sir. But, let's say all of this goes well. Keating gets the logic and wants to fast-track the follow-up. He agrees to keep it quiet until we have conclusive IDs. How are we going to point it at Fletcher, and Sawyer?'

'I'll talk to Keating. He's a fisherman. He'll understand. First, though, we move on the IDs, and quick.'

Another loud laugh from the cyclists.

'And then what?' said Moran.

'Then we bait the line.'

18

Sawyer took the scenic route out of Putney, swerving south into the bright afternoon sun, glued to the A3, with Wimbledon Common and Richmond Park hidden on either side by billowing sycamores and converted Edwardian semis. He set his Spotify Favourites playlist to shuffle, and the algorithms obliged, transporting him back to the Peaks by association: Art of Noise, Yeasayer, Friendly Fires.

As the suburbs thinned into the boxy deadlands of New Malden and Surbiton, he called up the phone panel on the Mini's CarPlay and tapped in a number. After a couple of rings, a deep male voice filled the car. Estuary accent.

'Jake Sawyer.'

'Tony Cross. Can you talk? Are you busy?'

'Very well, thanks for asking. How are you?'

Sawyer reached into the glovebox and took out a red Starburst chew. 'Are you in the UK?'

'Just got back. Security gig in France. Please don't tell me you need help with that Fiesta geezer again.'

'I'm in London.'

'What the fuck has dragged you back down there?'

'Consulting on a case. Sort of. Talk to me about telazol.'

Cross blew out a sigh. 'Not a good idea, mate. Safer to get yourself a crack habit.'

Sawyer smiled. 'I know it's used to tranquilise animals. But let's say I'm a psychopath—'

'Finally! A moment of clarity.'

'And I want to use it on humans. How would I get access to it?'

'With great difficulty. It's heavily controlled. When I've been called out by zoos, for dangerous animal response, there's usually one person who signs off all the darting gear. Paper trail would be hard to avoid as it's all individually logged, with monitored usage. They use it in sanctuaries, too. Vets, some pest control. Dangerous dogs, mostly. I've been called on a couple of those. Not the most glamorous.'

'What about the guns that fire darts to administer the tranquiliser?'

Cross clicked his tongue. 'Same, really. Specialist. I've got my own JM air rifle, but you can also use pistols. The darts are fifty cal ballistic syringes. They release the drugs using gas compression, and the decent guns have valves to let you control the level of pressure, depending on the size of the animal.'

'And they're quiet?'

'Practically silent. You got a drug rapist?'

'If only.'

An incoming call alert flashed on the CarPlay screen, along with the Caller ID.

Eva Gregory.

'Thanks, Tony. Got to take another call.'

'Who can possibly be more important than me, Sawyer?'

'Short but sweet.'

Cross laughed. 'Doesn't sound like your type, mate. Talk to you later.'

Sawyer took a breath and ended the call, automatically connecting the second.

'Jake? Can you speak?'

'Yeah. You okay?'

A pause. 'I need you... Uh, I need your help.'

'I'm in London. Is it Dale?'

'It's Luka. He's fine. But...' Eva took a drink of something. 'He *stabbed* someone, Jake. In the leg. A seventeen-year-old boy. He's okay, but we have a meeting at the school on Monday.'

'What happened?'

'He was playing football on Bakewell Rec this morning. Three older lads tried to take their money and phones. Luka says they pulled out knives. He took one off them, and...'

Another drink.

'Was he interviewed?'

'They sent a couple of officers here and took him back to the station. They *arrested* him, Jake. On suspicion of GBH. Took his clothes and did swabs. When are you back from London?'

'I don't know. Complex case. The Luka thing sounds like self-defence to me. How did he get the knife from them?'

She sighed, long and slow. 'He says he lifted it.'

Sawyer squeezed his eyes shut, opened them again. 'We don't know the full story yet.'

'Yes, Jake. We do.'

The road opened out, yielding to suburban Surrey; a bloodless wilderness of franchise hotels, golf courses and low-rise country estates.

'It's hardly a revelation. Testing the boundaries. Teenage hormones kicking in.'

'Questionable male role models.'

'Absent father.' He floored the accelerator and swung out into the fast lane.

'For one.'

Sawyer sighed. 'Let's not.'

Another drink. 'Dale wants to be... present again.'

'Really? I assume he's given you the speech about how he's left his dark side behind now he's an upstanding civic representative.'

'Dale's not a bad person, Jake. He's just made some poor choices.'

'People who make poor choices with partners often say that about their partners. I think Sonia Sutcliffe set the standard.'

She scoffed. 'Okay, if he used to be a bad person then

bad people can get better, right? Broken people can be fixed, or fix themselves.'

'I'm not sure I believe either of those things.'

'Well, aren't you the bundle of positivity today?'

Sawyer chewed on the sweet, prised it away from his teeth with his tongue. 'I'll talk to Luka when I'm done here. It'll be fine. He'll be fine. It's definitely self-defence. There's a thing called instant arming, where you're entitled to use a weapon against an assailant. Loads of case law. CPS won't be interested. They might get the youth offending team on it, but it's nothing. In the greater scheme.'

Another drink from Eva, longer this time. He braced.

'Don't be a ghost, Jake.'

The road straightened and he flipped down the sun visor, blinded for a second.

Sunlight patterns. A churn of nausea.

His eyes flicked up to the rear-view mirror. Empty back seat.

'I'm just busy, Eva.'

'Luka asked after you.' He steadied his breathing, left her hanging. 'So, you're saying that Dale isn't showing me the full picture?'

'I'm just saying it's not a good idea.'

'What isn't?'

'Going back.'

19

TWO YEARS EARLIER

Dennis sat facing the wall, head tilted back, eyes fixed on the small barred window high above. He let his hands fall by his side and tapped the chair's cheap plastic with his fingernails. A tangle of freshly healed score marks ran along the inside length of both forearms.

'You been hitting the gym?' A twentysomething man with a fiftysomething face sat up on the bottom bunk and set down his *How It Works* magazine.

'I've been working out, Earl, yes.'

'No pain, no gain.'

Dennis stopped tapping and pivoted his hefty frame towards the bunk. 'Are you referring to the scars?'

'No! I mean, the work. You're looking good. They got a gym in Healthcare, yeah?'

He turned back to the wall. 'Of sorts.'

Earl checked his watch. He got up from the bed and filled the plastic kettle, wedging it lengthways in the tiny sink. 'Making a brew.'

'Not for me.'

'Trackie means you're on basic, yeah?'

Dennis looked down at his olive-green boiler suit, as if noticing it for the first time. 'Yes, it's the governor's cloak of shame. Naughty boy. Do not approach.'

'What's it like up there, then? In Healthcare. Better than here?'

'Worse. By definition.'

Earl emptied his pockets out onto the shelf and clicked the switch on the kettle. 'How do you mean?'

'You're surrounded by people with severe mental health problems. At least here everybody can understand and follow the rules. It's predictable.'

Earl nodded. 'Not you, though, eh?'

Dennis turned again, further this time.

'I mean... I've only been here a few weeks, but you don't seem too great at making friends, yeah?'

'Are you my friend, Earl?'

'Yeah! Course. I'm just saying...'

Dennis trained his shining blue eyes on his cellmate and gave him a deadly smile. 'Are they saying things about me?'

Earl shrugged. Steam built from the kettle behind him. 'One or two, yeah.' He checked his watch again. 'This is my third time inside. There's the rules, yeah? And then there's the code. You bend the rules, but you don't mess with the code. It's what helps us survive in here.'

'You keep your mouth shut. If you know what's good for you.'

'That's right, mate. Don't be telling the kangas what you've seen, yeah? Sorry. Kangas. Screws. I'm from Oz.'

'I'd noticed.'

'So, yeah. I'm sorry, mate.'

Raised voices outside. Angry shouts, crashing.

Footsteps on the landing, running.

'What for?' Dennis stood upright. He had at least a foot on Earl, and around fifty pounds.

The kettle clicked off.

Earl stood in front of the shelf, blocking Dennis's view. He filled his large tea mug with boiling water and emptied several sugar sachets into the mix. 'Some things aren't pleasant, but they've got to be done. Yeah?'

More shouts from outside. The alarm sounded.

The door flew open.

Two of them stayed outside, on watch.

The other three ran in. Big, young. Two white, one black.

One of the watchmen slammed the door shut.

Dennis backed off and stood beneath the window. The three attackers held their ground by the door as they each produced a toothbrush with the handle sharpened to a point.

One of them yelled to Earl. 'Do it, you silly cunt!'

Earl picked up the tea mug and turned.

Dennis ducked his head and charged at Earl, forcing

him backwards. As he clattered into the shelf behind, Earl's arm jerked up and the boiling hot syrup splashed into the face of one of the attackers, sticking to his skin. The man roared in agony and scraped at his face, dropping his toothbrush as he collapsed to the floor. Earl dived past him and banged on the door.

Eyes at the peep hole.

The scalded man screamed and pushed Earl aside. '*Open it!*'

The door opened and the scalded man shoved his way out, pushing Earl back into the room where he clunked his head against the shelf and dropped to the floor, unconscious. The scalded man fell forward onto the landing, clutching his face and howling for help.

Dennis snatched up the sharpened toothbrush. The bigger of the other two attackers landed a solid punch to the side of his head, but he sprang up and drove the point into the man's neck once, twice, digging deep with each blow. The man cried out and swiped with his own weapon, but couldn't connect. He stumbled back and snatched a towel from the bunk, pressing it over the bleeding wound as he scrambled out of the cell door.

The remaining attacker dropped his toothbrush and picked up the plastic chair, waving it in the air.

Dennis smiled. 'You look like a fucking lion tamer.' He held his scarred arms wide, in crucifix pose.

The attacker stood firm, his expression melting from fury to fear.

Dennis stomped his feet and gave a comical animal

roar, baring his teeth. His attacker startled, then dropped the chair and bolted out of the door.

'What the *fuck*, man?' One of the men posted on the door took a look inside and slammed the door shut.

Thunderous footsteps, screams, shouts.

Dennis righted the chair, then reached down and lifted Earl from the floor. His cellmate stirred, but remained semi-conscious as the door opened again and two officers entered, wearing combat helmets and padded ballistic jackets.

Dennis fixed a beefy arm round Earl's slender neck and backed into the wall by the window. Earl opened his eyes wide and grappled with the arm, but it was futile. He gagged and kicked his feet against the floor as Dennis lifted him up.

The officers took out side-handle batons and snapped them open.

'Let him go and face the wall with your hands behind your back.'

Dennis turned to face the wall. He gripped Earl's head with both hands and tilted it back.

Earl spluttered and sobbed. 'Mate. I'm sorry. They made me do it.'

'Last chance! Let him go.'

Dennis spoke into Earl's ear. 'See the window, Earl? You're going on a wonderful journey.'

'I've got a little girl, mate. Please. They said it was you or her.'

Dennis rested a finger on Earl's lips. *'Shh.* You shouldn't be scared. You know why? You don't matter,

Earl. Your little girl doesn't matter. None of us here counts for much, on the grand scale. We're just vulgar little blips in time. An impermanence. But you've done a good thing here today. You've given me the chance to restore a tiny bit of balance in the universe. So, thank you.'

Dennis gripped Earl's hair, then raised the sharpened toothbrush high and thrust it into the side of his neck. He managed three deep stabs before the officers got to him.

20

PRESENT DAY

'That's the last one.'

Everett Asher double-checked he'd locked the door behind them, and walked ahead of Sawyer down a wide corridor with a low ceiling and walls lined with wooden security doors, all closed. Tables with rounded corners and integrated seats were fastened to the floor at regular intervals, and the colours never strayed from muted or pastel: grey floor, mauve bench between each door, a row of lockers with olive doors. It smelled palatable, untainted, with a soft tang of disinfectant.

Asher looked over his shoulder at Sawyer and smiled. 'High dependency ward. I'm guessing it's not what you expected.'

'It looks like a Premier Inn.'

Asher laughed. 'You're not the first to say it. The place got redeveloped, not too long ago. People think of Broadmoor as some kind of Victorian nuthouse with screaming and crying, and zombies shuffling round, drugged up to the eyeballs. But it's a hospital. We have patients, not inmates. The idea is to get them better, not make their lives miserable and difficult. Nobody behind those doors planned to be in here.'

'Maybe they did. Maybe they thought it'd be easier.'

'Does it feel easier to you? Six locked doors to even get you close to this ward.'

Four uniformed orderlies stood up from a table and nodded to Asher. They approached the door at the far end, near a vast window recessed behind steel bars.

'Maxwell is a five-man unlock. Nobody can dream of even touching his door unless they have four ranked colleagues at their back.'

'Has he been violent?'

'Not recently. But he was PIA for the first couple of years. Pain in the arse. Most of his aggression is directed at the other patients, but the multi-unlock is policy for a guy with his story. You can never really relax. I had a patient last year who'd been a dream for six months. One day, he just turned. Got his hands on a forensic psych, tore out a big chunk of his hair. Poor bloke needed a scalp graft. Here...' He handed over what looked like a mini rugby ball with a thumb button. 'Panic alarm. Use it if anything feels scary. Maxwell is fairly decent with me. I think because I'm the same with him. I indulge most of his requests. But, like I say, he has shown no violence for a while. Just... keep your distance, try not to provoke him, and certainly don't directly challenge him.'

'You mean he's not behind glass, in a straitjacket? No item delivery tray?'

Asher stopped at the door and took out his key. 'He's not a Hollywood villain, and he's not an idiot. Since he had the life tariff removed from his sentence, he at least has a hope of parole. I expect he'll be on his best behaviour. And I expect the same from you.'

———

Sawyer took a look at the clock above Taylor Maxwell's bed.

Almost five minutes of silence now. Maxwell sat at the fixed white table in the centre of the consulting room. Head bowed, strange little smile. He had short grey hair, thinning on top, and wore a woollen cardigan despite the heat. A tightly coiled rat-tail bobbed on his shoulder as his head and shoulders undulated, as if moving to imaginary music. Heavy-lidded eyes, doughy arms and hands, uneven shave. He looked like a 1980s darts player.

'What are you listening to, Taylor?'

Maxwell raised his eyes and studied Sawyer. 'We interrupt silence as we interrupt speech.'

'Of course. Silence isn't necessarily an absence. A deficiency.'

'Many of our problems come from an inability to tolerate silence. It's all... space. And it has to be filled. With desires, for product and content. Nobody respects the idea of *emptiness* as a good thing.' Maxwell's speech was low, almost murmured. 'We feel vague and disillusioned and disappointed, and so we chase distraction. Dopamine hits. Anything to make us feel good. Feel *something.*'

'Did you get a dopamine hit from strangling young women?'

Maxwell reeled. 'Oh! We were getting on so well, Mr Sawyer. But it's a fair question. I'd say, yes. For one, I was adding to the silence.' He gripped the underside of his chair, shuffled out from under the table, and pointed himself towards Sawyer. 'It sounds like you know about me. I did some reading about you, too. It's only polite.' He crossed his legs and held his palm face up, reading from an imaginary notepad. 'Your mother's death was appalling, but it made me wonder how you could have built a relationship with your father afterward. Surely, he must have closed himself away emotionally?'

Sawyer took off his jacket and draped it over the back of the chair. 'You hated your father, Taylor.'

Maxwell smiled, bearing stained teeth. 'Is this an interview or a therapy session? My father was a fucking god-botherer, like yours. He turned my mother onto it, too. I think they actually looked forward to going to church. He beat me, held me underwater. Don't remember seeing that in the Bible. He used to scream in my ear, about the meaning of life.'

'Did he tell you? The meaning of life.'

'He wasn't about the easy answers.'

'Damn. I was about to take a note. So, was your

interest in Satanism a rebellion? Something to piss him off?'

Maxwell smiled again, shook his head. 'Perhaps. I mainly found it to be a release.'

'Or a justification?'

Maxwell held his head in his hands and gazed down at the floor. 'I didn't just use it as a badge. I read LaVey, Crowley. I had my battered little copy of *The Satanic Bible*. The core values of Satanism are about *vital existence*. Undefiled wisdom. Responsibility to the responsible.'

'All that stuff about indulging the ego, though. Sounds close to good old-fashioned libertarianism to me. The freedom to act without accountability. And that's working out so well for everyone, these days.'

'Well. At least there's none of the sacrificing virgins nonsense... That's just as performative and juvenile as the holy sacrament, or *Christening*.' He shuddered and sipped from a glass of water. 'Dare I ask? Is this visit part of my parole assessment? Are you Cabrera's emissary?'

'No. And I'm not sure you should be pinning your hopes on him. He's hardly a cheerleader for reform.' Sawyer leaned forward, resting his elbows on his knees. 'I might be able to help you, though. You've expressed remorse. There are mental health mitigations. You were young.'

'Getting on for twenty years younger than I am now. It's not that I've changed my outlook. I *am* changed.'

Sawyer took a slip of paper from his pocket. 'Have

you been involved in any correspondence recently, Taylor?'

'I receive letters. Some I reply to. Everett and my therapist advise me to hand over anything hateful or triggering.' Maxwell threw back his head and inhaled. 'I get a lot of love, though. Proposals of marriage.'

'Fan mail? Pictures? Sketches?'

Maxwell eyed him.

'I'm wondering if you've encountered these symbols before.' Sawyer passed over the paper.

Maxwell stared at it for a moment, raised his eyes to Sawyer. 'You've seen my sketchbook.'

'Not personally, but I know about the sketches, and if your muse arrived in the mail, then it's a pretty abstract marriage proposal. We can do a legal dance if you like, but I'd rather help you avoid another twenty years in here. In exchange for a bit more detail.'

'You can't guarantee that.'

'No, but I can put my foot on the pipe. Throttle your chances of freedom, or at least Cat-D, down from slim to none.'

Maxwell smiled. 'I can't decide if that's a threat or an offer.'

'Column A, column B.' Sawyer shuffled his chair from behind the desk and faced Maxwell directly. 'Did you see the symbols in external mail? When? How many times? What else was in the letters?'

Maxwell bowed his head again and stayed silent for a long time.

Sawyer focused on his breathing: a slight whistle as he

inhaled. 'You strangled three women,' he said eventually. 'You broke into a family home, strangled the mother and suffocated the father with a plastic bag. While the kids slept through it all.'

Maxwell kept his head down.

'You took photos to relive the thrill later. How did you select the victims, Taylor? Why the home invasions? Can you at least help me with that?'

Maxwell sighed. 'According to EEG recordings, hearing is one of the last senses to fade upon death. Many of us will hear the pronouncement. The doctor recording the time. And then, the great silence. The infinite bliss of oblivion.'

'The anaesthetic from which none come round.'

Maxwell looked up. 'Is that Auden?'

'Larkin.'

Fire rose in Maxwell's eyes. 'I have a question for you, Detective Sawyer. Why did you become a detective?'

'To catch people like you.'

Maxwell laughed. 'The psychologists call that *splitting*. You hunt down the people who have acted out the wrongness you feel in yourself. Maybe you're seeing a future version of yourself. Something you might become. And so you catch it, stop it. And that feels good. It's a proxy way of addressing this wrongness in yourself. It externalises your pain, because it's too intense to bear internally. All that *noise*. Have you ever tried to find some peace from it yourself? Some silence?'

'Where did you see the symbols, Taylor? Go on. Give me a clue.'

'As a boy, I had a den in the woods near my house. I built it in an overgrown copse from corrugated metal. And I covered it up well, so it was hard to discover, even in winter. I didn't tell anyone else. I didn't go there to read dirty magazines. I went there for the silence. Some days, it was so quiet I could sit there and listen to my body. The breaths. The gurgling and squelching. Everything in motion. Nothing at peace. The people I killed, they call them my victims. But I see them more as lucky receivers of a gift. The gift of silence.'

'I'm sure they would have preferred money. Or chocolates.'

Maxwell took a plain white envelope from his back pocket. 'You see her, don't you?'

'Who?'

'Your mother. I used to see my mother. She died when I was young, too. Not in the same circumstances, but I remember that feeling of impotence you mention in your newspaper interview. I watched my mother deteriorate and there was nothing I could do to help. You couldn't save your mother, either, because you were a child. And so you bring her back to watch over you as an adult. It gives a meaning to the loss. But one day, you won't see her. Not because you've *processed* it, or come to terms with it. But because you've accepted that you're beyond salvation, Mr Sawyer.' He leaned forward. 'You've accepted that internalisation of the agony. It's become a part of you.' He opened the envelope and handed it over. 'You can't save yourself. No more than you could save your mother. I'll tell you why you do this.

Because, like me, like the killers you catch, you don't believe in change. You don't believe that things can get better, that people can get better. You don't believe that *you* can get better.'

Sawyer locked his green eyes into Maxwell's grey. He shook his head. 'Yes, I do feel that inner wrongness. But the difference is, I'm prepared to work on myself. I do this to catch people who think the way you do, Taylor. Damaged people who *aren't* willing to work on themselves, and who self-medicate by projecting their pain onto the weak, the unsuspecting. And if I didn't believe that people could change if they were willing to work on themself, I wouldn't be here asking for your help, because I would never believe that the version of you twenty years ago would want to help. So, you can spend the rest of your days in here watching criminology TED talks and then submit to that "great silence", or you can begin your own work, your change, by helping me.' He nodded to the envelope. 'Is this new?'

Maxwell nodded.

'When did you receive it?'

'This morning.'

Sawyer took a slip of plain white paper from the envelope. It was blank, apart from the same symbols in the centre of the paper in pencil.

ᛁᚾᛁᚠᛗ

Sawyer got to his feet. 'How many have you received?'

'Two others. Two days ago, and one on the eighteenth.'

'Do you still have them?'

'I threw them away. These symbols are meaningless, Mr Sawyer. Whoever this is, he isn't a true Satanist. He's read a few Wikipedia pages. He probably thinks he's referring to a well-documented term for a demon. *The dweller in the abyss*. I live. I dwell. It almost fits. But these runes are Anglo-Saxon. Anyone with a genuine interest in Satanism would use the Theban alphabet, or something bespoke.'

'And this is all he sends? No other messages.'

'Just the symbols. No contact details.'

Sawyer banged on the door, gave the thumbs-up to Asher. He turned to face Maxwell. 'Thank you, Taylor. I can't promise to get you back out there, among the noise, but this will act in your favour.'

The door opened.

Maxwell stood up. 'Before you go... Can you answer my father's question?'

'Which one?'

He shrugged. 'What *is* the meaning of life?'

Sawyer thought for a moment. 'It ends.'

21

Dale Strickland hurried down the hall, past an oversized portrait photograph of a woman with long white hair, lounging on the wooden floor of a studio, holding toddler Luka high with both hands. Both laughing and shoeless; both a decade younger.

Eva Gregory, now with shoulder-length black hair, sat at the kitchen table, opposite Luka, staring into his phone. She looked ragged and displaced in a lightweight hoodie and joggers. As Dale entered, she dabbed at her smeared eyeliner with a tissue and put on a pair of brown-rimmed Tom Ford glasses.

Strickland moved to embrace her, but stopped short. 'I'll talk to the school first thing Monday. Before your meeting.'

'What are you going to say, Dad?' said Luka. 'They'd better not expel me, or you'll close the school?'

'I don't have the authority to do that. Not in this county, at least.'

Luka scoffed and looked up at the ceiling. 'You could tell them you'll beat up the teachers.'

Strickland pulled out a chair and sat down.

Eva caught his eye. 'The police say they will need to interview Luka formally once they've established the facts from the other boy's perspective.'

Luka refocused on his phone, shaking his head. 'Unbelievable. They attacked us!'

'And you were defending yourself.'

Luka glanced up at Strickland. 'Yes. They tried to take our stuff. Am I supposed to just let them?'

'Yes,' said Strickland. 'You just got lucky. It could have gone so differently. What if the other boy had got the knife back off you?'

'He didn't,' said Luka. 'What if he had been carrying a gun? Well, he wasn't.'

'Hey...' Strickland spoke softly as he reached out for Luka's phone.

Luka sighed and set it down on the table, flipped it over. 'Screen is cracked.'

'Luka. I know things have been tough. But this is an important time for you. GCSEs aren't too far away.'

He rolled his eyes. 'They're not for *ages*.'

'Ah, but you're getting older now. Time seems to move more quickly. They'll be here before you know it.' He reached out a hand, rested it on Luka's. 'And I want to be here, too. I haven't been the best dad. But that can change.'

Luka glared at him. 'You never change.'

'I've just been preoccupied with my work, Luka. But

I was always trying to provide for us. To protect us, bring us more stability. And to give you options for your future. I've made some mistakes, but I have a very good job now. I *can* change.' He laid on a second hand. 'You're my number one priority. Your health and wellbeing.'

'He still gets dizzy spells,' said Eva. 'From the crash.'

'I don't!'

'I've seen you, my darling. Unsteady.'

'I'm fine.'

Dale took out his wallet. 'I'm going to buy you a new phone. It'll be good for helping us stay in touch more.'

'Am I one of your gang now, then?'

'Don't be silly, Luka,' said Eva.

'Luka, I did some stupid things and I went to prison. But now I have a good job and I think I'm about to get an even better job. I've gone from being inside the prison to being in charge of it. See? That's change, isn't it?'

Luka thought for a moment, then pushed back his hair. 'You don't like Jake, do you?'

Strickland flashed a look at Eva. 'Jake Sawyer? It's not that I don't like him. We've had some disagreements. He's accused me of things I didn't do.'

'I think he's brilliant.'

Strickland nodded, forced a smile. 'And where is he now? Is he here, offering to help get you out of this situation? Is he buying you a new phone?'

'No, but he's taught me more than you.' Luka snatched up the cracked phone and left the room. He stomped up the stairs and slammed his door.

'He's having nightmares,' said Eva.

'About the kidnapping?'

She nodded. 'Flashbacks. He seemed fine for such a long time. It's come out more recently. Claustrophobia. Sleeping with the light on.'

Strickland set his phone down on the table and navigated to an image gallery. 'Look at this.' He swiped through the images: a beach bar; a rustic-looking villa set back from the shore; an artfully ramshackle restaurant overlooking an aquamarine sea. 'This is the Treasure Beach Resort, on the southwest corner of Jamaica. Russell knows the owner.'

Eva swiped through the rest of the image gallery: sun-bleached sand; a jetty restaurant; tanned bodies leaping into clear water at the base of a shining waterfall. 'Russell?'

'Russell Hogan. The mayor.' Strickland shifted his chair around the table, closer to Eva. 'Sweetheart. We only go round once. We can *rebuild* something here.'

'What's this about you getting an even better job?'

Strickland moved the phone aside, held Eva's eye. 'Russell's health isn't good. I'm next in line.'

'For mayor?'

'There's a process. But if he stepped down, and I think he will soon, then I would be acting mayor. And, given the close election last year, and my drug initiatives—'

'So, this is your plan, Dale? The three of us jet off to Jamaica to play happy families?'

He leaned in and took her hand. 'It's a start. It could be more than that. We do it for Luka, and we see what

153

happens with us. Or we can stumble along like this and watch Luka repeat his father's mistakes, and continue with this ill-advised idolisation of a man who's served a suspension on suspicion of murder, and who disappeared for six months rather than face an internal enquiry following a suspect's death in his custody.'

Eva lifted Strickland's hand away. She took off her glasses and dabbed at her eyes with the tissue. 'Luka pickpocketed the knife from the other boy.'

Strickland threw up his hands. 'There! I take it this is Sawyer's influence?'

'Jake thinks you're a narcissist.'

'Pot, kettle.' His phone vibrated with a call. 'Look, let's get this knife thing sorted, finish the school term, get away. Russell can secure us the biggest villa on the complex. Half price.' He looked at the screen: *No Caller ID*. 'Sorry, sweetheart. I have to get this.' He picked up the phone and declined the call, then walked back down the hall. 'Let's speak again later.' His phone rang again, this time with a caller number displayed. 'They do fishing trips at the resort. River safaris. We could cycle into the Blue Mountains. There will be other kids there. The seafood will be incredible.'

He stepped out of the front door and walked towards a white Mercedes S-Class, parked on a verge at the end of the road. A stocky man in the driver's seat looked up and started the engine.

Strickland answered the call. 'This is Dale.'

'The fuck? You declined me.'

'Sorry, Curtis. Had to finish a meeting.'

'Well, I thought you'd want to know. Our mutual friend is no longer of this world.'

Strickland slowed his pace, looked back at the house. 'Fast work.'

'Nothing to do with me. Someone else got there first. Wilmot was shifted from VP and put in with a new cellmate. The toilet bowl was blocked, and this fella held Wilmot's head under, drowned him.'

Strickland winced. 'Not top of my list for ways to go.'

'Sort of fitting. He always did talk a load of shit.'

'How do you know this, anyway?'

Mavers paused. 'You're not the only one with contacts, Dale.'

'So... Who?'

'Doesn't sound like a beef over who gets the most nudie pictures on the cell wall.'

'But he's definitely dead?'

'He isn't breathing any more. That usually does the trick.'

Strickland reached the Mercedes; the driver got out and opened the rear door for him. He turned and walked a few paces back towards the house, keeping his voice low. 'Stokes. Doyle.'

'No doubt. Like I say, they want me. Probably tortured him first. Poor bastard didn't know where I was, though. So he couldn't tell them much, even when they had him gargling piss.'

'Surely they'll try Sawyer next, since you mentioned his name.'

'Have they really got the balls to go nose to nose with CID? If I was them, I'd tail Sawyer and take us both down when he finds me. Make it look like he did it.'

'I like it. The way to bind people is to give them a common enemy.' Strickland turned and climbed in to the car. 'And if you were mo, would you pass on that excellent idea to Stokes and Doyle?'

Mavers laughed. 'As if you'd want Sawyer finding me, Dale. Given what I've got on you. Let's not insult each other's intelligence. We both know that the fuckin' Happy Mondays aren't going to work it out, so I'd really appreciate a private passage to Naples, like, ASAP, before our friendly neighbourhood Detective Inspector pays me a visit.'

The driver idled the engine; Strickland held up a hand.

'Give me a day or two.' He hung up, checked the call log, and passed the handset to the driver.

22

'He's a fan.' Sawyer walked out to the front of the briefing room and stood beside Hatfield. 'Our killer is sending the symbols to Taylor Maxwell. A fledgling killer's acknowledgement of someone he sees as an inspiration. Something about Maxwell has lit him up. Maybe the strangulation method, the choice of victims, the Satanic dabbling.'

'And the mail to Maxwell contained nothing but the symbols?' said McHugh.

Sawyer shook his head. 'Just the runes. Anglo-Saxon. *I LIVE.* The thing is, Maxwell didn't buy it as a Satanism thing. He said that a true aficionado would use custom runes or a specific alphabet.'

Hatfield took off his glasses and cleaned the lenses with his shirt sleeve. 'So, it doesn't seem like he's seeking a relationship with Maxwell. It feels more like a deferral.'

'He's a mentor,' said Conway.

'Possibly.' Sawyer unwrapped a yellow boiled

sweet and popped it into his mouth. 'He might even view the whole thing as a fantasy connection to Maxwell. The letters with the symbols, the symbols at the scenes. Perhaps even the killings themselves.' Sawyer pointed to the pictures on the board. 'Maxwell says he's received three letters with the runes. One on the day of the Prior family murder, one on the day of the Carters'.' He sighed. 'And the other, today.'

'Fuck,' said McHugh.

'If the pattern persists, then we have to assume he's planning another killing for this evening or the early hours.'

'That's insane,' said Conway. 'He's narrowing the gap to one day?'

Sawyer perched on the edge of a table. 'Like I said, he's planned everything. I think he's selected all his victims already and, for whatever reason, he can only satisfy himself by killing in a burst like this. Maybe he'll run out of victims soon and go to ground, work on his next batch.'

'We can't be sure the messages are from the killer,' said McHugh.

Hatfield paced. 'The detail of the symbols at the scene weren't made public. It's too specific to be a coincidence. We have the third letter. London postmark. Forensics are on it, but I don't imagine they'll find anything. Did Maxwell have any ideas on what the phrase might mean?'

Sawyer turned his face to the window. The golden

glow of sunset cast otherworldly shadows around the briefing room.

The nausea rose in him.

He squinted, then closed his eyes.

Barking.

Vivid silver squiggles wormed at the edges of his vision, fading in and out. He reached a hand to the table edge but missed and jarred forward, checking his fall with an elbow to the tabletop.

'DI Sawyer?'

Hatfield's voice.

He would need to open his eyes again soon.

'You alright, son?'

Sawyer stepped up from the table, refocused on the room, now with one or two concerned faces.

Hatfield rested a hand on his shoulder. 'Do you need a moment?'

His mother's hand, reaching out, fingers buckled by a wayward hammer blow.

'Yeah. Just... not sleeping well. I'm okay.'

'You're missing the country air, mate,' said McHugh. 'You'll soon acclimatise to the smog.'

Sawyer caught Conway's eye. 'I was going to say... He's received three letters.'

'You told us that,' said Shah, in his usual corner.

'Yeah. Of course... The phrase. Perhaps *I LIVE* because the killings make him feel *alive*? Could he be terminally ill? An outpatient?'

Hatfield glanced at Conway. 'We need a bit more than that. Did you look into the tranquiliser drug?'

'Yes. It's hard to get hold of. Same with the guns and darts. Carefully controlled. If he's getting access to it because of his job, then it could be several professions. Vets, zoos, pest control.'

'We already know that,' said McHugh. 'DC Bryant and I checked on it, like you asked, sir.'

'They call the guns Remote Delivery Devices,' said DC Bryant. 'Easy enough to buy online. It's getting hold of the drug that's the difficult part.'

'Let's zoom in hard on those lines of work with potential access to the tranquiliser drugs. Cross-ref with criminal records. Narrow it to local.'

Sawyer eased further back onto the desk, letting it take his full weight. The edges of the room shimmered, and he lowered his gaze, sending his mind back to Thor's Cave: the feel of the rain-slick rock; the earthy scent of the inner chamber; the view across the valley.

DC Rodgers waved her pen in the air. 'Perhaps *I LIVE* comes from a feeling that he wasn't living an authentic life before the killings? Could he have recently transitioned, or turned his back on a toxic lifestyle?'

Hatfield replaced his glasses. 'It's good thinking, DC Rodgers. Look into local gender support services for clients with relevant previous. Quite a few dots to join up, but you might get a couple of hits. How did you get on with the burglar alarms?'

Rodgers flipped open a notepad. 'As we said last time, the systems at both the Prior and Carter houses were code entry. The alarm activates quietly and gets louder if the code isn't entered within one minute. Not a lot of time for him to get in and deactivate them.'

'Could he have hacked the system? Found the codes somehow?'

'Possibly, but the companies told me the system is tamper-proof, and it triggers if it detects anything unusual. They do have remote monitors that can tell if an alarm is active, but they're specialist.'

'Maybe he works for the alarm people,' said Conway.

'Different companies,' said Rodgers. She checked the notepad. 'Both families employed cleaners who had access to the codes. I spoke to both, sort of.'

'Sort of?' said Hatfield.

'Not great English. Both young. One's a student, originally from Bulgaria; the other moved here from Brazil a couple of years ago, does full-time cleaning. They're both on the books of a few agencies and work for several properties. They swear they don't share the codes with anyone, no records. Checks out.'

The voices bled into each other, coalescing in the muggy air. Sweat prickled Sawyer's brow; he slowed his breathing, fixated on Rodgers. 'Who else might have the codes? Any other family?'

Rodgers hesitated, looked at Hatfield. 'I...'

'You know what?' said Shah. 'Maybe *I LIVE* suggests more than just transitioning. It could be religious. Maybe he feels reborn? As if he was dead before and the new version of him commits the murders.'

McHugh blew out a sigh.

'Keep going,' said Hatfield.

'We shouldn't dismiss that psychology. Many traumatised people rebuild themselves to achieve distance from who they were when they were traumatised. Most Hindus believe that humans are in a cycle of death and rebirth called *samsara*. When a person dies, their *atman*, or spirit, is reborn in a different body. Some believe that rebirth happens directly at death, while others think that an *atman* may exist in other realms.'

'Can we stick to the earthly realm?' said McHugh.

'Again,' said Hatfield, 'I like the thinking, but it doesn't really help us at this stage. We can't do house-to-house on Hindu temples.'

Shah smiled, sheepish. 'I do have something more scientific, about the compound we found at both scenes.'

'You're such a tease,' said Conway.

'We originally thought the material was just waterproofed. But it's actually chlorinated. And it's not rubber. It's latex.'

'What's the difference?' said Rodgers.

'Not much. Latex is basically the intermediate stage before rubber is vulcanised to make practical clothing. It isn't elastic. It maintains the altered shape after stretching. It's popular as fetish wear because it's skintight. Have we heard of the magazine, *Skin Two?*'

'Sounds like you have,' said McHugh.

Shah forced a smile. 'So, there's an illusion of nakedness, or being coated in a shiny substance like paint. And, uh, some people enjoy that.'

'Why the chlorination?' said Sawyer.

Shah held a finger up in the air. 'That's the

interesting bit. Chlorinating the latex makes it easier to wear. It's a specialist process.'

'So, you don't find it in standard gloves?'

'Medical gloves are usually made from nitrile, which is like latex but without the complications of allergy, which is common.'

Hatfield paced again. 'Right. Now my head hurts. How can all that help me catch this bastard?'

'He's into BDSM,' said Sawyer. 'Maybe he has to wear something to help him shift from his everyday character to the version who kills. A restriction. Or as the thinnest possible barrier between himself and the suffering.'

'Are we really talking about a murderer who wears a fucking gimp suit?' said McHugh.

'Maybe not a suit. Maybe just gloves. Perhaps a mask or face covering. I've seen this psychology before. It serves the killer's psychology and also denies the victim a true vision of the human being behind their torment. Both things together might excite him.'

Sawyer's phone vibrated with a text message. Maggie.

Coming home early. Mia missing social life. She wants to go to some festival with a friend and her parents. It's fine. Got a few days out of it. Call you when we land. x

He looked up, to meet Hatfield's glare. 'This is all very interesting, Sawyer, but it's only useful for narrowing things down when we get sight of a few suspects.' He gathered his things. 'Get busy. DI Conway, co-ordinate. Professions with access to the drug, cross-ref with offenders. I want more on the Prior and Carter cleaners. Any associations, anyone with records or relevant previous. Let's revisit Maxwell and get a fix on what our killer might find appealing. I collared the fucker, so I'll look into that myself. DI Sawyer, take a break.'

'Sir?'

Hatfield headed to his office. 'We have enough solid lines of enquiry. Good work with the Maxwell element. Hopefully that will develop. I'll see you here for the morning briefing. Eight am sharp. Have a night off.'

'You need all hands,' said Sawyer.

Hatfield turned. 'I'll decide what I *need*, Detective. If he does pop up again tonight, then we've got a busy day tomorrow, and I want you fresh.'

Sawyer followed him into his office and closed the door behind them. 'Sir. The pattern is clear. Each letter to Maxwell has signalled a killing the same day. We might get a break on something in time to stop him. I want to help.'

Hatfield pulled out his handkerchief and took his time blowing his nose. 'I appreciate that, DI Sawyer. But it's my job to assign tasks to detectives I feel will be fully focused on them. I'm not doubting your ability or insight. I'm just seeing a few too many flashes of the old you. Don't take it as a slight. Maybe this is more of an... adjustment than I expected.'

Sawyer took a step forward. 'I know you have a full team on this, but he's building up to something. Shorter time between the murders, assuming he strikes again today. It's a crescendo. He has momentum now. We have to pull out all the stops to catch him before another family dies.' He kept his voice steady, but raised the volume slightly. 'So. Assign me a task. Sir.'

Hatfield glared at him. 'I already have.'

23

Leon Stokes leaned back in the purple sofa and sloshed liquid round a heavy crystal glass.

He motioned to the armchairs opposite. 'Take a seat, boys. But only if you bring good news. I'm not in a bad news mood.' He took a slug of his drink and propped his legs on a low velvet footstool.

Jakub Malecki stepped forward, ahead of Wes Peyton. 'We have something.' He sat down; Peyton remained standing.

Boyd Cannon, seated at the dining table, puffed out his lips and made a raspberry sound. 'Doesn't sound like much of an early birthday present.'

'Wilmot was tougher than he looked,' said Malecki.

Stokes tapped his glass. 'Your boy was tougher, though, I assume.'

Peyton took out his grenade and spun it round in his open palm. 'He's the one still alive.'

'Our guy was a full lifer,' said Cannon. 'They'll do

anything for a bump in the pecking order and a few grand on their account.'

Stokes stared into his glass. 'So. All square?'

'He's good,' said Peyton.

'Tell me more about this "something".'

'Wilmot told us that Mavers is back in Liverpool,' said Malecki.

'Keep talking.' Stokes looked from man to man. Cannon opened his laptop, deflecting.

'That's it,' said Malecki. 'He bit out half of my man's cheek.' He shrugged.

'And he's never heard of turning the other one?'

'Lost his temper,' said Peyton. 'Drowned him in the toilet.'

Stokes closed his eyes. He drained the glass, rolled it around in his fingers for a few seconds, then hurled it at the wall behind Peyton, where it shattered. A few shards rolled back and settled near Cannon's feet. He barely flinched, keeping focus on the laptop screen.

'Okay,' said Stokes. 'That's progress. We've narrowed it down to about two hundred and fifty square miles.'

Cannon looked over. 'Doyle can put the feelers out. Zoom in.'

'I was hoping for a fucking postcode, at least.'

'We know the kind of places he would feel comfortable,' said Peyton. 'He's not going to be in Mossley Hill.'

'Or Woolton,' said Cannon.

Stokes leaned forward and rested his hands on his knees, breathing deeply. 'This bin-dipper cunt came into my house, beat me unconscious, stole my money. I made him a promise that he would suffer, and I don't like to break promises. The competition hears I got smacked down and did fuck-all. I look weaker, they feel stronger. Boyd, get Doyle for me. Tap up anyone else we know up there. Ports, including Ellesmere and the container terminals. Train stations. Anywhere we know Mavers has links. And get people-watching nearby private airfields. I doubt he's stupid enough to jump on an EasyJet, but keep eyes on John Lennon, anyway.'

'Sawyer,' said Malecki.

Cannon exchanged a look with Stokes.

Peyton spun the grenade. 'You said we might need his help. Mavers named him. Must be a reason.' He sat down, opposite Stokes. 'I saw my brother again. He reckons Mavers got the intel from Sawyer.'

'Intel?' Cannon smiled at Stokes.

'Yeah. He's a copper. He had all the info, but he couldn't build legal cases, so Mavers was the direct route. Shut us down with intimidation, robbery, set us off against each other. So, Mavers comes here, gets his money, tries to throw us off the scene by naming Sawyer. But now he's fucked because he's stuck in Liverpool, trying to buy his way out to fucking Barbados, or wherever he's from.'

'Jamaica,' said Cannon.

Peyton pocketed the grenade. 'They've had a falling out. Mavers is hiding, but Sawyer will be easy to find.'

'He might be just as eager to get hold of Mavers himself,' said Malecki.

'And you're the man for this job, Wes?' said Stokes.

'Too fucking right, I am. Copper scum.'

Stokes shook his head. 'I know you're keen to impress your family, but we need Sawyer to stay alive if we want him to spill on Mavers.'

'I can convince him,' said Malecki.

'Let's see if Doyle can help first,' said Stokes. 'Then we'll have to hold our nose and bring home the bacon.'

24

Farrell shoved his way out of the lift, jostling the young woman in front of him, and strode out onto the top floor of Broadhurst House, the GMCA headquarters on Manchester's Oxford Street.

'Excuse me!' called the woman from behind.

Farrell held up a hand, but didn't turn, muttering under his breath. *'Fuck off.'*

The open-plan office was almost empty, and the automatic night lights flickered on as Farrell hurried across to a vast recessed reception area furnished with bespoke sofas in primary colours, contrasting with the polished glass and steel of the rest of the floor.

He stepped over a divider onto a cherry-red carpet and spoke to the back of a young man in a headset, typing at a standing desk.

'Can I go straight in?'

The man turned and beamed, struggling to sustain the expression at the sight of Farrell.

'Yes, Oliver. He can.' Dale Strickland opened the door to his office and ushered Farrell inside.

Early evening Manchester revved and hooted outside Strickland's open window.

'Noisy in here,' said Farrell, settling onto the silvery-grey sofa and placing a black folder at his side.

'You mean out there.' Strickland sat at his desk, shut down his computer.

'Well. Yes.' Farrell took out a canister of breath mints, waved them at Strickland, who offered a weak smile and an oddly sorrowful shake of the head.

'It's warming up,' said Strickland. 'I need the window open.'

Farrell slipped a mint into his mouth, shrugged. 'Use the aircon.'

'Time marches on, Robin. We do all we can to mitigate the effects. Did you know that your body loses its ability to produce sweat when you spend a lot of time in an air-conditioned room?'

Farrell sighed. 'No.'

'So, you lose a lot of moisture from your skin, which reduces its elasticity. That causes your wrinkles and fine lines to look more exaggerated.'

'Is this advice you've taken from Mr Metrosexual out there?'

Strickland smiled. 'With respect, Robin, I'm a man in the spotlight. I have appearances to keep up. Your work is mostly done in the shadows. Particularly at the moment.'

'It won't stick.'

'The suspension?'

Farrell got up, walked to the window. 'It's not a suspension.'

'You know, you really should give Oliver a little more notice before—'

'This couldn't wait.' Farrell turned, swept back his oily hair. 'Are we one hundred per cent private here?'

Strickland sat back in his tall chair, looked up and around the room in mock panic. 'Why? Have you come to tell me I'm under covert surveillance?'

Farrell crunched his mint.

'Yes, Robin. The room is soundproof, and I'm not wearing a wire. What's on your mind?'

Farrell picked up the folder and approached the desk. 'Late this afternoon, we discovered the remains of three people in a small patch of woodland near Ashbourne.' He laid out several sheets of scene photography showing three bulky items wrapped in black bin liners.

'Who's we?'

Farrell bristled. 'Derbyshire. Under my independent consultation. A private investigation that's borne fruit.'

'You sound like Russell Brand,' said Strickland, smiling.

'I have hard evidence that links one of these deaths to one Detective Inspector Jake Sawyer, in collusion with...' Farrell pulled out a passport shot of a scowling blond man with a tight ponytail sticking out behind his thick neck.

Strickland glanced up at Farrell. 'And who's this?'

Farrell crunched his mint again, swallowed. 'Come

on, Dale. We'll need to be frank with each other if we're going to make this work.'

Strickland shrugged.

Farrell pressed on. 'I believe that this man, Austin Fletcher, met with Jake Sawyer at an abandoned abattoir close to the woodland.' He brought out another picture. 'This is Scott Walton, an ex-worker at the abattoir who was suspected of a series of murders, including a teenage boy, Darren Coleman, whom Sawyer had been looking for on behalf of the boy's mother, despite serving a suspension.'

'Ah. So you have something in common with Sawyer.'

Farrell sighed. 'It's not a suspension. Now, I have an item of evidence that puts Walton at the abattoir that evening. It's exciting enough that I can track Sawyer and Fletcher's movements to connect them to Walton's death, but here's the fun part for you, Dale. The other two bodies.' He slid two head-and-shoulders photographs from the folder: a heavyset man in a sleeveless vest, and a shorter, neater character with mean little eyes.

'Marian Baros. Marco Hewitt.' Farrell held Strickland's eye. 'Hewitt was your campaign manager, wasn't he? And Baros worked for you briefly last year. I know you've had a busy time, Dale.' He waved an arm around the office. 'But... didn't you *miss* them?'

Strickland studied the photographs for a moment. 'How did you identify them so quickly?'

'NDNAD. They all had profiles. These days, we have

173

a thing we call a magic box. Portable, rapid DNA analysis for scene of crime. Results in less than two hours. It used to take days.'

'So, why the rush?'

Farrell sat down opposite Strickland at the desk. 'As you say, Dale. Time marches on. We can follow the standard procedure, and sit back as Sawyer wriggles out of this again, or we could be lateral. Clever.'

Strickland took off his glasses and regarded Farrell down his nose. 'Get you. A cunning plan.'

Farrell obliged by lowering his voice. 'I know you're into your *Art of War*, Dale. So, I found a quote for you.' He checked his phone and recited. *'Direct confrontation will lead to engagement, and surprise will lead to victory.'*

25

Sawyer faced the dressing table mirror, his green eyes muted in the lamplight. He bent his knees and fell into Wing Chun horse stance, tucked his fists in to the side of his chest, and fired out a series of centreline punches. Alternate arms, volley of ten, rest, repeat. He slowed his breathing and executed the second form: *Chum Kiu* ('Searching for the Bridge'). Precision pivots, blocks, open-handed strikes.

I LIVE.

The dweller in the abyss.

He'd spent an hour with a takeaway dinner, stumbling through the online rabbit holes. Crowley and his demons and magick. His self-styled religion of *Thelema*: the Greek word for will. *Do what thou wilt.* The concept of the abyss as an unknowable limbo. Gnostic cosmology. The leviathan. The Book of Enoch. *Paradise Lost*. Psalms.

Sawyer showered, head spinning. Was all this just

warped speculation? Misguided hero worship? Maxwell currying favour ahead of his hearing? Two disordered minds caught in an unfathomable loop?

Elaborate fantasist killers were vanishingly rare. Much more common were killers who legitimised their shameful sexual sadism by manufacturing fantasy or supernatural influence. It wasn't me; it was the voices. The word of God. The devil inside.

He dressed casual: T-shirt, jeans. Hatfield may have stood down Jake Sawyer, but he had a spare persona, more suited to the febrile evening.

Sawyer cleansed his thoughts of esoteric nonsense, and headed out to pursue a more likely driving force behind the killer's actions: sex.

―――――

'I've got a surprise for you, Mr Sawyer.'

'Robbins.'

Poppy Fuller turned off the engine and pushed her face close to the door window. 'Sorry. Mr Lloyd Robbins. Isn't he the guy who does the pasta sauce?'

'You're thinking of Loyd Grossman. My inspiration is a sleight-of-hand artist. Apollo Robbins. They call him an awareness manipulator. Have a look at YouTube. He's a genius. Your guy sells sauce and snoops around houses.'

Fuller kept her face to the window. 'So, you've named your alter ego after a genius? I'm learning more about you all the time.' She turned, smiled. 'And who doesn't love a bit of snooping?'

'Can I have my surprise now?'

'Lloyd, my love. You really are no fun.' She opened the glovebox and produced two gilded Venetian masks: one silver, one gold. 'The parties are all different. Strict rules here, because it's where the hosts live. Everyone keeps the masks on until midnight. It's an evening of two halves. First, a sophisticated little soirée where you make connections, arrange something for later. And then the masks come off, and then—'

'You realise the person you're planning to hook up with is an ex. Or an ex-colleague. Or your sister.'

Fuller laughed, held up a hand. Fake red fingernails, long and polished. 'Don't say "hook up". That's very policey. Here, we *play*.' She handed Sawyer the silver mask; he slipped it on, covering the top half of his face. 'Oh, yes. Very you. The silver makes those green eyes pop. You'll get plenty of attention. Keep your head down if you don't want it. Or stick close to me. Then we'll only be approached by single guys, who are all tightly vetted. You'd never get in here without me, do you realise?'

'I doubt it's the kind of club that would have someone like me for a member.'

Fuller put on the gold mask and got out of the car. She took the lead, her heels clip-clopping on the winding garden path of the enormous detached house. 'It's funny. I always feel more like me when I'm wearing this. It's not like I'm hiding my true self. More the opposite.'

They approached a cluster of masked people milling around a white-columned portico at the front door.

Fuller slowed, squeezed Sawyer's shoulder. 'You've gone quiet, Mr Robbins. How are we feeling?'

'Just getting into character.'

———

The house interior didn't deliver on the promise of the exterior. There was good taste here, in the choices of art —Blake, Miro, de Kooning—but there was too much of it, as if it had been bought in bulk. The furnishings were frilly and adorned: scalloped lampshades; textured wallpaper; shagpile rugs; gigantic bay windows smothered by blousy curtains. A new-money stab at a sensual wonderland, fumbled into sensory overload.

Fuller linked arms with Sawyer and led him through a hall-like sitting room with the furniture pushed to the sides, and an enormous double bed in the centre.

'I assume that's not for sleeping in,' said Sawyer.

She squeezed his shoulder again. 'You're catching on quick, Mr Robbins. They have a live bed show later on, when the masks come off. There's a mini cinema round the back which shows porn, but they also play different movies on all the TV screens around the house.'

A short man in a burgundy dinner jacket and glossy white eye mask barred their way, offering a tray of champagne. Fuller took a glass; Sawyer declined. He diverted to another couple hovering awkwardly at the entrance. Most of the guests looked to be in early middle age, with the men in thin summer shirts or designer T-shirts and the women in fitted dresses and heels. Diffusers scented the air with a subtle citrus, and the music—downtempo electronica—throbbed at low volume. A sign mounted beside a full length wall mirror read: *Not only do I dance like no-one is watching, I drink like I'm not working in the morning.*

'It's like a suburban cocktail party,' said Sawyer.

'What were you expecting? Guests strutting round in full fetish gear? As I say, it livens up once the masks come off.'

Sawyer caught the eye of a passing woman in a leopard-print wrap dress and black lace mask. 'I've been to the location of one of these parties before. Just never seen them happen live.'

Fuller sipped her champagne. 'You kept that quiet.'

'I thought Max might have already told you. It was a few years ago. Part of a case we were working. Tell me about the hosts here.'

'They used to work in the City. I think the guy, Graydon, inherited something and they both decided to live a life of leisure.'

'And Mistress Zhia?'

'AKA Kendra. She's Welsh. Chinese mother. Pretty sure she changed her name for exotic appeal. You'll never guess her original name.'

'Enid?'

Fuller spluttered on a sip of champagne. 'You're not that far off, actually.'

'Hilda?'

She looked at him. 'No.' He shrugged, shook his

head. She leaned in to whisper. 'Glynys.' She pointed to the window. 'Ah! I can see her out back. Follow me.'

Fuller pushed through the crowd and exited through a side door onto a slim decking area that ran along the back side of the main building. By the time Sawyer caught up, she was air-kissing a tall, elegant woman with long, shining black hair and lurid red lipstick. She wore a black PVC catsuit with a front zip, and a thick chain belt draped around her waist.

'Kendra,' said Fuller, 'this is my friend, Lloyd. Be gentle with him.'

Kendra stepped forward and held out a gloved hand. As Sawyer shook it, she leered at him over the top of her blue-tinted half-moon shades. 'Fresh meat. Always welcome. What are you into, Lloyd?'

'I'll try anything once. Twice if I like it.'

Kendra smiled. 'You don't have a drink. You're not religious, are you?'

'Far from it. Just not my poison.'

'You should put some fizz in your life. It's later than you think.' She eased herself back down into the corner of a curved lilac sofa, which overlooked a glass-fronted barn converted into an indoor pool and sauna. A steady flow of guests in towels and bathrobes padded in and out of the pool, along a raised walkway.

Fuller whispered into Sawyer's ear. 'Going for a quick wander. Careful you don't get eaten alive.'

'Are you playing with us tonight, Lloyd?' Kendra patted the sofa next to her. 'You should try the playrooms. And the cinema. You could start by joining someone in a private area, build up to the grope room.'

'That sounds intimate.'

'Pitch black,' said Kendra. 'With a partition for roaming hands.'

Sawyer sat down, in the red glow of a wall-mounted light. He looked up at the sconce: an octopus tentacle holding a bulb aloft. 'Can I ask you about your...'

'Services? Well, of course. At the moment, I'm Kendra. But once the masks come off, so does mine.' She held her arms out wide. 'I *transform*.'

'Into Mistress Zhia?'

Kendra beamed at him. 'Poppy has briefed you well. I trust she isn't expecting a commission.' She reached out a hand and ran it along the top of Sawyer's thigh. 'I do hope you'll commit yourself tonight, Lloyd. We have a fabulous pole dancer booked for the pre-midnight spot. She always raises the temperature.' She sat back. 'I have a feeling we'll be welcoming you for one of our legendary early breakfasts.'

'I'm a cereal and toast type. Not great with oats and avocado.'

'We need to bring you up to date, Mr Robbins. You're stuck in the past.' Kendra rose to her feet, catsuit creaking. She held out a hand. 'Let's go for a walk. You should see a bit more of how we enjoy life here.'

Sawyer followed her along the decking and across the walkway, her laced stiletto boots raising her close to his height. They passed a recently built single-storey outbuilding with a small raised window that flickered with light from within.

'That's our cinema. Last used yesterday afternoon by our two young children. *Kung Fu Panda 3*.' She turned and grinned at him. 'Don't worry. They're with their grandparents at weekends.'

They joined a straight path leading to a long low-rise building set apart at the back of a gravel courtyard.

'Do you keep horses?' said Sawyer.

She laughed. 'I think the previous owners did. We've refitted the stables into various playrooms. The dual doors fit our rules. Leave both open if you're happy to welcome participants. Top door only for viewers. Both closed for private. So, go on. I need more. What services were you interested in?'

'Poppy said you're a dominatrix.'

Kendra winced. 'I prefer the term *domina*. From *mea domina*. My lady. So this is why you're here on Kinks & Queens night?'

'How do you normally introduce new clients? Do you vet people?'

She glanced at him. 'Of course. I try to keep to a small contingent of regulars, though. Lower maintenance.'

'And do you see people from all over London? The UK?'

'I have clients who fly in from New York, sometimes at short notice. The majority are ageing executives with more money than they can spend. I know that world, because I used to be a part of it myself. I bossed young men around for an obscene salary. Now I boss middle-aged men around for even more.'

'You worked in finance?'

'Yes. I used to be *respectable*. I toed that tedious line for way too long. But then I changed. We can all change, can't we? We don't have to be the same thing forever. A slave to the same old impulses.'

Two topless men in polished black eye masks passed Kendra and Sawyer and headed into the pool.

'We're literally not the same people we were,' said Sawyer.

'Oh. Yes. You're right. Our cells die and renew, don't they?'

'Not all of them, but enough to make us distinct from the previous version.'

Kendra stopped and angled her head at Sawyer. 'What's your work, Mr Robbins?'

'I'm a writer. I want to set some... stories in this kind of world.'

She carried on towards the courtyard. 'Interesting.'

A burst of shrill female laughter drifted over from one of the stables.

'Sounds like someone couldn't wait to get the second half of the evening started,' said Sawyer.

'No. Some can't. We call them early risers.'

They stopped at the end stable. The top door was open, but it was empty and dark inside. Plumes of incense wafted over the courtyard from cones placed on tables around the edge of the building. Kendra opened the lower door, turned on a light—more red bulbs—and they stepped inside.

Apart from the wooden fittings, there was little evidence of the room's previous function. The floor was tiled in grey marble, and the walls painted midnight blue and hung with erotic ephemera. A tall black upholstered chair sat against the far wall. The centrepiece was a heavy-duty platform on raised legs with two jutting side panels. Hooks around the walls displayed costumes and accessories: straitjackets, harnesses, hoods, muzzles.

Sawyer walked over to what looked like a red leather hammock in the corner, suspended from the ceiling by straps and reins.

'That's a sex swing. It's a bit off-theme for here, but it's popular. I call this the House of Pain. I sometimes bring clients here for play, before the party gets moving. I'm leaving for a private booking elsewhere tonight, though, so it's open to all.'

'And the chair is for restraint?'

'It's customisable. Doms can use it as a throne to be worshipped by their subs, or they can incorporate the restraints for enslavement, humiliation. The platform is a whipping bench.'

The laughter again, filtering in from the adjoining stable. Screechy this time, fading to a moan.

Sawyer nodded to a studded iron door. 'What's through there?'

Kendra smiled. 'Have a look.'

He opened the door and stepped through into a windowless chamber with black padded walls. A huge wheel, also padded and black, loomed in the centre, mounted on a supporting frame. Sturdy restraints formed a spreadeagled human shape across the wheel's surface.

'I take it this isn't the crèche?'

'It's a soundproof room, mainly for hardcore deprivation, isolation. The wheel revolves.' Kendra pointed to an upright human-shaped metal frame suspended from the ceiling. 'I like the wheel, but I prefer the gibbet cage. I have a client who likes to spend hours in there.'

Sawyer pressed a thumb into the padding on the wheel. 'Is this all custom-made?'

'No. We get it from John Lewis. Of course it's custom-made. Most things are manufactured in Amsterdam and Germany and stored by wholesale companies. I use a place called Fetworld. Their showroom is quite a spectacle.' Kendra walked over to a wall-mounted cupboard with a glass front. She took out a contraption with a vacuum cleaner-style tube and bag. 'This is an aroma rig. Fill the bag with your favourite gas, strap it on, and release at will. Or surrender that decision to your dom.'

'And this is part of breath play?'

'It is. I do offer that, but you have to set strict rules. It's pretty niche.' She replaced the rig and walked out of the room; Sawyer followed and closed the door.

'How niche?'

She shrugged. 'It's not something I'm keen on. There are people who can't get off without restricting their own breathing. Others fetishise it as the ultimate form of control. The ones who need it themselves often find it difficult to get willing partners. It's why you see so many deaths from auto-erotic asphyxiation. They feel too much shame to visit sex workers.'

They walked back out to the gravel courtyard.

A *thunk* from the adjoining stable, followed by the female shriek. A male voice responded, in an admonishing tone.

Sawyer took a few breaths, unrefreshed by the scorched evening air. 'And... your clients. What's the psychology behind their fascination? Their fetish.'

Kendra sighed and tidied her hair. 'I feel like I'm being interviewed, Mr Robbins.'

'Sorry. Just... fascinated.'

Another *thunk*. Another scream. Then the male voice, more aggressive this time.

Kendra took a seat at a table on the edge of the courtyard. 'Restricted airflow can lead to heightened orgasm, but breath play is about the power, the eroticism of extreme trust. Particularly with smothering breath play. There might be something in the person's past that has allied itself with the thrill of restriction, deprivation.'

'Suffocation,' said Sawyer, joining her at the table, struggling to keep his own breathing steady.

'The mistake people make with BDSM, Mr Robbins, is they see it as someone indulging a sadistic or masochistic side. It's more about trust, an exchange of roles. With breath play, I find that it goes deeper still.' She leaned forward, shadows flickering on her face from a candle on the table. 'There can be something god-like about it. An absolute dominion over a fundamental function of life. To deny someone's ability to breathe is to deny them access to the air that's keeping *you* alive. You could almost say it's a way of celebrating your own aliveness.'

'Extreme mindfulness.'

She smiled. 'Sort of.'

They were still for a moment.

Another *thunk* startled Sawyer, and as the scream followed, he raised himself from the chair, as if ready to investigate, intervene.

Kendra rested a hand on his wrist. 'Don't interpret that sound as a cry for help. Seriously. That's not a damsel in distress. For me, a lot of BDSM is about the management of *fear*. How it can be constructed and destroyed. How it can be used as a tool for healing both environmental and inherited trauma. As Mistress Zhia, I introduce fear, then soothe it with relief. A consolation. For many of my clients, the sessions aren't about indulging a kink. They're therapy.'

Thunk.

Sawyer's breaths grew short, jagged.

Scream.

His vision compressed and crumpled. He flushed hot, sweaty. The Venetian mask stuck to his skin and he raised it for a moment, wiping his forehead.

His dog, barking and barking and barking.

Concern on Kendra's face. Her hand on his shoulder.

Thunk.

Scream.

His mother's scream now, as the hammer fell, shattering her cheekbones, collapsing her eye socket.

Sawyer sprang to his feet, stumbling, steadying himself with a fist on the gravel. He scrambled back to the stables, towards the source of the noise.

Kendra grabbed at him, but he shrugged her away, and shouldered through the double-closed door of the adjoining stable. His hearing had fuzzed over and he tore off the mask, gasping for air, clawing at the space in front.

A topless man in skin-tight trousers and heavy work boots stood over a woman facing the wall, her wrists locked in the clasps of a wall-mounted punishment rack.

The man backed away, brandishing a thick black paddle.

Outraged shouts, ruptured and vague.

A miasma of lilac, pheromone, choking incense.

Kendra's hands on him, as she implored.

Sawyer dropped to one knee, his knuckles on the cold marble floor. The man approached him, pointing, shouting.

The scene greyed out, slid away.

26

Deon Kinsella swerved in from the street and ran down a set of uneven stone steps. He had a thumb pressed to the bell beside the basement door with three steps to spare.

Inside, a dog barked, rabid and furious, and a male face appeared at the window. The door opened, and Kinsella shoved past the two goons and knelt to pet Doyle's pit bull, who whimpered and rolled over.

'Is he in?'

'Gym,' said the taller goon.

Kinsella let the dog play-bite his fist, then walked across the member's bar area to a set of double doors marked *PRIVATE.* The doors opened to a wooden-floored gymnasium marked out for basketball, but repurposed with resistance machines, spin bike, treadmill. Mickey Doyle stood beneath a wall-mounted TV, landing flurries of punches to the face of a free-standing torso dummy.

He paused to look up at the football on the TV.

'Never a fuckin' penalty. Not in a billion years. These officials have got one job, Deon. Get the decisions right.'

Kinsella looked up at the screen. 'Can't imagine your boys are looking forward to next season after the last derby.'

'Get fucked.' Doyle rocked the dummy with a decisive haymaker and yanked a towel down from a wall rack.

Kinsella took a can of Red Bull from a fridge and handed it to Doyle. 'We've found Curtis Mavers.'

'Who's *we*?'

'One of my lads got word. Mavers likes a bet, so I had all the bookies on the lookout in his old stomping ground.'

'Birkenhead.'

'Yeah. Cocky bastard went to the Ladbrokes down the road from his hotel. Small place.'

Doyle padded his forehead with the towel. 'I'd do the same. Nowhere posh. He's keepin' his head down until he can spend Stokes's money somewhere better than the knocking shops of Tranmere.'

Kinsella took a Diet Coke for himself, cracked the ring pull. 'We giving him to Stokes, then?'

Doyle slurped his drink and sat down on a workout bench. 'I'm curious.' He tapped his forehead. 'So many questions about Mavers and his detective pal robbing Stokes's boys. But I like to get my info nice and pure. First hand. I want to know if there's any plan to expand the operation. Do we need to throw out a few warnings to our big boys?' He held Kinsella's eye. 'I'm not running a fucking charity here. Wouldn't hurt to have a private chat with Mavers before we feed him to the Mancs. You could stay over. Must be a couple of salubrious saunas up in New Brighton.'

Kinsella lifted a dumbbell from a rack and tried a few bicep curls. 'I might do that. There's a place called the Dolphin. Bit of a dump. T-girls, though. And I might piss off up to Crosby when we're done. See the Gormley sculptures.' He replaced the weight. 'I'll go first thing.'

'No, you won't. You'll go now. Solo. Dawn raid. Don't fucking call me until nineish, though. I'll have a little FaceTime with Wolf Boy, then give Stokes a bell for the handover.'

Kinsella sipped his Coke. 'I had a look into this Jake Sawyer fella.' He took out his phone, scrolled through the Notes app. 'He witnessed the murder of his own mother when he was six years old. Father was an ex-copper turned painter. Topped himself a couple of years ago.' He looked up from the phone. 'Sawyer was there for that, too.'

'Jesus Christ.'

'Also, he's been on the fucking run for murder, Mickey. Few months ago. They dropped the case when a key witness changed testimony.' He slipped the phone into his back pocket. 'And he supports the mighty reds.'

Doyle balked. 'For a minute there, he almost sounded like someone we could work with.'

'Still, though. Easy to imagine why he'd be bezzies with the likes of Mavers. Are we missing a trick here? Maybe Sawyer is also keen to find Mavers. We could play them off. Bit of leverage. Just slapping Mavers around before handing him to Stokes and his merry band... Feels like we're leaving something on the table.'

Doyle headed for the wet-room at the back of the gym. 'I get it. But keep it simple for now. Find out from Mavers why he dropped Sawyer's name to Stokes. Go from there. And make sure he gets to Manchester with all his limbs fully functional. I don't want to start a war.'

27

Sawyer trudged down the narrow corridor of Waterfront House. He paused at the half-open oblong window and pushed his face into the gap. A lukewarm breeze, loaded with river stink and takeaway grease. He screwed his eyes shut, and the images reared up, tumbling and blending, replaying it all: a kick aimed at his body but clipping the side of his face; Kendra, frantic and fearful, hauling him away; scattered guests observing his exit, emotion hidden behind their masks.

He let himself into the apartment and walked straight through to the kitchen. Microwave clock: 1:30am. He leaned against the door frame, head pulsing, bones tender with exhaustion.

Sawyer opened the fridge and took out the last of Maggie's brownies. Peanut butter. He kicked off his boots and padded into the bedroom, cueing up the smart speaker with music from his phone. Burial. Eerie and beatless soundscapes to quiet his mind. Snatches of processed vocal. Desolate, estranged.

Hold me close.

Footsteps in snow, disfigured sirens.

He chewed the brownie. There was interest in the texture, but the taste had been muted by time.

Make me feel like I'm in love.

Sawyer sat on the bed and opened the bedside table drawer. He took out the orange notebook and rested it on his lap. It was marked by his mother, with his mother's name, but it was not his mother. It was cardboard, paper. Dead trees. Plastic. Pigments and solvents.

Night has come.

For the first time, he was angered by the book's permanence, its lack of potential. It would only ever exist in its current state, squatting at the end of a severed timeline, holding its comfort out of reach.

I've been in a bad place.

His nose twitched with a familiar scent. Dark, smoky.

He held the journal to his nose. Not that.

Not the open drawer, either.

He sighed, replaced the book, walked through into the unlit sitting room. He tugged at the bottom of the window, grinding it open another few inches. 'How did you get in?'

'Old lock.'

Sawyer fixed his eyes forward, keeping the sofa and the man in his periphery. 'I thought we were good.'

He turned.

Austin Fletcher got to his feet, with caution, his face in shadow, framed by his scraped-back blond hair. He drew in a slow breath. 'We are.'

Fletcher walked over to the window, his booted footfalls heavy on the wooden floor. He stopped a few feet from Sawyer, marking more territory with the aroma of exotic tobacco. He held up his phone screen.

Text message.

Housing development in woods starts in three days.
Full ground excavation.

Sawyer reached out to the phone, scrolled the message to see the final line.

YOUR SECRET ISN'T SAFE

Here by the window, Fletcher's hollow eyes seemed to swallow the gauzy moonlight. He raised his head, and at last Sawyer caught signs of life.

Fletcher pocketed his phone. 'You?'

'Not me.'

'Who, then?'

Sawyer flicked on a corner lamp. Fletcher retreated to the sofa while Sawyer took a chair beneath the window.

'Withheld number, I assume?' said Sawyer.

Fletcher nodded.

'So, who knows? About Walton.'

Fletcher raised his index finger towards Sawyer, but kept his hand rested on the sofa arm.

Sawyer got up and dragged the chair over by the coffee table. He sat and leaned forward. Fletcher barely flinched, tracking Sawyer's movement with his eyes alone. 'Is it just Walton you put there?'

Fletcher's gaze fell.

'Jerome? Sorry, Marian.'

Fletcher nodded.

'The Scottish guy?'

'Marco,' said Fletcher, nodding.

Sawyer dropped his head. He traced the knot patterns, soothing himself with their concentric geometry. 'That it?'

Fletcher paused, nodded again.

'Who knows your number? Dale?'

Fletcher nodded. 'A few others.'

'It must be Dale. But how can he know? Trackers on his men?'

Fletcher caught Sawyer's gaze again. 'Naked.'

'All of them?'

A single nod.

'Could they have something internal? Implant? Earrings?'

No response from Fletcher.

'However they know, they know. So you have to move.'

'We.'

Sawyer gave a slow, decisive shake of the head. 'I can't go back until I'm done here. Keep watch on the location. Don't move until there's sign of preparation for this excavation.'

'Too late by then.'

Sawyer got up from the chair, paced. 'I'll check with the local station. They would need to be informed if there's work planned. Potential resident disturbance, traffic issues.'

Fletcher scowled. 'They find something—'

'I know,' said Sawyer. 'It comes back to you.'

'*Us.*'

Sawyer sat on the chair again, waited for Fletcher to look at him. 'It's bait. Do you know poker?'

Fletcher nodded.

'You need to check. See if you can find out more about the cards the other players are holding. I'm out of favour down here, anyway. Give me a couple of days. I can help, but—'

'Now.'

Sawyer stared him out. 'Soon.'

28

Martha Dumas let herself into the house and slid her duffel bag along the hall floorboards. As ever, her aim was true, and the bag came to rest at the bottom of the staircase. She turned, by muscle memory, and reached up to the alarm control panel. She lifted the glass covering, reached an index finger to the keypad...

And paused.

Normally, her entry would trigger the near-silent pre-alarm, giving her a minute to enter the code before the system activated the main alarm and relayed an alert to the police.

She strained her ear. The pre-alarm was subtle, but distinct.

Nothing.

Dumas walked through to the vast dining room and unlatched the French windows. She stepped out onto a tiled patio overlooking a modest but immaculate garden, bordered with coral peonies, basking in the morning sun.

She took a seat, placed her paperback on the tabletop, and lit a cigarette. A quick chapter, then coffee, as she did the kitchen surfaces. Then each floor in turn, starting with the second, working down because it gave her a sense of direction, cleaning her way back out through the front door and on to the next job.

Dumas scraped her chair forward, out of the shade, and tapped her ash into the soil at the edge of the tiling. The angle gave her sight of the wooden double doors that led to the storage outhouse and the inner door that connected to the side of the kitchen.

One of the doors was ajar. She walked over, past the outhouse window, propped open by a rusted casement stay.

'Hello?'

She checked her watch. 8:30am. The Healys were normally consistent: all out for work and school by the time she arrived. It was one of her favourite calls. She hated having to clean around occupants, ushering them in and out of rooms, being treated like an inconvenience.

No answer. Dumas checked the lock—intact, key on the inside as ever—and closed the door.

She finished her cigarette, listening to France Inter on her phone's radio app, and walked back into the house. It was too warm for coffee, so she shouldered the duffel bag and climbed the stairs.

At the top of the second flight, she set her phone down on a shelf outside the bathroom and restarted the radio app.

She turned back toward the stairs and bent down to

open the duffel bag. Pink rubber gloves, Harpic, Elbow Grease, Cif.

Dumas frowned at the dim light seeping through the ajar door of the master bedroom on the floor below. She descended the stairs, surprised to find herself tiptoeing.

She rested her fingers on the bedroom door handle and took a breath. Normally, Alison would warn her by text if one of the family was still in the house. Dumas was heading home for summer next week, then driving with her boyfriend to Liguria. If someone was sick, she couldn't afford to catch it.

She hitched up her work blouse, covering her mouth and nose, and walked into the room.

The iron from the blood hit the back of her throat, even through the fabric.

She stared up at the defaced back wall. The bodies beneath it, propped in chairs, side by side. The dark patch beneath Alison Healy's chair.

The silence: dismal, endless.

Dumas yanked the blouse further up her face, covering her nose, as if by obscuring one of her senses she might will all this away: the barren eyes, the tilted heads, the fissure across Alison's neck.

She found the strength to turn, and ran, up the stairs to her phone, jabbering in her mother tongue, calling for a god she didn't believe in. She closed the radio app, dialled 999, ablaze with terror, with nausea. Her inhales were sharp and snatched, her exhales moans of panic.

The operator patched her through to the police responder.

'Hello. My name is Martha. Please help. They are… they are *dead*.'

'Okay, Martha. Try to stay calm. Are you safe right now? Are you in any immediate danger?'

'No. I'm okay.'

'Right. You're breathing quite quickly, Martha. Try to calm yourself. You've done the hard bit. I just need your location. Then I can get you some help, okay?'

Noises from behind, across the landing.

Movement. A door opening.

'Is there anyone in the house with you?'

A shard of fear ripped through Dumas, and she turned.

A young boy in Spider-Man pyjamas emerged from a walk-in airing cupboard between the two bedrooms. He stared at Dumas with wide, wild eyes.

'Martha? Is there anyone else there with you?'

The boy ran to her, wrapped himself round her legs.

'Yes, there is.'

PART TWO

SEA OF TEARS

29

He learned to ride the dark.

She didn't know that. She thought the dark was a preview of death, that its presence would somehow accelerate his end. And for a while, it pressed on him, walled him off.

And she thought the dark was where he should have stayed. She gave him many names: all foul, usually hissed into his face, imprinted by her stinging saliva.

Accident.

Shit Stain.

And then *he* came along, and added his own.

Stillbirth.

Dead Boy.

And the dark gave the names form, defined his reality.

But then he learned to ride the dark. It became like soil. The ground that grew him.

When he was sent out in the world, when they had to

send him out, he made them regret it. And so, they put him back in the dark.

'Don't worry,' *she* would say, as she pushed him in. 'You'll be back where you belong soon.'

And then the door, and the dark.

And always the shouting and screaming elsewhere in the house. The damp crack of the punches. The keening remorse.

His visits would always follow. Stale bread, brackish water. A dog dish of leftovers tossed in, usually spilled, forcing him to gouge it out of the filthy carpet.

His face at the door, crumpled with hatred, outlined by the torch propped on the basement floor behind.

'You are not here. You don't exist.' On a good day, *he* would stay outside and jab a finger at him. 'Your mother had no choice. They had to cut you out, like a tumour. But this is your life now. She gave you life, but you will never *live*. *Dead Boy*.'

And on a bad day, *he* would crawl inside, filling the tiny space with sour breath. And *he* would take his neck in his rough hands, and squeeze, forcing a stubby thumb into his windpipe, numbing his limbs, muffling his hearing. *He* would always time it just right, sending him deeper into the dark before releasing him, pulling him back.

'See?' *he* would say. 'I decide. Not God. I'm your god, *Shit Stain*. You can have another day. But you'll need to work for it...'

He learned fast from then. He learned to accept the

agony, to claim it as his right, as evidence of his existence. His sole source of sensation.

He learned that his continuing aliveness fuelled the shouting and screaming, telegraphed the pain.

He learned that he wasn't supposed to survive, and yet he did.

And so, he renounced his god, and learned to ride the dark.

30

'The Healys,' said Conway, climbing the stairs in front of Sawyer. 'Mother and father. John, Alison. Two boys aged six and seven. Noah, Isaac.'

They squashed into the wall to make way for two suited forensic officers heading down to the ground floor.

'And the other boy?'

Conway sighed. 'Nathan Carroll. Turned seven last week.' They reached the landing, showed their warrant cards to the officer at the door of the master bedroom. 'He was here on a sleepover. The cleaner, Martha Dumas, discovered everything early this morning. According to her, Nathan was hiding in the airing cupboard between the boys' bedrooms. He came out when he heard her voice.'

'Same kind of place,' said Sawyer. 'Three floors, similar area. What did they do?'

'Alison was a consultant. Urology. John lectured at Roehampton. History.'

Sawyer walked into the larger of the two bedrooms. Iron-frame bunk bed; stacked shelves of action figures and picture books; laundry basket hung from the bed post; peg rack on the inside of the door hung with comic character costumes: Batman, Captain America, Hulk. A silvery-grey sign above the bunk bed read *ADVENTURE AWAITS*; another above the figure shelf read *HEROES*. The furniture was upmarket; more Heals than IKEA.

He inhaled. Sweet polish, synthetic fruit fragrance from a scented candle.

Conway hovered in the doorway. 'This is Isaac's room. The cleaner says Nathan has slept over a few times before, but he usually sleeps in here. Noah's room is smaller, no bunk.'

Sawyer walked out to the landing, nudged open the door of a small bathroom at the top of the stairs. 'Maybe he got up, saw the killer, but the killer didn't see him. Made it into the cupboard before he was spotted.' Sawyer opened another door next to the bathroom: a small but deep utility room with stacks of towels and bedding. He crouched. A compartment unit at the back held more bedding, pillows, freshener sprays.

'Oh,' said Conway. 'Forensics came back on Maxwell's letter. Nothing.'

Sawyer walked into the master bedroom. Neil Shah stood with his back to them, gesticulating to a grim-faced junior officer as he tapped something into a tablet.

As with the other families, the Healys sat bound to chairs, all in nightwear, side by side in front of the far wall. Noah had slipped to the left, tilting his chair into Isaac, resting his head on his brother's arm.

Sawyer crouched before them. 'Same deal. Eyes untaped, but only the mother's nostrils left free. Mother's throat cut. All the others suffocated.' He looked up at the wall. Same pentagram, same runes. 'He's almost finished.'

'What do you mean?' said Shah, moving in from behind.

Sawyer stood up. 'He can't sustain it. Daily attacks of this complexity. The planning required. The stress on him. Two-week gap, then two-day gap. He's speeding up. You'll only catch him if you up the pace, too.'

Shah scoffed. 'Shall I tell my officers to do their work more quickly, DI Sawyer?'

'Yes.' Sawyer walked out, trailed by Shah and Conway. 'And get more officers. Use agencies. Retirees. Better labs. Faster labs. The room's on fire and you're running round with a water pistol.'

'We're flat out,' said Conway.

'Get flatter. There's a family out there who might not see another sunrise. Can I talk to Nathan?'

'Significant witness,' said Conway. 'Tier threes have done the initial video interview.' She dropped her voice. 'Sawyer, this boy's older brother Ollie was killed in a coach crash on an icy road last year. Nathan survived it. Four other lads were also killed. I'm hearing the tier threes are getting next to nothing. He won't even tell them what happened before he got into the cupboard.'

'Parents?'

'He's under guard at the family home. Social services protection, FLO. Tier threes will be in contact to see when he might do a second interview. It'll all go through social protection now, though. His wellbeing comes before the enquiry.'

Sawyer dug his fingers through his hair. 'Maybe he'll talk to the cleaner.'

'She's in a state herself,' said Conway. 'Tier threes are with her, too. She said that Nathan sometimes sleeps in the cupboard when the boys clash about who's having the top bunk. Calls it his den. His mother Alison warned her he might leave rubbish in there, but he's always left it tidy.' She looked at her phone. 'Hatfield is calling us back for a briefing.'

'If he wants forensics fast-tracked,' said Shah, 'I'll have to decline.'

Conway shook her head. 'He knows that. He's asking for me.' She looked up. 'And Sawyer.'

———

Conway weaved her Skoda around the stop-start traffic and turned onto Putney Bridge. Low morning sun flashed off the Thames, and she flipped down her visor.

'That's only just the second worst thing I've seen all day,' said Sawyer, looking back to the junction.

'The traffic?'

'Bar on the corner. *Tequila Mockingbird*.'

She winced. 'It's a chain. Cocktail bar. We did

birthday drinks there a few weeks ago. One of the FLOs on the current case, actually.'

Sawyer looked around the car interior. 'Is this your vehicle?'

Conway scowled at him.

'Madam.'

'Pool car. General purpose. I'm not sure if that's a genuine question, Sawyer, or a passive-aggressive dig at my taste.'

'What do you think?'

'Well. Glass houses.'

He nodded. 'I don't drive a Mini ironically. I love it. My mum used to have one.'

She shuffled in her seat and dropped the driver's window. Sawyer did likewise, as Conway accelerated over the bridge. The wind swirled in from the river, tousling their hair.

'He's spent a long time on this,' said Sawyer.

'Who?'

'Our killer. The increased frequency of attacks. The families have been staked out way in advance. We still don't know the logic behind his selection.'

Sawyer fished a tube of Starburst from his pocket and unwrapped one. 'Do you mind?'

'What? The rustling? The chewing?'

He slid the sweet into his mouth. 'The rustling is over. And I'm a quiet chewer.'

'Normally, I get detectives asking if they can smoke in my car.'

'Inner child. He needs a lot of sugar.'

She glanced at him. 'It's the worst thing for you. I don't have it in the house.'

'Your boy must love that. How old?'

Side-eye. 'Nine.' She sighed. 'Christ. Those boys. And that young lad.'

Sawyer chewed, silently, gazing across the river to the dense clutch of trees bordering Fulham Palace. 'He'll need a lot of care and attention. His old life is over. It's like a broken bone. You can't just leave it to fix by itself, because it'll be misshapen, weaker.'

'I'm so torn. We need his testimony, professionally, but personally, I hope he didn't see or hear too much.'

Sun flare.

Streaks of red, shining among the grass. Beads, extending and dripping.

He dropped his visor and twisted it over the top of his passenger window. 'Did Hatfield say why I was off his naughty list?'

'No. I didn't know you were on it.'

'He thinks I'm...' A beat of silence.

'Struggling?' said Conway. 'I thought you were mainly here for your experience. Research, consultation.'

Sawyer turned back to the window. 'The DSI in Buxton said he was considering me for DCI. At first, I didn't see how Hatfield needed me. But things have been colourful up north, lately. This gets me out of the way, checks on where my head's really at. Hatfield and Keating are old friends.'

'And you think Hatfield isn't liking what he sees?'

'No. That's why he put me in the corner. It's

probably been relayed to Keating already.' He took out his phone, browsed for something.

'So, what do you think he's seeing?'

'History repeating.' He turned to her. 'You know my story.'

Conway kept her eyes on the road. 'Mostly.'

'Before I transferred back to Derbyshire a few years ago, I found out that the man who had been convicted of my mother's murder was due for release. It tripped a wire in me. I wasn't at my best. Poor judgement, over-indulgence, self-medicating. Erratic in briefings, taking on too much, trying to hold too much in my head. I screwed up a relationship I had down here. And I almost cost an armed officer his life when I missed something during a trafficking raid.' He glanced at her. 'And Hatfield looked the other way when I covered something up, to save Reeves's marriage.'

'Max Reeves?'

'Yeah. It didn't directly affect the case, but it was a misjudgement. I asked for the transfer and Hatfield was only too happy to accept. I was being groomed for greatness, but he made his case and the Chief Constable obliged.' He unwrapped another Starburst. 'But I assume you know all of this. Hatfield must have briefed you when he assigned you as my babysitter.'

Conway sighed, deeper, buying time. 'He didn't think you'd miss that, either. But does any of it matter now?'

'No,' said Sawyer, chewing. 'That's why I'm back in the tent pissing out. With Hatfield, it's... Columbo

214

Syndrome. He thrives on being underestimated. He's a mess on the outside, but he's *sharp*.'

Conway smiled. 'He taught you all you know.'

'Most of it. Now he's done his favour for my boss. But the situation is getting worse, and he's no closer to making it better. So, his pragmatic side has kicked in. He's switched from obligations to necessities. He used to say to me, "There's no time for nice-to-haves. We focus on needs".'

Conway turned off the bridge and slipped into the lane leading to the MIT office car park. 'So, what does he need?'

'The best man for the job.'

31

'*Sawyer!*'

Hatfield beckoned from his office, then walked inside and held the door open.

'Doesn't look like I'm top of his list, after all,' said Conway. 'I'll send in help if you're not out in fifteen minutes.'

Sawyer shoved his way through the detectives packed in for the briefing. The bodies smelt earthy and unlaundered. Sleep-starved eyes tracked him as he crossed to the office.

Hatfield closed the door and flopped into his chair. 'I have twelve people dead. We're fucking *nowhere* with this.'

Sawyer lingered by the door. 'There are two key people. One, a witness. Nathan.'

'We *might* have a witness.' Hatfield pulled out his handkerchief, mopped his forehead. 'If he opens up. The lad has gone limp. He's not even hugging his parents.'

'Tier threes are good, but they take time. My father told me it took them two weeks to get anything out of me after my mother's death.'

Hatfield rested his chin on his hands. 'I'm not sending you in with him, Sawyer, if that's where you're going. I know there's a parallel, but—'

'Not me. I know someone who could help. She's a trained FLO and counsellor. And a mother. DSI Keating will vouch for her. Just give her some time with him. We lose nothing trying, and we might gain something.'

'Give me the details. She'll need to drop everything now, though. So, who's the other key person?'

'The Healys' cleaner.'

Hatfield stuffed the handkerchief back into his pocket. 'Halle-fucking-lujah. A traumatised kid and an adult who barely speaks English.' He sighed, slurped his coffee.

Sawyer sat down, found Hatfield's gaze.

'All hands,' said Hatfield.

'He's planned all of this too carefully to leave anything to chance. There's nothing random. He's laid it all out for himself. I just searched for the cleaner who discovered the Healys. Martha Dumas. The cleaners for all three families work for several agencies, but they share only one.' He held up his phone; the screen showed a bright but corporate-looking website with testimonials and a header in a sober font: *KwikClean*.

Hatfield squinted at the screen. 'I know it. Mainly covers the Barnes, Hammersmith and Fulham areas.

Makes sense. Two of the vic houses in Barnes, one in Hammersmith.' He shrugged, waiting for a pay-off.

'I'm wondering if he got to the cleaners. Made them give him the codes. That would explain how he deactivated the alarms once he'd got in. He's staked these places out carefully. No cameras, older alarm systems. The cleaners would be a good way to gain access to security, the families' routines and rhythms.'

'We've checked the first two, Sawyer. There's precisely zero evidence that they're being squeezed. And I've heard Martha Dumas's emergency call. Seriously. This was all news to her.' Hatfield groaned as he sprang up from his chair. 'I'm happy for your counsellor friend to talk to the boy, though. Right. Move your arse. Briefing.'

Sawyer's phone rang; he looked at the Caller ID. 'Sir. Need to take this.'

'Is it the pope?'

'No.'

'Then you don't need to take it. We've got a briefing.'

Sawyer checked the screen again, gave him a grave look.

Hatfield stopped at the door. 'Who is it?'

'Everett Asher. From Broadmoor.'

32

Deon Kinsella smiled at the receptionist and turned into the gloomy ground floor corridor of the Birkenhead Premier Inn. The carpet crunched beneath his feet, and he grimaced at the breakfast odours leaking from the vents. His lower back throbbed from the drive and he ached for a hot shower and a warm body. The sauna could wait. After the job, he'd head back to the city and call on an old Norwegian chef friend. His favourite combination: clean eating, dirty mind.

Kinsella stopped at Room 7 and looked back down the corridor. Empty, quiet. He slipped the revolver from inside his belt and pushed his ear to the door.

Silence.

He took the universal key card from his back pocket and slipped it into the lock. The light flashed green. Holding the gun at his hip, he turned the handle, eased open the door, and found himself eye to eye with a silenced Glock pistol.

Curtis Mavers grinned and nodded down to the revolver. 'Easy now, soft lad.' He held out his other hand. 'Let's have your little friend.'

Kinsella handed over his gun. Mavers nodded to the window and Kinsella walked past, into the room.

Mavers closed the door, keeping his eyes and the Glock fixed on Kinsella. He edged forward, turning slightly, revealing the tattoo on his forearm: a wolf with wild eyes, breathing fire from its open jaws. He was tall and broad, bulked with muscle, fully dressed in a grubby white T-shirt and jeans. The room was sterile and modular, undisturbed but for the messy bed.

'Took your time,' said Mavers. 'I clocked the fella at the bookies yesterday.' He laughed. 'Shifty as fuck. I assume he gave you the room number.'

Kinsella stood at the window, head down, eyes fixed on the Glock. He glanced back at the partially drawn curtains. 'We can work this out, Curtis. Just lose the gun. Please.'

Mavers stepped forward. 'I never thought Dale's cleaner would be a Scouser.'

'I'm not a cleaner. I came armed because I knew you would be.'

Mavers sat down in a padded chair beneath the tiny wall-mounted TV. 'We're in the Premier Inn, not the O.K. Corral.'

'Who's Dale?' said Kinsella.

Mavers studied him for a few seconds, then pointed. 'You're good. But the guy with the gun gets to ask the questions. You red or blue?'

'Red.'

Mavers grinned. 'Correct answer. Next question. Who, then? If not Dale.'

Kinsella dropped his gaze.

'Don't be thinking about a dramatic exit, by the way. The windows don't open without a key.' He shuffled the chair closer to Kinsella. 'Taurus revolver. Bit of a girly gun. And you're too pretty for hired muscle. And *metro*. I'm getting a whiff of something expensive. Too early for cologne.'

'Vitamin E. Hydrator.'

Mavers nodded, shuffled closer. 'You'll have to tell me the brand.' He smiled and aimed the gun at Kinsella's knee. 'Okay. Let's go again. If not Dale, who?'

Kinsella stared him down.

Mavers rocked in the chair, angling his head. 'You're knocking on a bit. But you look after yourself, don't you? I'd wager you like the gym, maybe a bit of running, cycling.' He leaned forward. 'Do you know what happens when you get kneecapped? Most likely you'll get a joint fracture. A lot of them are so severe they cause neurovascular damage. Hospital food for weeks. Physio for months, maybe years. If they can't fix it, they sometimes amputate below the knee. Forget never walk alone. You'll never walk again.'

'Jake Sawyer,' said Kinsella.

'Go on.'

'He sent me. The fella who followed you was police. They're getting ready to pick you up. Sawyer intercepted the intel and sent me to get you out first. He wants a reset.'

Mavers beamed at him; gold glinted from a gem in one of his front teeth. '*Bless*. You think I spilled Sawyer's name to Stokes because we were working together and we've had a row or something.' He stood up. 'It's a good effort. I'm not having it, though.' He jabbed the gun at Kinsella and pointed with his other hand. 'You're on Leon's books, somehow. I reckon our next stop was the Polish psycho he told me about. And if you're on Leon's books, that makes you a drug dealer. And I really fucking hate drug dealers.'

Kinsella shook his head. 'I don't know what you mean by "Stokes".'

Mavers laughed. 'You *are* good. You got a car here?'

Kinsella nodded.

'Looks like a nice day. Let's go for a drive up to Wallasey. Bit of sea air will do you good.'

33

Hatfield stood in silence at the front of the MIT briefing room, head lowered. The chatter subsided, and he looked up. 'Ladies and gentlemen. As you all know, we believe the perpetrator of the Prior and Carter family murders is also responsible for the deaths of a family of four whose bodies were found by their cleaner at their home in Barnes earlier this morning.' He stepped to the side of the whiteboard and pointed at the third column of photographs. 'Alison and John Healy, and their two sons Noah and Isaac, aged seven...' He lowered his head again, gathering himself before he looked up. 'And six.'

Sawyer stepped up to the board and referred to his phone as he sketched four new rune symbols beneath a drawing of the previous four. 'Taylor Maxwell received another letter this morning at Broadmoor containing the same symbols, again translating to *I LIVE.*' He turned to the team. 'I did feel that the killer was looking up to

Maxwell because of his crimes or some kind of Satanist connection. But now I'm not so sure.'

'Great,' said McHugh. 'Something else we don't know.'

Hatfield glared at him. 'Let's look at what we *do* know. Three home invasions. Twelve people dead. Maxwell gets a cryptic letter on the morning of each attack. There's no doubt in our killer's mind about the outcomes. The confidence tells us a lot.'

'He's staked out these people over time,' said Sawyer. 'There's nothing left to chance. Whatever he's getting out of the murders personally, sexually, is only a small part of the picture.' He stepped to the side of the whiteboard, turning his back on the glimmers of sun at the window. 'We have enough information now to focus on connections between the victims.'

'There's a lot of work on that already,' said Conway. 'The only real link is the houses are all in the same area of London.'

'We should think more about type,' said Sawyer, 'rather than direct links. The victims were well heeled. Upscale, moneyed. As far as we can tell, they were happy, thriving families. Is there a resentment there? They all had domestic cleaners employed by several agencies, with one shared by all. A company called KwikClean. We think we know how he got into the houses, but if he knew the codes to deactivate the alarms, he might have got them from the cleaners. We need to talk to all three and probe for individuals who connect to them personally or the KwikClean company as a whole.' He stepped forward. 'I want to know about the KwikClean employees. Not just the cleaners. Admin staff, everyone. Any criminal records, sentences, acquittals.' He took another step, and stood ahead of Hatfield, gesticulating wildly. 'And I want to know about the people and companies KwikClean do business with. Affiliates, partners. Any hits in their employees for previous, prison. Cross-reference with companies who might have access to the drugs we've seen in the victim's systems.' He raised his voice. 'Our killer must have had the codes to deactivate the alarms, and so the systems weren't a surprise. He knew those houses had those types of alarm systems. So, tell me about the estate agents, sale histories, alarm installation histories. Who might have access to them? We need some names to work on, before we get another family with a bright future *snuffed out.*'

He took a breath, caught Conway's gaze, her barely suppressed grimace.

DC Rodgers waved her pen in the air. 'Why are you not so sure about the link with Maxwell?'

Sawyer turned to her. 'The communication feels personal. First person. He never refers to Maxwell himself. It's all focused on him. *I* live. Maybe Maxwell's crimes are irrelevant. The methods, the strangulation, the link with suffocation, the occult nonsense. Maybe the messages are all about the killer's relationship with Maxwell. Maybe he's not an admirer, after all. Maybe the letters are taunts.'

'That's a lot of maybes, DI Sawyer,' said Conway,

holding his eye, her critical tone tempered by a tiny nod of solidarity.

Hatfield shifted forward, bringing himself into line with Sawyer. 'We should have drilled down into Maxwell earlier. I pursued and arrested him. I'll dig out my files, talk to Dr Cabrera. There could be something in his past that might help us understand the nature of the messages.' He looked at Rodgers. 'Any joy with the gender support line?'

She shook her head.

'We may only find out the deeper meaning later,' said Sawyer. 'As DCI Hatfield says, we should focus on what we know. Build on that. He always kills on the day of communication with Maxwell. We have to assume that will continue.'

'That's insane,' said McHugh. 'First, a two-week gap, then two days. Is he going to do this every fucking day? How are we going to keep up?'

'Rowan,' said Hatfield in warning.

McHugh opened his desk drawer and pulled out a copy of the morning's *Mirror*. 'The press will have a fucking field day when they get word of the third family.' He waved a hand at Sawyer. 'Usual Met bashing. They already think we're hopeless or corrupt and *he's* been sent as some kind of expert saviour.' He threw the paper to the floor.

Sawyer picked it up. The cover showed a huge picture of himself and Conway entering the MIT office the previous day, with a screamer headline.

Sawyer skimmed the piece. It featured quotes attributed to him on how he'd been brought in to assist because the Met had never seen anything like these crimes before. He looked up; all eyes were on him. 'I didn't speak to anyone. This is all made up.'

'None of this matters,' said Hatfield. 'This time, we might have got a break. A young lad, Nathan Carroll, seven years old. He was on a sleepover at the Healys and was hiding in a walk-in airing cupboard. Came out when he heard the cleaner calling it in. He's slept over there before. The cleaner says he sometimes stays in the cupboard if there's an argument over a bunk bed in one of the boys' rooms. Nathan's older brother was killed in a recent road crash, so he's not in the best state to start with. He's with officers and social service protection at his family home, but he's given us nothing so far. I've authorised an interview with an FLO and counsellor who has significant history with trauma. We just don't know what he knows yet.'

Sawyer stared at the newspaper photograph, struggling to connect his own reality with the man next to Conway. The surrounding room, the light, the people, the consternation. It seemed dreamlike and intangible, simultaneously important and trivial.

The nausea flared in his core.

'I hate to interrupt,' said Shah, 'but can I interest you in some science?'

Hatfield parked on the edge of a desk. 'Always, Neil.'

'Same forced entry at the Healy scene. No new trace, apart from a tiny bit of a chemical called melamine. Nitrogen-based. Pretty standard. It's used for lots of things. Coating pans, cookware. But it's strange to find it in a bedroom. And there was also some of it at the Prior scene. Two hits is interesting. There's also more of the chlorinated latex residue. I repeat, this is not the kind of substance you find on the high street. I had the previous samples compared to latex we manually chlorinated. We're still working on that, but I imagine it'll be the same result.'

'Which is?' said McHugh.

'It's specialist latex. The DIY chlorination process is actually quite complicated. Chlorine fumes are bad news. You can get pre-chlorinated outfits commercially, but if someone was into this enough to care, then they would definitely go specialist.'

'Most of this stuff is fetish wear,' said Sawyer. 'It's manufactured in Europe. Holland or Germany.' He looked up from the newspaper. 'Apparently.' He smiled, giving them the dimple. 'I have the name of a distributor. I'll check it out.'

'I bet you will,' said McHugh, to muted laughs.

Hatfield turned, stormed back to his office. 'Get busy. Names and leads. Briefing at three.'

34

ONE YEAR EARLIER

'How have you been, Dennis?'

The silence lingered. At last, Dennis lifted his head and pushed out a smile. 'You're new.'

The man nodded. 'That's right.' He took off his suit jacket and hung it across the back of his chair. 'Your previous counsellor has moved to another part of the hospital. My name is Dr Harvey Delgado. I'm a forensic psychiatrist. You seem to have made significant progress of late. When we first met you, things weren't going quite so well.'

'We?'

'The unit.' He consulted his laptop screen. 'There's been little self-harm. You're more civil to the staff. And I believe you were a great help during a recent disturbance?'

Dennis tapped on the tabletop and looked around the interview room. The usual pale blues, soft greens. Beige wooden floor. Realist-style painting of a stork swimming over still water. Delgado's desk was clean and empty, apart from his phone and laptop. Fake flowers. A strong smell of wood polish, with a hint of vomit.

'And you're accepting the risperidone and clozapine. Do you still think you're unwell, Dennis?'

'Of course. I always will be.'

Delgado took off his silver-rimmed glasses, cleaned the lenses with a tissue. 'And why's that?'

'Because of my past. It can't be changed. But I can shape a better future through my choices in the present.'

'Do you really believe that? It sounds like something you've read.'

Dennis's glinting blue eyes drifted over Delgado as he replaced his glasses. 'It's based on ideas I understand because I've read about reframing and triggers. I'm a product of my past, but I refuse to let it define me.'

'You feel you have a more positive purpose now?'

'Yes. Nietzsche said that if you have a why to live, then you can bear almost any how. We find meaning not in circumstance, but in the pursuit of objects, people or activities that give us purpose.'

Delgado typed something. 'I'm going to recommend a move to the asserted rehab ward. That should accelerate your progress even further. I'm also pleased to see that you've applied for positions of increased responsibility.'

Dennis took a deep breath, let it out slowly. 'I've done some bad things, Dr Delgado. But I'm finding a way back. I'd like to help some of the people in here who aren't quite so lucky.'

'And you think you have a strong "why to live"?'

Dennis smiled, more sincere this time. 'Absolutely.'

35

PRESENT DAY

Sawyer drove west, out of Putney, happy to have the mid-morning sun at his back. The trip could have been covered with a phone call, but he needed to decompress and reboot himself with music, distracted by the mechanics of steering and navigation.

He surged through the terraced suburbs of Richmond, windows down, blasting his favourite album: *Loveless* by My Bloody Valentine. Seismic, distorted drumming; vague vocals drowned by melting guitars.

In a brief gridlock outside Twickenham rugby stadium, he paused the music and rewatched Shannon Carter's TikTok video on his phone.

The ponytail.

'No fucking mercy.'

The girls' bathroom. Pink, purple, yellow.

There was something there, but it was unreachable; an itch he couldn't yet scratch.

The traffic thinned, and he moved off, with Kevin Shields singing about how you can't hide from the way you feel.

———

He parked at the end of a row in front of the main building: a giant hangar in light and dark grey. He got out and checked the site map beneath the elevated entrance sign: *HANWORTH TRADING ESTATE.*

Unit 6 was round the back, opposite a monolithic blue-and-white slab devoted to a self-storage company, complete with tempting proclamation above the reception: *WE SELL PACKAGING MATERIALS.*

He walked through a wedged open door into a bland anteroom connecting to a warehouse area, low-lit and steeped in an unmistakable scent.

'Can I help?' A young woman with a side-sweep of pink and blonde hair leaned out of a storage room. Sawyer held up his warrant card and she stepped forward, smiling. 'Jesus. What have we done now?' She brushed her hands down the front of her fitted T-shirt.

'I prefer cornflakes,' said Sawyer.

She nodded and glanced down at the T-shirt design, which bore the word *SEX* in large letters above a pencil outline of a reclining, semi-nude woman and a sub-line: *BREAKFAST OF CHAMPIONS.* 'Very good. I've had scrambled eggs, bacon and eggs, Weetabix, one or two Pop Tarts.'

Sawyer smiled, sheepish. 'Originality is overrated. This is Fetworld, right?'

She beamed. 'At your service. The rubber smell gives it away, right? I'm Jen.' She jabbed out a hand; he shook. 'We're more supply than retail, though. I can recommend some brilliant shops in the area. First-timer? Oh... Unless you've come to take me away. At least you won't have to worry about forgetting your handcuffs.' She nodded to his pocket and winked. 'Let's have another look.'

He held up the card again.

'So, is this about business or pleasure, Detective Sawyer? I assume you're not just stopping off to break up the journey to the Staines reservoirs.'

'Just a few questions. About your more specialist products.'

Jen raised a pierced eyebrow. 'Yeah. We have those. Which ones?'

'Breath play, deprivation.'

'No problem. I can show you round. We have shackles and restraints, hoods, muzzles, harnesses, bridles, playsuits. I bet I can guess one of your questions. Maybe the one you're too embarrassed to ask.'

Sawyer looked across the room at the racks of rubberwear, whipping tables, cages. 'You're thinking it's *why?*'

'That's the one.'

'I'm good with that. It's all about conditioned reflexes. Trigger points in your sexual development.'

'Yeah,' said Jen. 'That was on a podcast about addiction I heard the other day. Pavlov, isn't it? He used to think we need repeated exposure, but these days they reckon fetishes and fixations can be built off a single moment or experience. The repeated exposure gets it really hardwired, though. We all have loads of non-sexual conditioned reflexes. Did you know that? For me, whenever I cut cucumbers, I *always* think of this guy I knew who only ate cucumber sandwiches for lunch.'

Sawyer nodded. 'You could say we like to think we're sophisticated social animals, but we're actually just the sum of our conditioned reflexes, with a bit of social skill on top.'

Jen puffed out her lips. 'You could say that, yeah. You know... I won't lie. This doesn't feel like a conventional arrest, Detective Sawyer. So, I definitely haven't done anything wrong?'

'No. I just wanted to ask about specific suppliers. Products with pre-chlorinated latex.'

'Well, yeah. It helps the fit. You don't want to do that yourself, though. We only sell chlorinated latex wear to order. It comes in from a supplier in Westpoort. Amsterdam.'

'And is the chlorination restricted to skin-tight fetish wear?'

'Usually.'

'What about melamine? Does that go with chlorinated latex?'

Jen glanced up to the high ceiling, thinking. 'They

use that in some of the padding, for the furniture, cages, boxes. We have to know this because of allergy advice.'

'Furniture?'

'Yeah.' Jen took a brochure from a glass cabinet and handed it to Sawyer, open at a section near the back. 'Stools, spanking horses, bondage boards, play wheels, isolation boxes. The padding is coated in melamine.'

Sawyer studied the items. 'I saw a play wheel recently.'

'Did you now?'

'So, chlorinated latex and melamine...'

Jen laughed. 'Someone's having fun. Deprivation play, I'd say. Something snug and skin-tight, and probably one of these toys.' She tapped the brochure.

Sawyer's phone vibrated in his pocket. The sound was audible in the quiet space.

'Just a phone,' said Sawyer.

Jen narrowed her eyes. 'Right.'

He took it out, checked the Caller ID.

Conway.

'Thanks for your time, Jen.'

She winked again. 'Take a card. Call me if you need anything else.'

Sawyer slid a business card from a dispenser on the cabinet and walked back out to the car park, squinting at the sun, ducking into a patch of shade by the wall.

He answered the call.

'Where are you?' said Conway.

Sawyer looked back at the squat warehouses, the skips, forklifts, pallet stacks.

'A long way from Mam Tor.'

'Found something that might be interesting. The cleaning agency KwikClean has a relationship with a company called Pestaway. Sort of an indie Rentokil. Both are owned by the same holding company, so they probably have access to each other's records. I suppose they're both types of cleaning company. Here's the thing. Pestaway reps have attended all three of the family homes in the last month.'

Sawyer hurried to his car. 'While the cleaners were there?'

Conway paused. 'Yes. We contacted all three and they recognised the company logo and remembered the visits.'

'And the families weren't present?'

'No. The visits were all during the day. None of them are logged on Pestaway's system. The Prior and Carter cleaners don't remember much, apart from letting a guy in for a few minutes. But the Healy cleaner, Martha Dumas, says that the guy claimed to be responding to a report of a carpet moth infestation. He was only there for five minutes, then left, saying he'd update the Healys. We don't know if there was any actual follow-up. Martha said the guy was legitimate, with ID and everything. And, no. She doesn't remember his name. Or at least the name he claimed. But she did say he had some kind of scar on his top lip. We could probably confirm an ID with her, though. Maybe the other two cleaners.'

Sawyer slid into the Mini and started the engine. 'Reverse-engineer. Check all the cleaners on KwikClean's books, narrow them down to similar houses in the same area. Barnes, Hammersmith, Fulham.' The phone transferred to the in-car audio as he drove away. 'Once you have names and houses, show them all the Pestaway logo and ask if their cleaning sessions have been interrupted by a similar rep in the past two or three months. And rake through the Pestaway employees to see if you hit any nominals. With a fair wind, we might give Hatfield his names, and the potential addresses of planned future victims. One of which might be getting a visit tonight.'

36

Sawyer parked the Mini in the pick-up zone outside Putney Bridge Tube Station. He opened all four windows and tipped back his head, sipping a cherry smoothie, eyes fixed on the exit barriers. The crowd swelled every few minutes, synchronised with District Line arrivals.

He closed his eyes, took himself away, carried by the sultry air.

To the cave, a hundred and fifty miles away. Ten thousand years old.

And again, he was a child, grazing his knee on a jutting rock at the mouth of the cave, howling for his mother.

An elderly couple comforting him. The woman's jacket hood flapping around her ears in the wind as she asks him his name, and the man leans into his eyeline, having misheard.

'Where is she, Jack? Is your mummy inside the cave?'

A seven-year-old boy, scrambling away, cheeks hot with tears, holding on to the cave wall, sinking into the cool comfort.

His father's voice, echoing from behind as he reaches the top of the trail.

'Jake! Wait for us. Don't go too far.'

The boy, hunkering down in a dark, damp corner, wallowing in the limbo between lost and found. Here, his mother's absence didn't hurt as much because the cave had formed way before she had existed. Before anyone currently alive had existed. They all receded to a tiny point, like the blip in the centre of his old portable TV screen.

Here, his mother was still gone, but it was okay because so was everyone.

There was just the boy, and his snot and tears and the ache from his knee, and the peaty aroma of the past. Forever fixed. Before love, before pain. Before fear.

'Wakey, wakey.'

Maggie Spark climbed into the passenger seat and shoved a backpack onto the rear seat.

She brushed back her rust-red hair and gazed at him. 'Are you with us, Mr Sawyer?'

He smiled. 'I thought you didn't tan.'

'I know! I think I found my sunscreen brand.'

She leaned over and kissed him. Pursed lips. Coffee taste.

His brain de-fogged. Maggie looked flushed, but unflustered. Crisp white blouse, sleeves pulled up slightly. She leaned back, held up the head of a new necklace. 'Do you like? Mia bought this for me, in the old town. A place called Chania. Well. I gave her money to buy something for herself and she got me this because she couldn't find anything she liked.'

Sawyer leaned in to get a close look at the heart-shaped pendant with dancing male and female stick figures etched either side of a sun symbol.

'It's handmade. Silver and candlewick. Mia says the shop woman called it the Relationship Optimism Necklace.'

He raised his eyes to meet hers. 'I love it. The shirt looks English, though.'

'Nearly. Zara, at Luton Airport. Got the message from Keating to call Hatfield at baggage reclaim. Justin was due to pick us up. Mia and Freddy are staying with him for a few days, before Mia's festival.'

Sawyer started the engine and moved off.

'This is all very exciting, Jake. To be summoned like this. It's nice to feel wanted. Hatfield seems decent. He sent a car, and I can claim hotel expenses. Found a nice place off the Goldhawk Road.'

'I'll take you there first,' said Sawyer.

She tilted her head.

'To freshen up. But I need to get you to Nathan straight after. Have you read the case notes?'

'God, yes.'

He glanced over. She had turned to face him, resting the side of her head on the seat back. 'It's urgent, Mags. The killer has been sending cryptic messages to a patient

241

at Broadmoor. They've all arrived on the day of an attack. He got a new one today.'

She faced the front, nodding. 'Have Nathan's parents been briefed by Hatfield's FLOs?'

'Yes.' Sawyer overtook a van to jump a light on Fulham High Street. The driver sounded his horn, in chorus with a car that had already entered the junction and had to stop to avoid him.

'Christ, Jake. Remember, you don't have to impress me with this kind of thing anymore.'

'I'm not trying to. This is the baseline for London. You get worse abuse if you go slow.'

Maggie frowned at the pulsating kick drum, muffled by the city noise. 'What are we listening to?'

'It's a reissue. *The Fires of Ork*.' He glanced at her. 'Collaboration between Pete Namlook and Geir Jenssen of Biosphere. Too many *Blade Runner* samples, but I like it.'

'So, you've gone native?' She turned again.

'Hardly.'

'And how are you?'

Side-glance. 'Been too busy to notice.'

'That's not a good plan. Distraction. You look sleep deprived.'

'Yeah. That is an issue.'

Maggie stayed silent, waiting.

'Can we not run a session right here? You haven't been in the country for five minutes.'

Maggie squinted at him. 'What's an issue? You said

your mind had sped up since you got here. That you're feeling overstimulated.'

He hesitated. 'I remember back when... in the days after...' He took a breath. 'I had to sleep with the light on for a while. Then, when I finally stopped needing it, I used to get these strange episodes, where I thought I could see things moving on the walls. Creatures, insects. I'd turn the light on, and they'd be gone. Sometimes, I couldn't move to turn the light on, and I'd just lie there and watch. I knew I was awake, but I couldn't move.'

'Sleep paralysis,' said Maggie. 'It can happen with anxiety disorders, PTSD. Have you had this again?'

'Yeah. And a few... moments. Sort of minor blackouts.'

Maggie held up a hand. 'There's no such thing as a minor blackout, Jake.'

'They're not actual shutdowns. More like vagueness. I used to have them when I was in London before. Sometimes headaches, too.'

'Could be your schwannoma. You should see your brain doctor again.'

He looked at her, smirking. 'Neurosurgeon.'

'Yes, yes.' She waved the hand, turned back to face the front.

'No visions?'

'My mum? No. But the sun isn't a good thing. Sometimes the patterns... When it dapples.'

Maggie checked herself in the visor mirror. 'Reminds you of the day it happened.'

'It's more than a reminder. It's like a sort of... emotional rewind, filling me with the sensations I had at the time. Panic, horror. It's the old cliché. *Like it was yesterday.*'

She flipped up the visor, rested a hand on his knee, squeezed. 'You should have come with me.'

37

Nathan Carroll shuffled back into the far corner of his bed and toyed with a grey-and-white plastic buggy. He was slight, with straight and glossy brown hair trimmed to a fringe. Maggie pulled over a chair but stayed near the door, giving him plenty of space. The room was huge and lit by a vast single-panel window, half-open, which looked down on a row of tidy back gardens. The walls were papered in midnight blue, speckled with cartoonish stars, and the curtains continued the theme, with matching duvet: shooting stars, rocket ships, planets.

'Hello, Nathan. I'm Maggie. What's your truck?'

He flipped up the hood of his dressing gown, kept his eyes on the toy. 'It's a rover. For the moon. And the sun makes it move. That's this bit.' He tapped the panel.

'Oh. It's solar powered.'

He didn't reply, glanced at the careworn man and woman sitting on the sofa beneath the window. 'That means the sun gives it energy,' said the woman, reaching out to Nathan, rubbing the back of his hand.

'Does it move?' said Maggie.

He frowned at her. 'Yeah. Course. In the sun, though.'

'Do you like outer space, Nathan?'

He nodded, lowered his gaze again. 'My stars glow in the dark.'

'The duvet cover,' said the man. 'And the curtains.'

Maggie smiled. 'Would you like to go on a rocket ship, Nathan?'

Silence. The question hung in the air for several seconds.

Nathan shrugged, keeping his attention on the rover. 'My dad says you have to be good at maths to be an astronaut.'

'You have to be strong, too,' said the man. 'You're strong, aren't you, Nath?'

Nathan drew in an exasperated sigh, raising his shoulders and holding them high for a moment before letting them drop. 'My brother was really strong. But he died. His name was Ollie.' He rocked a little, detaching and reattaching a radar dish at the front of the rover.

'That was an accident, wasn't it, sweetie?' said the woman, screwing up her eyes.

Silence again.

Sawyer hovered just outside the door, watching with an older woman in a crumpled blazer jacket. He whispered to her. 'Do Gareth and Sue have Maggie's questions?'

She nodded and whispered back. 'Parents approve the list, yes.'

Nathan hummed tunelessly as he ran the rover back and forth along a shelf at the side of his bed.

'You can take a break at any time,' said the woman with Sawyer.

'Rockets can go fifty thousand miles an hour,' said Nathan.

Gareth smiled. 'It's fifteen, isn't it?'

Nathan shrugged again. 'Still fast, though.'

'What's your favourite planet, Nathan?' said Maggie.

He stared up at the Milky Way spiral on the ceiling. 'Saturn. But I also like Mars.'

'What planet are we on now?'

He looked up at her, frowning. 'Earth. There are only two planets closer to the sun. Mercury and Venus.' He sighed again, struck by a sadness. 'But we couldn't live on them because they are too hot.'

'Tell me about your friends here on Earth, Nathan,' said Maggie. 'Noah and Isaac.'

He brightened and looked up, rocking from side to side as he spoke. 'Noah is my best friend, apart from Stefan. You can see the river from his house. Isaac is Noah's brother. He messes about a lot. His mum sometimes shouts at him when I go to his house. Sometimes he's okay, but sometimes he's mean and won't let me sleep on the bunk bed.'

'So, you go out to the little airing cupboard?'

'Yeah. It smells of clothes. I sometimes don't sleep well because you can hear the water in the pipes. But it is cosy.

Do you want to play chess? I'm learning it.' He took a chessboard from his bedside table drawer, laid it on the bed and scattered the pieces out from a pouch. 'The king can only move one square, and you have to protect him. The queen is the best, but my favourite is the knight because it looks like a horse.' He handed the white knight to Maggie.

'He's very smooth,' said Maggie, turning the plastic over in her fingers.

'White must always go first. Stefan cheats at chess because he sometimes goes first, even when he's black.'

Maggie shifted a little closer. 'In the airing cupboard, Nathan. Can you hear anything that happens outside? In the bedrooms. On the landing.'

Nathan began to set up the pieces. 'Yeah. There's a buzz from the water, but it stops and starts, and then it stops for ages. That's when I can sleep.'

'Did you sleep last night?'

He looked up at the Milky Way again. 'A bit.'

'I have children, Nathan. My son Freddy used to sleep under my bed sometimes. When he was little.' Nathan looked at her, eyes wide. 'I had to wait until he was asleep, then carefully take him out and carry him to his own bed.' She patted the duvet. 'Your bed here looks really cosy.'

Nathan looked down, rocked from side to side. He was silent for close to a minute, then looked up at Maggie. 'Are Noah and Isaac dead? Like Ollie.' He propped the pieces up in line, one by one, waiting for his answer.

'Which piece would you be, Nathan?' Sawyer took a step into the room. 'I'm Jake, by the way.'

Nathan thought for a while. 'I would be... the pawn.' He held one up. 'They are not very strong, but if you're clever, you can make them change. You can turn them into the other pieces.'

'You move them forward, don't you?' said Sawyer. 'And when they get to the end—'

Nathan threw his hands up in the air. '*Boom!*'

Maggie startled at his volume.

'You can make them a queen, and then *everyone* is in trouble and has to run away.'

Maggie gave Sawyer a look, drawing a weak smile. He retreated to the door.

'Remember when you were in the little room last night?' said Maggie. 'Why did you only sleep for a bit?'

Nathan pondered. 'I didn't like the noises.'

'The water in the pipes?'

He shook his head. 'Funny noises. Someone shouted. I think it was Noah and Isaac's dad. So, I hid under my duvet.'

'Any other noises?' said Maggie. 'Did you hear anyone say anything?'

Nathan completed his set-up of the white pieces and moved on to the black. 'No. There were some bumps. But that was after the breathing.'

Sawyer stepped forward again. 'What kind of breathing, Nathan? Was it snoring?'

He shook his head, firm. 'Stefan has got asthma. It

was sort of like that.' He looked up. 'I thought it was Isaac, but it wasn't.'

'You're doing really well, sweetie,' said Sue, rubbing Nathan's hand again.

Sawyer crouched by the bed, level with Nathan's eyeline, helping him set up the board. 'Did you hear any alarm sound, Nathan? Even a really quiet one?'

Nathan pivoted the chessboard. 'We've got it the wrong way round. There has to be a white square in that corner.' He looked up; Sawyer smiled.

'Can you remember an alarm, Nathan?' said Maggie. 'Like when you hear a car alarm. A siren. It might have been quiet. Just for a few seconds.'

He shrugged. 'I just heard the breathing. And one of my friends went to the toilet.'

'When was that?' said Sawyer.

'It was when the pipe noises had stopped. And they hiss when someone goes to the toilet.' He yawned, rubbed his hands across the top of his head. 'I'm really tired.'

'That's okay,' said Sue. She turned to Maggie. 'I think he needs a break now.'

Sawyer got to his feet and retreated to the door as Maggie moved in closer, sitting on the edge of the bed.

'Hey, Nathan. You've done such a good job.' She leaned forward, held his eye. 'I think you're strong enough to be an astronaut one day.'

Nathan looked down at the board, rearranging the pieces. 'Are Noah and Isaac dead, too?'

'Okay,' said Sue. 'Please...'

Nathan kept focus on the chess pieces. 'Do you want to play chess with me?'

Maggie caught Sue's eye. 'I... don't know how to play, Nathan. I think Jake does.'

Nathan shrugged. 'He's gone.'

Maggie looked over her shoulder. The door frame was empty.

38

Leon Stokes pushed a button on the arm of his cushioned chair. The seat back reclined a few degrees, slow and steady. He gazed up at the glittering image on the hundred and fifty-inch screen, beamed from a ceiling-mounted 4K projector.

He'd dropped twenty-two grand on the cinema room, to indulge his passion for art films. Painterly cinematography, layered characters, stately pacing. Ozu, Bergman, Bresson.

Today, though, it was a guilty pleasure: *Terminator 2: Judgment Day*. The climactic chase scene had reached the moment of pay-off, and Arnold Schwarzenegger's benign cyborg faced off with his more advanced counterpart, gazing in predatory wonder as a spillage of liquid nitrogen froze the antagonist into a brittle shell.

The main door opened, and Boyd Cannon slipped through, closing it behind him. He hovered at Stokes's shoulder, wincing at the Dolby Atmos sound roaring from the wall and ceiling speakers.

Cannon tapped Stokes on the shoulder, but he held up a hand, ordering him to wait.

On-screen, Arnie aimed his pistol at the helpless mass of frosted bio metal.

'Hasta la vista, baby.'

'Yes!' said Stokes, leaping up from his seat as the blast shattered the target into thousands of pieces. He gripped Cannon's neck in the crook of his arm and ruffled his hair. 'I fucking *love* that scene.'

He paused the film and turned to Cannon, who sat on the edge of a U-shaped sofa, grim-faced.

Stokes closed his eyes. 'No?'

'No,' said Cannon. 'And Doyle wants to talk.' He twisted a wall switch, turning up the lights, and laid an open laptop on the footrest before Stokes. 'He'd been there. Not there anymore.'

Stokes sighed and took a slug from a bottle of water. He nodded to the laptop. 'Bring him on.'

Cannon activated a Zoom call and sat just out of shot as it connected. Doyle's heavyset, under-lit face filled the screen.

'Mickey,' said Stokes.

'I'm gonna park the pleasantries, Leon. Nothing personal. I'm just not feeling too pleasant at the moment.'

'Sorry to hear that.' He glanced at Cannon. 'What's going on?'

Doyle took a breath. His pit bull panted, off-screen.

'Mavers likes a bet. One of my boys clocked him in a bookies in Birkenhead, followed him to the Premier Inn. I sent my top man, Deon, to bring him in, deliver him to you. And now he's not answering his calls. It's not like Deon to go dark.' He rolled his head around, cracking his neck muscles. 'Please tell me this is nothing to do with you, Leon.'

Stokes looked at Cannon again. Head shake. 'Full disclosure, Mickey. We just had a look there ourselves.'

'What? When?'

'About an hour ago. We had an anonymous message giving us Mavers's location. Not exact, but enough to give us the hotel.'

'That didn't come from any of my sources.'

Stokes nodded. 'I believe you.' He angled his head, beckoning Cannon, who moved into view of Doyle.

'Mavers had been there,' said Cannon. 'But he's long gone.'

'So, who tipped you off?' said Doyle. 'How could they be so exact about his location? You got someone at the hotel?'

Stokes pondered, shook his head.

'There are ways,' said Cannon. 'But you need some information to go on. Mobile number is the most likely. Even if it's a burner, as long as you know the number, there are ways of tracking the device. We did something similar with a rogue dealer last year. It's a custom cellular service. Call-trapping. Dead easy. First time they call, if they block their ID, you decline it. That lets the service redirect the number to their system, which unmasks the caller and sends you a notification with the exact number and some additional info. I set it up on Leon's phone here, in case Mavers got cocky and called. We don't have anyone at the hotel or in that area. Also, whoever sent us the tip-off used text message and masked their number by routing it through internet protocol. I tried a workaround but couldn't unmask them.'

'The point is,' said Stokes, 'this isn't some ex-con who's heard we're after Mavers. It's sophisticated. They would need specialist equipment to track his phone.'

'StingRay, probably,' said Cannon. 'Simulates a phone tower. But you have to know the number.'

Doyle rubbed his eyes with his thumbs. 'Fellas. I'm glazing over. Are we saying that whoever knew where Mavers was—'

'Probably had access to specialist equipment and surveillance techniques.'

'Police,' said Doyle.

Stokes looked up at the dimmed ceiling spotlights. 'I call Sawyer. Follow the logic. Whoever sent that message came to me because they know I'm after Mavers, and they want me to find him.' He looked back at the screen. 'They want me to find him because they want him gone, too. Because they're cleaning up. Whatever Mavers and Sawyer had going on, it looks like it's hit hard times. Seems we've got more of a problem with Sawyer than we thought.'

Doyle moved closer to his screen. 'No, Leon. *You've* doubled *your* problems. I fucking grew up with Deon Kinsella. I used to play kerby with him when we were lads. I did a bit of Googling about Sawyer. Proper psycho. He faced up to a fucking polar bear to save some suicidal fella. He's got to be pulling the strings. He's used his police connections, had some toerag steal your money and give you a beating. They've fallen out, and Sawyer has tipped you off about where he is, because he wants Mavers gone without having to get close himself.' The screen jumped as he bashed his table. 'This is *your* shit, Leon. And *my man* has got caught up in it.'

Stokes spoke in a low, even voice. 'Steady, Mickey. Keep it civil.'

The screen jumped again. Doyle was shouting now, waving his arms around. 'Get your fucking house in order. I don't give a shit if Sawyer is police. He's mugging you off, good and proper, and it's time you grew a pair of bollocks and did something about it. Or you and me are gonna really fall out.'

The screen went blank, as Doyle ended the call.

39

Sawyer sat in the Mini outside the Carroll house, head churning. He took out his phone and watched Shannon Carter's TikTok video at half speed.

Dora scrambling up the stairs. Ponytail.

Her hand over the lens.

Freeze-frame on Dora's face.

Captions, arrows.

Dora entering the girls' bathroom.

He paused the video at the half-second shot of the bathroom interior.

And called Conway.

She answered instantly. 'I was about to call you.'

'He's already in the houses.'

'What?'

'At the Carter scene, you said the girls' bathroom was private. No parents allowed.'

'That's what the cleaner told us, yes.'

'The toilet seat is up. Two girls. Our killer gets in

before the families are home. He disables the alarm and holes up somewhere until everyone has gone to bed. I've just been with Nathan, the boy who slept over at the Healys'. He said he heard a strange breathing sound. I think the killer was in the airing cupboard we saw. Plenty of room at the back. There will be similar places at the other scenes. He knows the houses well. He's done his homework.'

Conway took a breath. 'I don't get it. So, he breaks in when everyone's out, disables the alarm, hides... Why not just break in later?'

'He's meticulous. A planner. He's eliminating all risk. And there must be something about the act of hiding. It's part of his signature. Something he needs to do to fulfil himself. It excites him, charges him up. The practicalities, the way he gets himself into the position to subdue the families in the first place, that's his MO. I think this is a case where the method is serving the need. It's part of the package. What's missing is how he disables the alarms.'

'If you'll let me get a word in,' said Conway, 'I might be able to help with that. I cross-checked the cleaners on KwikClean's books with houses in the catchment area. One other said they had a visit from a Pestaway rep a few weeks ago. She's assigned to a house similar in layout to the others. Fulham. Three floors. Family of five this time. Sawyer, one of the kids is four years old. Again, this visit isn't on Pestaway's system, but the guy had ID and seemed legit. Sketchy description from three of the cleaners, but the new cleaner confirms Martha Dumas's description of the scar on the guy's top lip. She also said he was short but well-built. Maybe a cleft palate?'

'Could be,' said Sawyer. 'But we don't have time to go to Crimewatch with an e-fit.'

Maggie tapped on the Mini passenger window; Sawyer nodded and she climbed in.

'Check Pestaway and KwikClean employees for anyone matching the description. If that doesn't work, try affiliate companies who are on both Pestaway and KwikClean's books. Suppliers, agencies. Talk to the holding company. Our guy is posing as a Pestaway employee to stake out the houses. Tell Hatfield to get everyone together. I'm heading back.'

He disconnected the call and looked over at Maggie.

'Progress?' she said.

'Could be. You off to the hotel?'

'Nathan is taking a break. I'm going to hang around and talk to him again. I don't want him to get second-hand information about what happened to Noah and Isaac. It's hard for him. He isn't emotionally equipped for this. We have to help him build a bridge so it doesn't define his future, his adult life.' She turned, rested a hand on his. 'Do you remember what happened when you were being looked after? You were six, too.'

Sawyer bristled. 'Nathan heard some strange noises. I saw my mother's murder.'

'There's no grading system to this, Jake. Trauma is trauma. When we're forming, when that natural understanding of our world is interrupted by extraordinary events... It can be long-lasting. Lifelong.

See it as part of an old life, lived by a different version of you. And so, you take control by building a new life, focusing on what's best for you now. Redefining your future.'

'Mags. We've been round and round on this.'

'I know. I'm just trying to focus you on something tangible.' She squeezed his hand. 'Something you can feel, here and now. Building a new future often starts with choosing the people you want to share it with.'

Sawyer's phone rang, connecting with the car audio. He checked the Caller ID.

Matt Walker.

Maggie got out of the car. 'Let's get together when this is all done. Stay out of the misery.' She smiled, closed the door, and started back toward the house.

Sawyer answered the call. 'Matt.'

'Sir. Good to hear you. How are things going in London?'

He started the ignition, drove off. 'Busy. What's up?'

'It's Moran. He's crowing about a case he's been working on. Thought you should know.'

Sawyer pulled out of the junction opposite the cemetery and turned onto Fulham Palace Road. 'I'm braced.'

'Remember the murders from last year? We dug up remains by the old abattoir but never found the suspect. Scott Walton.'

His stomach dropped. 'Go on.'

'He's turned up. Dead. Moran put it together. His remains were buried in woodland near Mayfield. We have a knife found at the abattoir scene, which has his DNA all over it.'

'How was the body found?'

Walker cleared his throat. 'That's the thing. Moran is being cagey on how it all came about, but he says they ID'd the remains and left it there in sight of a CROP team. And someone appeared and tried to dig it up. Bloke called Fletcher.'

40

Hatfield parked himself by the whiteboard and raised a hand for hush. Sawyer stood off to the side, below the window, silhouetted in the vermillion glow of the sinking sun.

'Ladies and gentlemen,' said Hatfield. 'Some progress.' He nodded to the window.

Sawyer stepped forward. 'He stakes out the houses in person to make sure they're suitable. There has to be a lot of room. Three floors. Somewhere for him to hide. Because he has to be there when the family comes back from work and school. He gets in before they come home, and he hides and waits for dark.' He moved further into the room and leaned forward on a desk. 'I think he works for a company called Pestaway. All three cleaners of the murdered families are on the books of Pestaway's parent company, KwikClean. He visited the houses recently, claiming to be a pest control officer when the cleaners were present, saying he had to take a

look around to prepare for possible work. The Healys'
cleaner Martha said he told her carpet moths. She has
also told us that the man is short but muscular, and has a
mark on his top lip, possibly a cleft palate. We're looking
into Pestaway, KwikClean and the holding company at
the moment, cross-reffing for employees who fit that
description.'

'A pest control company would have access to the
drug,' said Rodgers.

'Exactly,' said Hatfield. 'It fits.'

'If he's staking out, would he really risk going there in
person?' said McHugh.

Sawyer shook his head. 'Extra risk if he has someone
else to do it for him. Plus, I think his needs are too
specific to trust to someone else.'

'Needs?' said Hatfield.

'Lying in wait. Somewhere closed and dark. The
young boy who slept over at the Healys' says he heard
strange breathing in the middle of the night. I think that
was from a utility room I saw when I visited the scene.
Our killer wants the families to be asleep and settled
before he strikes. That would make them easier to
subdue, but I think it's the waiting that's giving him
what he needs. Perhaps the dark space is a factor, the
isolation. All the houses had ideal rooms on the top
floors. He must have absolute control over the families.
Immobilising them, silencing them. But he doesn't want
drama or confrontation. He wants them all quiet so he
can enjoy the suffering with no excess,' he searched for
the word, 'humanity. We also have a new target.' He

tacked a Google Maps screenshot of a large detached house to the board. 'This is a similar property in the same area. Well-to-do family, the Pruetts. Two adults, three children. The cleaner is on KwikClean's books and remembers the same Pestaway man paying a visit a few weeks ago. Given the acceleration in the offences, we have to assume he's planning to attack this evening.'

Conway spoke up. 'The cleaner is due at the house in an hour for a three-hour session. The family has been contacted and informed, but we want the cleaner to carry on as normal in case our killer is watching. It makes sense that he'll wait for her to finish and then get in. If we don't see that, then we'll enter and search. Rowan?'

'I've arranged a safe hotel for the family while we surveil. They're due home in around four hours, and we should assume the killer has staked out carefully, so he'll probably know that.'

'I'd rather pick him up before he gets anywhere near the place,' said Hatfield. 'We have a team working on the employees and employee history now. Hopefully, we'll get a name and can bring him in.'

Rodgers waved her pen. 'So, how does he disable the alarms?'

'Still not sure of that,' said Sawyer. 'But, given his communication with Maxwell, and the lack of other properties that fit the bill, I think he's been building to this. He has something to finish.'

Movement through the window of Hatfield's office.

Hatfield coughed, ragged and ugly. He held up his hand, took a moment.

'You okay, sir?' said Sawyer, craning his neck to see who might be in the office.

'Something on my chest, I think. It's nothing.' He pointed. 'Rowan, triple-check all the other houses that tally up. Catchment area, no cameras, KwikClean cleaner. Brianna, take charge of the family protection and the Pruett house surveillance.' He turned and headed back towards his office, beckoning Sawyer. 'Make sure all your teams are full speed on those company links. Find me someone who fits the cleaner's description.'

Hatfield entered the office and Sawyer followed him in, closing the door behind them.

Dr Guillermo Cabrera rose from his seat and bowed his head. 'Detective Sawyer. Nice to see you again.' He wore a tangerine orange jacket and trousers with black polo neck. The room reeked of the same soapy cologne he had worn in his office.

Hatfield took his seat, dabbing at his forehead with his handkerchief.

'Are you okay, Colin?' said Cabrera.

'Yes. Bit warm for me. Feel like I'm coming down with something. Sawyer, I said I'd look deeper into Maxwell's background, given the killer's messages. I've briefed Dr Cabrera on the case.'

Cabrera nodded and leaned forward in his chair. For a moment, it looked like he was about to reach out and touch Sawyer's knee. 'I'm intrigued by your idea, Detective. That the letters to Taylor Maxwell are not appreciative. They are taunting.'

'Do you know someone who Maxwell might have

pissed off in the past?' said Sawyer. 'Someone who might connect to the case?'

Cabrera sat back. 'Connection is your job. I know of Maxwell's colourful background and psychopathology. One of his kills was a woman called Evelyn Frey. She was discovered at her home in Wembley after neighbours complained of the smell. Strangled, pre and post mortem sexual assault.'

'Maxwell has never confirmed it,' said Hatfield, 'but I believe he was also living at the address, and Evelyn Frey was his partner. He scarpered and I didn't get to him for two years, during which time he murdered five people.'

Cabrera smoothed down his beard. A trickle of sweat traced the snaking vein along his temple; he wiped it away. 'Evelyn Frey's mother Caroline died when Evelyn was thirteen. She was already being abused by her father Evan, but the abuse intensified when he was left to his own devices. He insisted on home-schooling her, off the back of a spurious complaint about bullying.' He shuffled in his seat. 'Now, there's nothing here so far to draw the attention of authorities or social services. There's no formal statutory powers to monitor home-schooling, but the parent does have to reply to any request for clarity on the nature of the education. Evan Frey worked hard to keep up on the admin, so the abuse could continue uninterrupted.'

Hatfield sighed. 'Evan Frey was last seen two years after we know that Evelyn took up with Maxwell. But someone drew his dole cheques for another three years.'

Sawyer closed his eyes, processing. 'So, Maxwell the

hero kills Evelyn's abusive father, disposes of the body, then moves into the house. Three years later, he kills Evelyn and runs. What went wrong?'

'The house had an old cellar,' said Hatfield. 'Tiny, no windows. It looked like Maxwell had tried to clean it up before he legged it. But not very well. There were Satanist and Crowley books in the main bedroom, but forensics found a couple of them stashed in a bricked-over crevice in the cellar. Fingerprints all over them. Maxwell's and one other person. Not Evelyn, not on the database.'

'No other DNA?' said Sawyer.

Cabrera shook his head.

The room was stifling. Cabrera took off his jacket and rolled up his sleeves to reveal his hairy forearms. Hatfield mopped his brow every couple of minutes. Sawyer angled his chair away from Cabrera, but the fug of cologne clung to him, forcing him to breathe through his mouth.

'We've got the surveillance covered,' said Hatfield. 'The family are safe. I want you to go back to Maxwell. Find out who was reading those devil books in the cellar. Was it just some weird ritual bullshit or could it be someone he was holding captive?'

Cabrera opened his arms wide. 'Along with the taunting messages, the killings could be their own form of cryptic communication. As you well know, Detective, a subject rarely directs his anger at the focus of his resentment.'

Sawyer got to his feet. 'I think we left the textbooks behind a long time ago.'

41

'Go straight in, Mr Farrell.'

Oliver took out his earpiece and replaced it, offering Farrell the briefest of smiles before returning to his computer.

Farrell flashed his practised sneer and pivoted away from the standing desk. Dale Strickland sat at his office desk, door open. He held up both hands in mock surrender and Farrell stalked in, closing the door behind him.

'That is not the gait of a man at peace, Robin.'

'I won't be at peace until our mutual friend is the wrong side of a prison cell.'

Strickland half-turned and opened his window. 'Any updates?'

Farrell flopped down in a chair. 'We picked up Fletcher. Easier than we expected. Rural Observation Post with a sightline on the woodland.'

'And he didn't put up a fight?'

Farrell pushed a thumb into his nostril and spun it around. 'It was like arresting a teenage dogger. Hands straight up. I'm surprised he didn't say, "It's a fair cop."'

Strickland smiled. 'Austin rarely says anything. He's more of a thinker and a doer.'

Farrell pulled up his chair with a screech. 'He'll have plenty of time to think. Fifteen to twenty if Buxton can put it all together.'

Strickland angled his head. 'Buxton?'

'Jurisdiction. Had to get Derbyshire MIT to wave it through. I worked it up with one of their DCs and he took it to the DCI. Fucking frustrating, not to get the credit.'

'It'll work in your favour. For the suspension.'

'It's not a suspension. Fletcher was carrying, though. Glock. Only his prints on it.'

Dale smiled. 'That's a shame. Is he in custody?'

'Buxton. No choice. Technically, it's their op, and the site is on their map.' He punched his knee. '*Fuck*. I could have him in the cells at GMP right now, with the tier threes.'

Strickland shook his head. 'I don't think even that would loosen him up. Like I say, he's not a talker at the best of times. He will have reckoned on arrest, too. You should be careful.'

Farrell worked his sneer again. 'And before you ask, no Sawyer.'

'Were we expecting him?'

'No. He's in London. But if Fletcher doesn't want to play, we don't have much of a route to Sawyer. The car footage is circumstantial. No new DNA on any of the bodies at the scene. Can you put pressure on Fletcher?'

Strickland laughed. 'I think that ship has run aground, Robin. He probably suspects me as the sender of the message.'

Farrell took out his breath mint canister, shook it. Empty. He lobbed it at a corner wastebasket, missed, didn't bother to tidy it. 'If... *fucking* Sawyer gets away from this clean again...'

'Keep working the interrogation magic. I said I had a few lateral ideas to make life difficult for him. This is only one.'

Farrell rubbed at his eyes. 'I can't get involved in any...'

Strickland raised his eyebrows, waiting.

'... *subterfuge.*'

'Good word. Don't worry. We won't have to get our hands dirty. Someone else can do it for us.'

42

Taylor Maxwell sat at the fixed white table, hands placed face down in front of him, thumbs touching. He kept his head down and his grey eyes fixed on a spot just beyond the fingertips, as if expecting something unspeakable to rise up from the Formica and engulf him. As before, he shifted his head and shoulders right and left in tiny, rhythmic turns.

Sawyer sneaked a look up at the clock above the bed. Twelve minutes of silence and counting.

He forced a cough. 'Tell me about Evelyn Frey, Taylor. The time before you killed her, I mean. Were you happy together? Can you remember a time when you were happy? Content? In love?'

Maxwell laughed. 'Like everyone else, we were in lust at first. That's the biology talking, isn't it, Detective?'

'Phenylethylamine,' said Sawyer. 'Dopamine. Bonding chemicals. They keep the species going.' He lowered his head, kept his eyes on Maxwell. 'You lived with Evelyn for a while. And her dad, Evan.'

Maxwell shifted in his seat. 'That's not a revelation.'

'Did you kill Evan, Taylor? He disappeared not long after you moved in.'

Maxwell leaned forward and studied Sawyer, looking him up and down. 'Do I need a lawyer, Detective? This is suddenly all very formal.'

'No. I'm sorry. I'm rushing you. It's just that I'm in a bit of a rush myself. We're trying to catch a killer, Taylor. Before he kills again. I'm hoping you can help. Last time we spoke, you said you were changed.'

Maxwell formed his hands into a tunnel and peered through at Sawyer. 'Evan Frey was vermin. A contaminant. Like David Bowman, the world is a brighter place without him. You did kill David Bowman, didn't you?'

'Yes. In self-defence.'

Maxwell smiled. He brought the edges of his hands together until his eyes were barely visible through the tunnel. 'Self-defence. With a well-aimed axe to the throat. I wonder, are you a detective or a Viking?'

'Enough about me. Taylor, I can influence the decision on your parole. Your outside time will be heavily managed, but there is a chance of feeling the sun on your skin again. It won't help you if I report that you were playing us, and someone else loses their life because—'

'*Enough.*' Maxwell slapped the tabletop with both hands and pushed himself to his feet. Sawyer remained seated, staring him down.

Everett Asher unlocked the door and entered. 'Are we being respectful, Taylor?'

'It's fine, Everett.' Sawyer held up a hand and Asher left. 'Sit down, Taylor. Please. Now. Enough of what?'

Maxwell dropped his head again. 'The future. You can stop. Let's be real for a moment. All this getting out business.' He took his seat. 'There is no *out* for me. I've made my choices. The tabloids called me sick and evil. They're right. I'll never be cured. I'm not... compatible with *out*. I wouldn't work. I don't aspire to any kind of brighter future, Detective. Somewhere with a nice view of a fucking waterfall. You know this all too well, don't you? Some of us are just too broken to be fixed.'

He lowered his head.

Sawyer held the silence. One minute, two minutes. They sat there and listened to the muted clunks and shouts on the ward outside, the electrical hum, each other's breathing.

'What happened at Evelyn's, Taylor? I'm going to assume you killed her father. None of this conversation is being recorded, and I won't be relaying anything that doesn't directly help me with my current case.'

Maxwell smiled and raised his eyes. 'Do you swear on your mother's grave, Detective Sawyer?'

'I swear on my mother's grave. I bought the headstone myself.'

Maxwell indulged in another minute's silence, then inhaled deeply, held it, exhaled. 'Evelyn's father sometimes raped her four times a day. When she thirteen, he caught her being sick in the morning and beat her until she miscarried. And then he got it into his head that he wanted to be a father again. So, the next time she got pregnant, he took her out of school. He delivered the baby himself, down there in that fucking cellar. A boy. And two became three. But he botched the birth. *Ruined* her. And when Evan saw the baby's scar, he was sure it couldn't be his, and he made her keep it out of sight. That child was born hated.'

'Scar?' said Sawyer.

'Birth defect. Cleft lip and palate.'

'Did Evelyn even register the birth?'

Maxwell shook his head. 'Not at first. Universally hated. Incestuous. Born of rape. Technically doesn't exist. That's quite a start in life.'

'So, did Evelyn care for the boy?'

'Evan forced her to, I think as a kind of punishment for the deformity. Maybe in his mind he'd recreated a hideous family unit. He kept Evelyn at home, insisted she keep the child in the cellar. It was sickly, though. Skinny, barely slept. In the end she had to register it, get healthcare. I think she said they set it up in the spare room for a visit from social services, but then Evan insisted she take it back down to the cellar.'

'What were the health problems?'

'Cleft lip, hole in the heart. She was told the growth rate would be slow, and the child might not make it past a year. But he survived. And he kept surviving.'

Sawyer took a sip from a plastic cup of lukewarm water. 'How old was Evelyn when she gave birth?'

Maxwell smiled. 'Thirteen. Evan started to let her out

when she was seventeen. She was too scared to tell anyone about home. She met me a couple of years later and we got close. She opened up. Evan wouldn't let her bring people round, but he got to know me. Tolerated me. She showed me the boy.'

'What did she call him?'

'Hayden. It was her mother's middle name.' Maxwell raised his hands, formed his tunnel. 'She told me more and more about the abuse. I argued with Evan. There were a lot of screaming rows. I'm sure Hayden heard it all.' He brought his fingers closer together again, narrowing the view. 'Evelyn and I bonded over our abuse, Detective Sawyer. My own father held little parties, passed me around. He also abused me personally, taught others how to do it better.'

Sawyer nodded. 'Cabrera told me you tried to kill him in his care home.'

Maxwell narrowed his tunnel to a tiny aperture. 'He used to strangle me during the abuse. He would apply the pressure with his thumbs, relieve it, squeeze again. Pure domination and control. Evan Frey was out of shape. I hit him with a heavy pan and strangled him, using my father's technique. Evelyn helped me to get him into a coal sack weighed with house bricks. We dragged him to my car, drove to Southend, dumped him in the Roach estuary.' He shrugged. 'Best place for him.'

Maxwell took a sip of his water. He sat up straighter, as if his burden had lightened.

'And after that?' said Sawyer.

'We kept collecting his benefits. Evelyn wouldn't let

me kill Hayden. So, we just kept him down there. He became a bit of a project for me. I practised my technique.'

'Strangling?'

He nodded. 'By now he was eight, nine. I wanted him to die, but Evelyn wouldn't let me. So, I used him for kicks.' He smirked at the memory. 'I gave him names. Shit Stain. Dead Boy. Because he was practically dead, surely soon to be physically dead. He had this fucking horrible rough sound in his breath. It came out when he was stressed.'

'Hole in the heart,' said Sawyer. 'And I doubt your near-asphyxiation was helping.'

Maxwell formed his tunnel again. 'I told him he was Dead Boy. I told him he didn't exist for anyone else. That only I had the power over his life and death.' He dropped the tunnel, raised a finger. 'I didn't abuse him. He was too repulsive.' He smirked. 'Not my type. The little bastard just wouldn't die. I mean, he was a fucking wretch. If anyone deserved the gift of silence...'

'What did he *do* down there all day? How did you keep him contained? How did he pass the time?'

'He learned to read. My occult books, some of Evelyn's.' Maxwell shook his head. 'She hated him for what he represented, but I know she went down there when I was out. She wouldn't just leave him to me. Evelyn studied computing at the library, when she could get some respite from Evan. I think she got him into it.'

Sawyer looked up at the clock. 'Numbers. Binaries. Certainties in a world of chaos.'

Maxwell pushed his shoulders back, took a big breath. 'And then I got bored. With Dead Boy. With Evelyn. I decided I would kill them both. But the fucker got out of the cellar one day, and out of the house. Evelyn didn't lock the door properly. So, I punished her.'

'Killed her.'

He nodded. 'So, all that trauma. It's passed on and on, down the line. Like a hex. Victims creating more victims. Evan's pain at his wife's early death. My father.' He leaned forward. 'Your mother, Detective Sawyer. And then your father. Once the curse is cast, can it ever be lifted?'

Sawyer stood up, headed for the door. 'I used to believe it couldn't. But I see myself now, and like you, I'm different. I've changed. And I'm still changing. As you say, you've made your choices, and so here you are. This is the future you created for yourself with those choices. You've arrived at your destination, Taylor.' He knocked on the door and smiled. '*Terminus*. I'm still travelling.'

43

Sawyer drove out of the hospital car park and sped past the row of handsome houses that lined the route towards the M3 and back to London. Buzzcut gardens, gravel drives, garages and greenhouses. He pictured the estate agent viewings, imagining the selective pitches. The Broadmoor escape sirens had last sounded by accident a few years earlier. These days, the job was covered with less drama, via cascade alerts and Twitter.

He connected to CarPlay and tapped Conway's number. It rang and rang, and he was close to giving up when the call connected.

'Sawyer?'

'Can you talk?'

Crackles on the line. 'Yeah. Just had to get out of the place where we have the Pruetts.'

'You *can* tell me where it is, you know.'

She sighed. 'Don't worry. We've ruled you out of the enquiry. What's up?'

'I've got a name. Hayden Frey. It's possible he might have changed it, but he'll probably retain the surname at least. Get the teams on it.' He reached over to the glovebox and slid the Fetworld brochure onto the passenger seat. 'Frey is the son of one of Taylor Maxwell's victims. She was raped by her father and he forced her to give birth in the house.'

'Christ.'

'I know. There's more, but just focus on that name and throw it into the cross-ref mix for employees of the Pestaway and KwikClean holding company. Also, affiliates. He has a cleft lip, which explains the cleaner's description of the scar. He'll probably be good with computers. Maybe he works on the admin side. Systems, IT. Get them on it quickly.' He looked out at the darkening sky. 'We're on a serious clock here.'

Conway made a noncommittal noise. 'I don't think we are.'

'What do you mean?'

'I was going to call. I asked the Pruetts about their plans for this evening. The daughter plays violin and they were due to attend an open-air recital at Holland Park, then on to a party in Kensington. Sawyer, they were due to stay there overnight. Surely the killer would know that, if he's so meticulous.'

'Maybe he doesn't know. Maybe he wasn't planning to attack tonight. This is our blind spot. The house just fits the criteria. We don't actually know his intentions. He might already have finished. Maxwell said Frey was kept in a cellar, abused, partially suffocated, denied agency. The killings could be some kind of dark celebration of his aliveness. The transformation from unwanted runt to a god-like character with dominion over life and death...'

Conway picked up the thread. 'And by targeting the kind of families he was denied, he proves his dominance.'

Sawyer flew over a mini roundabout and onto a slip-road marked with a sign for London. 'This is all good, but let's wait until we know more about Frey. Please jump on that straight away.'

'I will. And I'm afraid there's something else.'

'Is Hatfield okay?'

She paused. 'How did you know?'

'Poor health, stress, new granddaughter, wayward protégé detective to manage. He didn't look too good in the meeting earlier. What's happened?'

'Suspected heart attack. They're sending a new SIO from Hendon. DCI Eric Harding. I know him, though. He's alright. McHugh's old boss. He wants to keep surveillance on the Pruett house in case our man turns up in the night, expecting them back from the party tonight or in the morning.'

'It's a good call. Things might be about to get hectic, though. So, make sure he's properly briefed.'

She scoffed. 'Anything else? Can I get you a coffee?'

'*Hayden Frey.*'

He rang off and settled into the empty slow lane, glancing down at the brochure, checking the road as he turned the pages. He took out the Fetworld business card and called the number. A bright female voice answered, almost sing-song.

'Hello?'

'Jen? This is Detective Jake Sawyer.'

She thought for a second. 'Oh. Hello again. You're keen.'

'This is late for me. I usually crack within the hour.'

Jen laughed. 'So, what can I do for you? Be specific.'

'You said you're the key fulfiller of custom orders in the London area.'

'Yes, for the whole of the southeast. We don't do it all, though.'

'But if it's a big piece...'

'Probably us, yeah. All the key websites bounce off us. We're hard on the SEO.'

Sawyer slowed further to leave space for an overtaking van. 'Can you look at the order history for the piece on page twenty-five? A7.'

'Hold on... Okay. The isolation box.'

'Looks like a coffin.'

'Yeah. Similar size and shape. The inside padding is coated in melamine. I remember you asking about that. It's hardcore. Totally soundproof. All hand-crafted. Angled steel frame, coated wooden panels. The door is designed so that no light gets in when it's closed. Fresh air system to provide enough oxygen inside.'

He glanced down at the photographs, back up at the road. 'How does it lock?'

'Pins or padlocks. It's obviously a two-person piece. Usually, the user will enjoy that feeling of surrendering control to their partner or dom. Putting their freedom, and life, in another's hands. With sub-dom play, it's about as dark as it gets.'

'Literally.'

'Well, yes. No light. Quiet. Completely shut off. I'm just looking up the order history... We've fulfilled twelve in the past year. Doesn't sound much, but they are pushing two grand all-in. Takes at least eight weeks to make them, all to order.'

Sawyer waited, leaving some space, wary of appearing desperate. When Jen didn't speak, he added, 'Could you send me the names and addresses of the orders?'

She laughed. 'Of course not. I run the day-to-day, but the owner is feral about client confidentiality. I'd end up in a similar box myself.'

'Can you send me a private picture?'

'Right...'

'I'd like to see the warehouse. I'm interested in visiting but I'm anxious.'

She paused. 'But you've already been—'

'Let's pretend I haven't.'

'Okay. So, we're roleplaying.'

'I suppose so. But with sky-high stakes. I think one of the customers on your order list could be responsible for the deaths of twelve people. Six children. So... If you could allay my anxiety with a photo of the warehouse, without closing your fulfilment software?'

'It's not that fancy. Just a spreadsheet.'

'Okay. So, the focus of the photo is the warehouse,

but the screen with the name and address detail is still visible, zoomable...'

She sighed. 'You're a bad boy, Detective Sawyer.'

'It's not my fault. I was made this way.'

She lowered her voice. 'Someone needs to discipline you.'

'Join the queue. Look. Jen. I admit it. I'm at your mercy. I need you to help me join a few dots and catch someone who is way beyond roleplay. He was the product of incestuous rape. Held captive for his formative years, in darkness. Abused, beaten, strangled.'

'You make him sound like the victim.'

He paused. 'Have you heard of attachment theory?'

'Isn't that about parents bonding with children?'

'Yes. We need to form those bonds at an early age. But humans aren't as naturally instinctive as other animals. We have to learn how to behave. And so, when those early bonds are subverted by tragedy or abuse, our view of the world is ruptured.'

'Fucked up.'

His eyes moved to the rear-view mirror. Empty back seat. 'If you like. So, we don't read social cues in the appropriate way. We don't react to danger or kindness. Our empathy gets screwed. We become delinquent children, teens.'

'And violent adults.'

'Exactly. Abuse begets abuse. It's a cycle. Nature abhors a vacuum. So, when we're denied love, we fill the space with hate. And that often manifests as hatred for those who we feel *weren't* denied love. I think this applies to a name on that list. You're right. He is a victim. I'm just asking you to help me stop him creating other victims, other abusers. To break the cycle.'

A pause, then a shutter sound.

'Hope that helps,' said Jen.

She disconnected.

Sawyer checked his phone; a message came through with a picture attachment.

He laid the phone down on the passenger seat and opened the picture. It showed the Fetworld warehouse, with an open laptop on the reception desk in the foreground.

He zoomed into the screen and scanned the list of names.

44

A white Mercedes S-Class rolled onto the gravel drive of a vast detached house, triggering the security lighting. The build was contemporary, stylishly hideous. Sandy brickwork; gable roofs varnished with grey slate; matching skylights and floor-to-ceiling windows. The car pulled up beside an adjoining double garage and idled in the shade of a tall laurel hedge.

A bulky man, as broad as the door frame, emerged onto the stone-covered porch and lingered in the dusk, eyeing the car.

The driver killed the engine, got out and opened the back door, allowing Dale Strickland to step onto the gravel. Strickland was dressed for business, immaculately groomed in grey suit, white shirt, navy blue tie. The security lights caught his trimmed white hair as he walked over to the man at the porch, unaccompanied.

He smiled and took off his heavy-framed glasses. 'Dale Strickland. Here to see Leon Stokes.'

The man studied him. 'We're not expecting anyone, my friend.'

'I didn't say you were. Tell Leon the Deputy Mayor of Greater Manchester would like to see him.'

Voices from inside the house; the man looked behind him and stepped aside. Strickland strolled in.

'First left,' said the man, closing the door.

Strickland walked on without breaking stride and turned into the sitting room. He paused at the door, surveyed the room: Stokes on the purple sofa; Boyd Cannon and Wesley Peyton at the dining table. 'Gentlemen.'

The large man entered and hovered near the dining table.

Strickland turned to the wall and looked over the gigantic yellow-and-red abstract painting. 'Is this an Auerbach?'

Stokes got to his feet. 'It is. You a fan?'

'I am now. He's all about bringing order to the chaos of life, as I understand.' He turned, smiled at Stokes. 'I'll have my assistant look into it. The Broadhurst House walls are a little bare. A Rothko or two would do the trick, but... Bit depressing.'

Cannon tapped something into his laptop. 'I don't think painters sell their work by the yard.'

Dale stepped forward, shook Stokes's hand. 'Dale Strickland.'

Stokes nodded. 'This is Boyd. Wes.'

Peyton tugged at the brim of his Manchester City baseball cap. 'You canvassing, are you? Bit late for it.'

Strickland smiled. 'Wesley Peyton. Your brother's a bit of a celebrity. Is that one of his?' He nodded to the grenade on the table.

Peyton shrugged. 'Fake. The fuck do you know about my brother, anyway? You're the cunt who put him inside. Well, you're the boss of the cunts.'

Strickland sighed, sat down. 'Before my time, Wes.'

Stokes glared at Peyton, sat opposite Strickland. 'Drink?'

'I'll take a Glenfiddich, if you have some.'

Stokes nodded at the bulky man, who got busy with a drinks cabinet.

Strickland reclined in the chair, looked around the room. 'I have to say, Leon. I had you down as a Grade II man. This is all a tad... contemporary.'

'I try not to live in the past.'

Strickland nodded, deep in thought. 'Uhuh. You do have a score to settle, though.' The doorman handed him a tumbler of whisky. 'A man named Curtis Mavers came into your home recently, beat you quite badly, stole a lot of money. I know he's been responsible for other similar attacks on your employees.' He sipped his drink. 'Now. Mavers is clever and durable, but he would need insider help to access the addresses and security information required to take on those hits.'

'You mean police?' said Stokes.

'I mean CID.'

'Jake Sawyer,' said Peyton.

Dale beamed, pointed at Peyton. 'He's smarter than he looks.'

Stokes glanced at Cannon. 'Answer me this, Mr Strickland. What possessed Curtis Mavers to name Sawyer before he left?'

'A disagreement. Sawyer co-ordinated the attacks on your dealers, with Mavers as the muscle. Sawyer wanted to stop, have a cooling-off period. But when Sawyer gave him this address, Mavers saw the chance to take the bigger swag bag for himself. Sawyer got wind of it and tried to get Mavers out of the picture, but he was too late. So, Mavers dropped his name to you, to make trouble for him.' Strickland finished his drink, shuddered with pleasure. 'Now, let me tell you what I'm hearing. As the boss of the cunts, I occupy a unique position. One ear open to the underworld chatter, the other to police ops and policies. Word is, Leon, you've been double-fucked and you're still bent over, asking for more. They're laughing at you. Mavers, because he knows someone *told you where he was*, but you still couldn't get him. Sawyer, because he was the one who tipped you off. And of course, he knows where Mavers is now, but he's not going to volunteer the information again.' Strickland looked over to Peyton, spinning his grenade. 'Are you still following all this, Wes?'

Stokes rubbed at his eyes. 'The tip-off thing wasn't my fault. Someone got to Mavers first.'

'Well. The word is, you're a lame lion. All the young cubs in Moss Side aren't impressed. They're eyeing your spot as king of the jungle. You say you try not to live in the past. But before you know it, you'll be history. An irrelevance.'

'So, to what do we owe the pleasure? What's it to you?'

Strickland brushed at his shirt cuff. 'Cards on the table. I'm in line to be the Greater Manchester mayor soon. I'll have all the power, and I can make sure you're free to operate at an advantage over your rivals. Consolidate your position. But from now, I need to keep my hands nice and clean. In public, at least. Keep up appearances. A woman at my shoulder, easy on the eye.' He leaned forward, elbows on knees, and pointed at Stokes. 'But I need your help, Leon.'

'How?'

'I want Sawyer gone. Off the board. He's become too complicated for me, in too many ways. He was a sparring partner for a while, but he's an obstacle now. And anyway, he's corrupt. A liability. The brass will be happy to see the back of him.'

Peyton spun his grenade, hard. 'So, we your fucking hitmen now?'

Strickland rose to his feet and walked over to the dining table. He took a seat next to Cannon and stared Peyton down. 'Your brother blew up some low-ranking lowlife in his stolen car, Wes. Sawyer is a Detective Inspector. He's known. High profile. The newspapers call him *hero cop*. This would be like you bagging big game compared to your brother taking out a scrawny pigeon. *You* would be the one getting talked about. No longer in your brother's shadow.'

Peyton leered at him, spun his grenade again.

Stokes got up, walked over. 'Let's think this through.

You want us to tag CID in exchange for your influence. What about Mavers? I want that fucker's head on a spike.'

Strickland stood, headed for the door. 'I can give you Mavers. He's worked with me before. Ask around. He trusts me. He can't get out of the country without my help. Get me Sawyer and I'll get you the time and destination of the private airfield where I'll arrange for Mavers to fly out. Everybody wins, Leon. You balance your personal books, regain respect, get more freedom to operate.'

'And you?' said Cannon.

'I get Sawyer. At a safe distance. No blowback.' He paused, squeezed Stokes on the shoulder. 'Well. Something to think about.' He flipped a card onto the dining table. 'Call me. Thanks for the drink.'

Stokes, Peyton and Cannon sat in silence, listening to Strickland's unhurried crunch across the gravel outside, and the car pull away.

'What do we think?' said Cannon.

Peyton pocketed his grenade. 'I'm sure Eddie's mentioned his name. Shady fucker.'

Cannon shook his head. 'It's quite a risk. Coming here, unannounced. Unprotected.'

'It's swagger,' said Stokes. 'He's either fearless or stupid. Or he thinks he's untouchable. I'm not keen on trusting someone with any of those qualities.' He dropped back into the sofa. 'But if what he says about Sawyer is true, then he will surely be in touch with Mavers. He'll know where he is.'

'And we're in the red with Doyle,' said Cannon. 'This has become about a lot more than payback for Mavers.'

Peyton banged a fist on the dining table. '*Fuck* Doyle. Shithouse Scouser lost his bum-boy. So what?' He fluttered his fingertips around his eyes, miming tears. 'Boo fucking hoo.'

'Doyle's got reach,' said Stokes. 'It's not clever to make an enemy of him.'

'Way I see it, Leon,' said Peyton, 'if Sawyer's running the show with Mavers, taking down our dealers, attacking you, invading your home... That makes him fair game, too. However many stripes he's got.'

Cannon stretched, groaning with the effort. 'He's right. We can't sit on our hands forever.'

'This is the time,' said Peyton. 'We need to make it nice and clear. If you fuck with us, you're going to get fucked with.'

Stokes sprang up, strolled over to the cabinet, poured himself a drink. 'Before I throw my hat in with Strickland, I want one last go at finding Mavers myself.' He glanced at Cannon. 'Send Malecki.'

'Where?'

'Sawyer.'

45

'Mrs Frey?'

The woman—thirties, tall but heavy—hung back in the doorway, studying Sawyer. 'No.'

'You're not married? To Hayden?'

'No. Are you delivering something?' She stepped down off the porch into the fading light. Long false eyelashes; bleached blonde hair bunched at the scalp; talon-like nails, painted violet. She stood level with Sawyer, but almost matched his height. He looked down. Expensive-looking heeled mules. Purple.

He smiled, trying the dimple. 'I'm a detective, working with the Metropolitan Police. DI Jake Sawyer.' He produced his warrant card.

The woman glanced at it, then fixed her focus on him. Her eyes roamed, taking him in. 'Oh, god.' She covered her mouth with both hands. 'What's happened?'

'Nothing. It's fine. Can I ask your name? Are you the homeowner?'

'Charlotte Malone. I am, yes. What's this about?'

'Do you mind if I come in for a few minutes?'

Malone frowned.

'I promise I'll be quick. I can tell you were in the middle of something.' Another smile.

'I... don't mind, no.' She turned, led him through to a cavernous sitting room, untroubled by chintz. Period fireplace; window-sized wall mirror; framed monochrome prints spaced around the maroon and white walls. Cindy Crawford, Madonna, a topless man holding a car tyre in each hand.

'Herb Ritts,' said Sawyer.

Malone forced a smile. 'I was going to say... I don't mind, but I need to go out soon. I have a private lesson at a house on the hill.'

'Harrow-on-the-Hill?'

'Yes. Near the school. I teach music there.'

'What time is your lesson?'

She looked at her watch. 'Fifteen minutes. And it's a five-minute drive. Sorry... Can you tell me what this is about?'

'I was hoping to speak to Hayden. Is he here?'

Malone dropped her head to one side. 'No. He's out. With a friend. Somewhere in town.'

Sawyer nodded. 'Can you give me his number, Charlotte?'

'I'd rather speak to him first.'

'No problem. And Hayden lives here with you?'

'He lives and works here. He has a few health issues. Has he done something wrong?'

'I need to speak to him before I can say for sure. What does he do?'

Malone paused, as if listening for something. 'IT. Systems. He works for various companies. "Infrastructure", he says. No idea what that means, but he does okay.' She walked past Sawyer into the hall. 'Would you mind if I just check on something? I won't be a minute. Please. I was just... on a Zoom call.'

'Can I take a look around?'

She hesitated. 'I don't know. Can you? Can I stop you?'

'If you did, it would make me *really* suspicious.'

A loud thump, from the room above.

Sawyer looked up to the ceiling. 'Is there someone else in the house, Charlotte?'

'Just an overweight cat. She'll come through the ceiling one day.' She sighed, weighing options. 'Have a look round if you like, but just for a couple of minutes. And please stick to this floor. The workspace upstairs is private. I'll be down soon.'

Malone walked past Sawyer. He listened as she thudded up the stairs, hurrying. Heeled footsteps in the room above. A muffled voice: Malone's.

He headed through to the back of the house. Good-sized kitchen. Wooden dining table; red lacquered units with recessed lighting; vase of white lilies; framed photograph of a glossy blue dog figure made from folded balloons.

Sawyer muttered to himself. 'Jeff Koons.'

A small side room off the kitchen contained an

electric piano and a tall bookcase loaded with academic textbooks and sheet music.

He walked back up the hall and climbed the carpeted staircase quietly. At the top, he entered the first facing room: an office. Blackout blinds; brown leather office chair; a computer station with keyboard and multiple monitors.

'*Hello*. I asked you to stay on the ground floor, Mr Sawyer.'

He turned to see Malone exiting the room above the sitting room. 'Sorry. I need to use your toilet. Couldn't find one downstairs.'

She closed and locked the door behind her. 'Bathroom is first left.'

Sawyer pointed to the room behind Malone. 'Workspace?'

She folded her arms. 'Yes.'

'Hayden's workspace?'

'It is.'

Sawyer nodded, hoping for more.

Malone angled her head, impatient.

'Has Hayden lived with you here for a while?'

'Yes. Many years. We complete each other.' She forced a sarcastic smile. 'He finds social contact difficult. But he's really quite exceptional. That room has been his haven, for work and learning. He had a rough start in life.'

Sawyer turned back to the office. 'Can I have a closer look? At the things Hayden has been working on. Learning about.'

'As I said, it's private. I'm not comfortable with you nosing around in Hayden's absence.'

He smiled, turned to face her again. 'You probably think I need a warrant. We have a thing called Section 17, Charlotte. It gives me the right to search a property without a warrant if I feel there's a "danger to life or limb".'

'And why on earth would you think that?'

'In short...' He took a couple of steps across the landing; Malone stayed in front of the door. 'My spidey sense is tingling. I'm sorry to tell you I need to question Hayden about some serious crimes. That counts as Section 17. Also, I'm not happy with your demeanour. You're jumpy. You're seeing through me, not looking at me. As if you have something else on your mind. Pretty strange when a copper has just turned up at your door unannounced. I'm also wondering about this overweight cat, and why you would lock her in a room.'

Malone puffed out her cheeks and nodded to the floor. 'She's there. Dita. I just let her out while you were snooping in Hayden's office.'

Sawyer looked down as a portly black cat threaded through his legs and lumbered down the stairs.

'What serious crimes?' said Malone.

'I need to speak to Hayden, Charlotte. It'll all become clear soon.' He pointed to the room behind Malone again. 'And I'd like a quick look in there. If it's not too much trouble.'

She hesitated, then turned and unlocked the door.

'Fine. But please. I have to leave in a few minutes, and I'm still not ready.'

He walked past her into a wooden-floored bedroom with king-size bed, mirrored dresser, well-stocked bookcases. The window blinds were drawn behind a tall vase of fake white flowers in the centre of the ledge. Sawyer moved in and stood at the edge of a section of grey padded flooring built from interlocked panels. Several items of specialist fetish furniture sat around the edges of the flooring: a whipping bench, restraint chair with wrist and ankle ties, suspension rack. A black leather sex swing hung from chains connected to a reinforced ceiling block, and the black isolation box lay flat beneath a shelf of accessories. Sawyer stepped onto the padded section and looked along the shelf. Cuffs, gags, hoods, muzzle.

He stopped. 'Very strange.'

'It's just sex. Different strokes.'

'No. I mean the noise.'

Malone came over. 'What noise?'

'Exactly. There isn't any.'

'Soundproof windows. Acoustic glass. I have the same in the music room downstairs.'

Sawyer crouched down by the isolation box. 'Is this mostly used by Hayden?'

Malone retreated and sat on the bed. 'Yes. Some people have very specific needs. I like it, too, though.'

'The box?'

'BDSM. Roleplay. This all looks medieval, but that's part of the power play. Not everyone can get turned on by reciprocal desire, equal give and take. Makes for tedious sex. This is all done under strict conditions and principles.'

'Informed consent,' said Sawyer, running a finger along the padded black edges of the box lid. 'And I assume Hayden feels the same?'

'He does. The box is custom-made. It's extreme, but you'd be surprised by how many people find deprivation arousing. For some, it's the isolation, being removed from the world. For others, it's the quiet, the silence. I had a boyfriend who had nightmares about being in the womb. The box was only partially sexual for him. It eased his anxiety.'

'Can I have a look inside?'

'Sorry. Hayden keeps it locked. He has the key.'

Sawyer stood up, pointed to a long, silver cabinet on the wall in the corner. 'Is that a gun safe?'

'Yes. It's Hayden's. He shoots. There's a range up in Ruislip.'

'Shotgun?'

She nodded. 'A Browning. Licensed.'

'Your gun safe should be out of sight.'

'I know. I'm sorry. I told him.'

'Is that what you came up for? To cover it up?'

Malone eyed him. 'Yes.'

'And you mentioned a Zoom call.'

She pointed to a closed laptop by the bedside. 'Local music group.'

Sawyer's phone buzzed; he checked Caller ID— Conway—and screened it to Voicemail.

'Thanks for your time, Charlotte. Did Hayden say when he'd be back?'

She shook her head.

Sawyer held out his phone and scrolled to his own entry in the Contacts app. 'I'd be grateful if you could have Hayden call me on this number the moment he arrives.'

She pulled a notebook from the bedside table and copied the number.

'I'm sorry to worry you, but this is a serious matter and I'm hoping to eliminate him from the enquiry as soon as possible.'

She squeezed out a smile. 'Of course.'

———

Sawyer walked back to the Mini, parked at the corner of a side road opposite Frey's place. He climbed in and sat low in the seat, eyes fixed on the row of Edwardian semis, watching and waiting as the twilight dimmed to night. The street lighting flickered into life as he called Conway's number, setting the phone to speaker.

She picked up immediately. 'Sawyer. We have an address for Frey. And more.'

'Is it in Harrow?'

A pause. 'How did you get it?'

'Maxwell. Cross-reffed a couple of things. I'm there now.'

'Hold on.' She muted the phone for a few seconds, then came back. 'I'm trying to okay some support. Can't get hold of Harding yet and we can't allow anything without his sign-off. There's nothing happening at the Pruett place. We're standing by. That's we meaning you.'

'How's Hatfield?'

'Recovering. He'll live. Not sure when he'll be back at work.'

A light came on in Frey's first-floor window. Sawyer squinted through the windscreen, looking for movement.

'What's the more?'

'Huh?'

'You said, "and more".'

'Frey is clean, but his social service record makes for grim reading.'

The light went out.

'I can take it.'

'We got his name from a financial trace. Holding company payroll. He's not employed by them, but they keep him on a retainer. IT. Booking systems, website, app. Lots more. It's all in HOLMES.'

Sawyer rolled down the window. Still and muggy. No breeze. Chinese food smell from a takeaway opposite the houses. 'Could he access the KwikClean and Pestaway systems?'

'Well, yes. He wrote them. McHugh thinks he got the sedative drug via Pestaway. Maybe over-ordering slightly, syphoning it off. KwikClean has a closed server that holds all the cleaner records. Cleaners can access it like an intranet to update a personal profile area with their addresses, details of the properties they cover.'

'Updates of any alarm codes?'

'Oh, yes.'

An open-top car sped past, engine growling, music thumping.

'Do we have a picture?'

'Yes. I was shocked.'

'Because he looks so ordinary?'

The car noise faded. Only the dead air now. Drowsy birdsong.

'He looks like...'

'A mortgage adviser?'

Conway snorted. 'Not quite, but still... Yes. Ordinary. He has a marking on the left side of his top lip. Pale eyes. Almost translucent. Thick hair, slicked back. Black. Looks dyed, though.'

'Sounds like someone I know. Frey was brutalised by Maxwell when he was a child. Kept in the dark. Confinement and isolation is all he's ever known. It's shaped his paraphilia. Maxwell held a god-like power over him, and so he's exercised similar control over the families. And I think there's something transformative going on. The confinement fuels his urges, charges him up. And when he exercises his will, to free himself, he *changes*. The abused becomes the abuser. The jailed becomes the jailer. He's alchemised weakness and impotence into ultimate strength. Power, domination, control. The classic triad.'

'So why the suffocation? The suffering? Why kill the women outright?'

Sawyer tilted back his head. A warm breeze drifted

across his neck. 'The families represent a world he was denied. He got into the houses to spend time in that world for a while, as the confinement gave charge to his urges. Their happiness offends him and he draws intense pleasure from taking it away, forcing them to observe the appalling, drawn-out end of each other's lives. It's important to him that they draw no comfort from each other in their final moments. The tape seals off all communication, and they can only watch, as they die themself. Frey's mother Evelyn was the source of all his misery. She bore him after incestuous rape. She despised him for what he represented. She abandoned him as Maxwell's plaything. As proxies, he saved the worst for the women in the families.'

'The worst?'

'He killed them last, after they'd seen the rest of the family die. And he slit their throats for the blood to use in the markings, and because there was nobody left to suffer over their suffering. The markings are proclamations. Among other things, Maxwell called him Dead Boy. *I LIVE* is a rebuke to that. An affirmation of his aliveness. Again, a transformation. The old Hayden was as good as dead. The version who emerges from the dark and kills is a different beast, fiercely alive. He sent the notes to Maxwell as taunts, using incorrect runes to show contempt for his abuser's childish obsession with the occult.'

'And when will he be done? Will he ever be satisfied? Is there an end point?'

'I still worry about the feeling of crescendo. His god

complex would never entertain the idea of someone else deciding his fate now. He had enough of that in his early years.'

A shout of distress from somewhere. Female.

'Contact Harding,' said Sawyer. He got out of the car. Another shout. From Frey's house?

He ran across the road, forcing a car to stop and sound its horn.

Another shout. More like a scream.

'What was *that*?' said Conway.

'About to find out. Go over Harding's head if you have to. We're in Section 17.'

'Stand down. I can't send a team until—'

Sawyer disconnected the call and ran down the front path of the Frey house. He opened the letterbox, pushed his ear in close.

Thuds upstairs, movement.

He took a few steps back and shoulder-charged the door. The lock crunched away from the wood and fell onto the stone step.

'Charlotte?'

He paused, listening.

Nothing.

Sawyer climbed the stairs in slow, quiet steps, keeping his eyes on the landing.

More movement. Shuffling sounds from the bedroom.

He reached the top of the stairs and paused again.

Malone's voice. Ragged, stifled. Spluttering and gasping.

He crashed into the room.

Malone hung from the suspension rack, arms above her head, wrists cuffed and wrapped around the steel bar. She was just too short to reach the ground in this position, and she writhed and rocked, toes scuffing on the padded floor, kicking through a puddle of blood gathering at her feet. Her throat had been cut; thick gaffer tape bound her mouth.

Sawyer snatched up a pair of nail scissors from the dresser. He rushed over to Malone and cut through the tape, tearing it away. She gasped, choking, aspirating the blood flooding her lungs.

He turned to check. Heavy blood spatter on the bed, a few feet from Malone. Carotid probably severed, not punctured.

Sawyer took a step back and leapt up to the suspension rack, holding on with both hands, swinging. The fastener bolts broke free, wrenching the rack from the ceiling, dropping him to the floor next to Malone, showering them with plaster.

He scrambled to his feet, skidding in the blood, and tore a pink bathrobe from the back of the door. He wrapped the sleeve around Malone's neck, applying pressure, trying to steady her as she thrashed around in blind panic, eyes on him. Imploring.

He pulled down her handcuffed wrists, placed her hands on the sleeve of the robe.

'Push down, Charlotte. You'll be okay. It looks bad, but you'll be okay. I'm going to get help. Just focus on the pressure. Try not to move around too much.'

She lay there, trembling, eyes fixed on the ceiling.

Blood soaked into the padded floor, leaking over the edge onto the wood. Rivulets trickled through the grooves between the floorboards.

Sawyer wiped his hand on the bed, sat down, pulled out his phone.

He rattled out the details to the emergency dispatcher.

CALL WAITING alert. Conway.

He screened it, looked across to Malone. Trembling. Fitting?

For the first time, he noticed the open isolation box.

Gun safe. Open. Empty.

A noise from the back of the house. Ground floor.

'Charlotte. Is Hayden here?'

No acknowledgement. Eyes staring.

Definitely fitting now. Or at least in shock.

He sprang up from the bed, slipping again, steadying himself with a hand to the floorboards.

Warm blood.

He saw it all again. Lived it. This was more than memory. He had travelled in time.

Barking.

Malone, wracked by violent tremors. Feet thumping against the floor.

His dog, his Jack Russell terrier, on its back. Howling in pain and confusion. Thrashing its legs. Unable to flip over.

The blood, warm on his hand.

The blood, shining in the grass. Matted in his hair.

He wrenched himself away, out of the door, down the stairs.

'Run, my darling!'

Commotion on the street at the end of the path.

Blood drips and splashes on the stairs, in the hall.

He turned, ran through the kitchen past the music room, out through the wide-open back door.

The garden was small and untidy, fenced in on either side, with a taller fence at the back. A dilapidated tool shed crouched at the far end.

Dark out here. Sawyer switched on his phone light and ran through the clumps of thick grass.

More blood, glinting on the soil.

More flashes.

His mother's orange jacket.

His brother, in a heap.

His dog's raking barks; its final sounds.

Hands guiding him away. Soothing voices.

The back seat of a car, his face pinned to the window.

Everything receding into the distance.

Everything he held precious: defiled or destroyed.

Sawyer slumped forward, tried to slow his breathing. He reached the tall fence at the back of the garden, spun his phone light across the ground. No blood here.

He checked the fence. Rickety, but possible to scale.

An enormous *boom* from inside the shed. A howl of pain, male.

Shouts of alarm from neighbours.

Sawyer pushed open the shed door and aimed his phone light into the darkness.

The shed was crammed with utility clutter: rusted lawnmower; moulding garden furniture; a frail-looking shelf stacked with crusted paint cans. The back wall was splattered with fresh gore, blood dripping down from the narrow ledge of the shed's only window, opaque with grime. Dense smoke hung in the air, along with a pungent, sulphurous smell.

A man lay on the floor beneath the window, his body pushed into the corner, legs folded over each other at an unnatural angle. He inhaled quick and sharp, and exhaled in long, low animal moans.

Sirens out front. A vehicle pulled up, the blue lights flaring through the ground floor windows, illuminating the garden with a slow strobe effect.

The man twitched and trembled, flailing an arm to the side, raking the nails of the hand up and down the shed wall.

Sawyer crouched by the door, aimed his steady white phone light at the man.

Dark black hair, splayed across the floor behind his head. His other arm lay limp at his side, bleeding from a cluster of slash marks above the wrist. A Browning shotgun lay at the man's feet.

Bodies in the house. Running. Shouting. Boots on the stairs.

Sawyer passed the light up to the man's face.

Most of his lower skull had been blasted away, with only a jagged spur of bone protruding at the side of his upper jaw. His nose was a mass of smouldering cartilage, smeared across his cheek, and his eye socket had shattered, exposing a pulped eyeball.

Sawyer got to his feet, held the light up to the near wall, and read the markings, daubed in blood. Plain English, this time.

I DIE

46

'Did you know Frey was in the box?'

Hatfield winced as he reached over to his bedside table. Sawyer picked up the plastic glass of water and handed it to him.

'It didn't occur to me. I was focused on his girlfriend. What she was telling me. What she was trying to hide.'

Conway stood by the window, looking down on the Queen Mary Hospital car park. 'Frey had oxygen in there, or you might have heard his breathing. Like Nathan.' She drew the blind halfway down the window, shading Hatfield from the early morning sun. 'Just one of those things.'

Sawyer ruffled his hair. 'No. I should have done better for her.'

Conway looked up with a sympathetic smile. 'You're human, Sawyer. Despite what the media say.'

'This time they're right, though,' said Hatfield. 'He *is* a fucking hero. The evidence on Frey's office computer suggests he was planning to attack the Pruetts next, probably soon. Then he realised he was rumbled. You put it together. You clicked with Maxwell.'

Sawyer gave a grim laugh. 'Another name on my psychopath Christmas card list.'

Hatfield wriggled in the bed, trying to prop himself up. He leaned forward as Sawyer stacked the pillows behind him, then sank back with a contented sigh. 'To my mind, you saved five lives, son.'

Sawyer gazed at the water as it settled in Hatfield's cup. 'Shame it wasn't six.'

'Malone died at the scene,' said Conway. 'You did everything possible. She'd just lost too much blood. Frey is recovering after the first round of surgery. He's due for more later this morning. Lost the sight in one eye and they're not sure they can save the other. They're reconstructing his face with no lower jaw.'

'Fucking hell,' said Hatfield. 'Reminds me of one of my first call-outs. Bloke who tried to shoot himself with a vintage revolver. Blew a hole in the side of his skull but survived. I walked him to the ambulance, holding a cushion to his head, keeping his brains in. Poor bastard survived. Ended up paralysed down one side.' He looked round the room. Clean, quiet, well equipped. 'Tell y'what. Thank fuck for private healthcare. But I'd kill for some breakfast.'

'I'll ask,' said Conway.

A moment of silence.

Conway cleared her throat. 'Martha Dumas ID'd Frey as the Pestaway guy, staking out the Healys' house.

The tape used on his girlfriend was the same as the tape found there. The knife he used to cut himself in the shed matches the wounds on the mothers. We need more forensics and results from the analysis of his devices, but I'm confident, given the message on the shed wall.'

'Local police got there quickly,' said Sawyer.

Conway nodded. 'The neighbours called them before you. All the noise.'

Sawyer checked his phone. Missed call from Maggie. 'How about you, sir?'

Hatfield sighed. 'It was a mini heart attack. Temporary artery blockage. They're putting me on blood thinners. More veg, less sugar and salt. Stress management. Yeah, I know. Good luck with that. It's more of a wake-up call than cheating death. But, still, I need to change a few things. As the doc says. Build a better future for myself with the choices I make today.'

'Change is the only constant in life,' said Sawyer.

'Who's that?' said Hatfield. 'John Lennon?'

Sawyer smiled. 'Heraclitus.'

Conway walked over. 'You should consider early retirement.'

Hatfield gaped at Sawyer. 'Jesus Christ. I have a bit of a health scare and she's after my job. It's just... changes. You can't just keep doing the same thing and expecting different results.'

'That's the very definition of madness,' said Conway.

An orderly entered with a tray of breakfast. Scrambled eggs, toast, baked beans, pot of tea. Hatfield sat himself up further and gathered the cutlery.

'Is this the start of the new regime?' said Sawyer.

Hatfield sliced into the toast. 'I'm starting that tomorrow. Visiting my granddaughter tonight.'

'How is young Olivia?' said Conway.

'Awake,' said Hatfield through a mouthful of eggs. 'Most of the time. Listen...' He raised a fork, pointing at Conway and Sawyer. 'I'm off for a few days. Work together on the report.' He swallowed, sat back for a moment. 'Sawyer. Thank you for your help. You did alright, son.'

'You'll take it from here?' said Sawyer.

Hatfield laughed. 'Yes. We will.'

'Take care of yourself, sir. Don't keep doing the same thing. The city needs you. Make that... adjustment.'

Hatfield shook his head. 'You know, Sawyer, you were always high maintenance but I never expected you'd put me in hospital. That's the thing, though, isn't it? As your man says. Things change. You can't get too settled. You never know what's round the corner.'

47

Sawyer loaded his case into the boot and climbed into the car. He rolled down the windows and took a final gulp of the parking garage air: soot and ammonia, sun-baked rubber.

His phone rang. He switched to speaker and connected.

'Mags.'

'Mr Sawyer. I hear your work there is done.'

'Well. I had the last of your brownies a couple of days ago. There's nothing to keep me here now.'

She laughed, a little strained. 'Hatfield gave me access to the HOLMES file. Hayden Frey, Jake. My god. That's quite a life.'

'Yeah. And, despite his best efforts, it's not over yet.'

'Are you heading north soon? Just got back. Walker says Bruce is looking depressed.'

He rummaged in the glovebox. Empty Starburst

packet. 'Are you seriously suggesting that my cat is missing me?'

'Just projecting. I think of him as your avatar.'

'He washes himself more than I do.'

'Nice.'

'Sorry. Been busy. I need some fresh air. It feels like I'm breathing in everyone else's sweat around here.'

'Missing the manure smells?'

'I really am. How are the dogs?'

She sighed. 'A handful. But it's a joy to see them bounding around the fields now that summer's here.' She lowered her voice, almost to a whisper. 'I want to see you.'

'So do I. See you, not me.'

'Come over. Freddy went to some summer sports camp thing and he wants to carry on for the rest of the week. It's near to Justin's, so he's staying there. Mia's at her festival for another day. If you're really good, I might even cook you something.'

Sawyer rolled his shoulders. 'As opposed to letting me starve? Why are you back so soon?'

'Early train. Keating wants me to talk to this Fletcher character. He looks like the guy who was spying on me last year.'

'He's an old acquaintance. That was all about getting some leverage. He had nothing to do with the assault on you. What does Keating want you to do?'

Clatters and clanks in the background as Maggie prepared something in the kitchen. 'Apparently, he hasn't said a word since they brought him in. Different prospect to a seven-year-old, though. He's down for three murders, and they're close to charging him with one. Custody period is expiring, but Keating wants a three-day laydown to prepare the other two cases. He's hoping that Fletcher will take the first charge badly and open up about the other two bodies. They think there might be more, in other places.'

He started the engine. 'I could sit in, too.'

'That's for the boss to decide.'

'Driving up now. Exhausted. But the manure calls.'

Taps, kettle. 'Take it easy on the motorway, Jake. I'll come and see you when you've rested this off. You need a cooldown period. You might not feel you do, but you do.'

'Don't worry. I feel like I do. I want to get away somewhere.'

She sighed, theatrical. 'We've talked about this. Self-isolation will just amplify everything, with nobody else there—'

'For *emotional context*, yes.' He drove up to the security booth. 'Did I say I wanted to go alone?'

'Okaaay...'

'I'll see you soon, Ms Spark. Keep your hands away from Fletcher's mouth.'

He disconnected and leaned over to the open passenger window, waving up at the booth.

Milan gunned his intercom. 'You leaving then, lawman? Hey!' He held up his phone. '*Bullet Symphony*. Two hundred and twenty-five thousand. Some guy called

LloydR is top of the global table. Two-five-five. I mean, *really?*'

Sawyer whistled. 'You won't top that.'

He laughed, wagging his finger. 'Come back in another five years. I'll get there. Hey. Do you want half a protein bar? Tried a new flavour. Tastes like sick.'

'It's a hard sell, but I'm going to pass this time. Take care, Milan. Nice to meet you.'

Milan offered an exaggerated salute. 'So, was justice served?'

He shrugged. 'As long as everybody is videotaping everyone else, justice will be done.'

Milan balked. 'Judge Dredd did not say *that*.'

Sawyer shook his head, rolled up the window. 'Marge Simpson.'

48

TWO DAYS LATER

DSI Ivan Keating turned from his monitor and opened a paper folder. 'Do you know what you are, Sawyer?' He held up a hand. 'Before the smartarse reply, I'll tell you the answer.' Keating sat in full uniform, with his police hat resting on the desk. He kept his eyes on the folder. 'You're a hydra. One problem gets solved but another two grow in its place.'

'That's a spurious analogy, sir.'

Keating raised his eyes to Sawyer, standing at the window. He lifted a feathery eyebrow. 'Hatfield's back at work. Bloody fool.'

Sawyer looked across to the training session at Tarmac Silverlands Stadium. Three small groups of players in contrasting bibs, playing keep-ball. 'Did he leave me a five-star review?'

Keating clicked his chunky ballpoint. 'I'd call it four point three. He had some concerns about your wellbeing.'

Sawyer walked over, sat down. 'Unsettled by London. Don't worry, though. Not tired of life. Did I miss much?'

He fell back in the chair. 'It was quiet. Shepherd's up in Sheffield, helping set up a new MIT. A few holidays going round. Most of the bad people basting themselves in Dubai. The Costa del Crime days are over.' He sighed, clicked the ballpoint. 'But then the Walton thing floated up. Moran is all over it, but I suspect he's had unofficial support.'

'Farrell?'

Keating nodded. 'We have three bodies, including Scott Walton. CCTV. Fletcher was near to Walton's body when he was picked up, and there's DNA from Fletcher and Walton on the knife found at the old abattoir.'

'Hence the charge.'

'Yes. It went to the wire with the CPS, but we got it. Fletcher's brief is focused on how he had no items on him to dig up the body or dispose of it. No bags, nothing.' Keating frowned. 'It's almost as if he saw the arrest coming and wanted to force the issue.'

Keating held a silence, leafed through the papers.

'It's lively,' said Sawyer, 'but I'm not sure how I can help at this stage.'

Keating jerked up his head and fixed Sawyer with his death stare. 'Since we brought Fletcher in, he has said literally one word. To Maggie, this morning. "*Sawyer*."'

'We know he has a link with Dale Strickland. Maybe he's read about our recent issues and sees me as some kind of—'

'Here's what I don't want.' He pointed. 'I don't want you talking to Fletcher. I don't want him to know you're even in the county, let alone building. Make sure I get what I want. Maggie has one more session with him later, and then I've agreed to turn him over to specialist interrogators and get the other two deaths to stick to him. Fletcher is a man of few words, but I'm sure the prospect of a life term might loosen him up. You'll be pleased to hear that DI Conway's review was closer to five stars, but I'd like to know why a vicious bastard like Austin Fletcher has you on his mind before we start any movement for your DCI recommendation.'

Keating closed the folder and propped his elbows on the desk. He rubbed his hands together, eyes down, then raised his gaze to Sawyer, grim-faced.

'This one is bad,' said Sawyer. 'I can feel it.'

'Dennis Crawley. Transferred from Manchester Prison to a medium secure unit after showing schizophrenia symptoms. Paranoid delusions, self-harm, hallucinations. Eventually accepted antipsychotics and therapy. He also stabbed his cellmate up at Manchester after an attack in his cell. The bloke survived. Just. He got through the medium secure screening despite suspicions that he was intentionally alienating other prisoners to provoke the attack. You don't go from prison to secure hospital on violence alone.'

'Probably exaggerated his symptoms.'

'If he did, he fooled two doctors. Then, at the Cygnet place in Nottingham, he was on best behaviour, diligently taking his meds, co-operative, no agitational boundary breaches. He even helped during a patient disturbance last winter.'

Sawyer looked to the window. 'How did he get away?'

'Complained of eye symptoms, and they took him to an ophthalmologist near Derby. Overpowered a nurse as she dilated his pupils, got out of a back door. Manhunt has drawn a blank. If you're short of something to do, you could pop down to the East Midlands and offer your insights.'

'Crawley might have an eye on Strickland. He blames him for his mother's death, remember? Keeps the tooth he says that Strickland knocked out in a ring.'

'Hard to see how he'll get near him, these days.' Keating put on his hat and stood up; Sawyer did likewise, stepping aside as Keating opened the door to let him through. 'I hear your former *bête noire* is next in line for Greater Manchester mayor.'

Sawyer lingered by the open door. 'Proves the old chestnut about nice guys finishing last.'

Keating slapped him on the shoulder. 'Good work. You deserve a bit of playtime. Talk to Nottinghamshire about Crawley if you like, but take that leave soon. Climb a mountain. Lie on a beach somewhere. Read bloody *Ulysses*. Whatever keeps you from being tempted to talk to Fletcher.' He nodded to the office outside. 'On your way. I'm Zooming with the chief and he gets the arse if I'm ten seconds late.'

Sawyer walked across to the lift and pressed the call button. The doors opened and DC Ross Moran stepped out.

He smiled, without warmth. 'Good to see you back. *Sir*. I hope the big city wasn't too hard on you, mentally.' He moved closer, lowered his voice. 'We'll crack Mr Fletcher very soon. I'm looking forward to what he's got to say about the night he killed Scott Walton.' He leaned in, next to Sawyer's ear. 'I bet you are, too.'

49

Sawyer dropped two jagged sugar lumps into his latte and stirred. He raised his eyes and caught Maggie's quizzical stare. 'Brown sugar. Wholemeal.'

She smiled. 'No. It's not.'

He slurped at the froth and looked around the cramped but cosy interior of The Nut Tree café, buzzing with the late afternoon tourist crowd. The main door was propped wide open by a large rock, drawing a modest breeze.

Maggie sat back on her matching brown leather sofa. She pointed to the plate on the table before Sawyer. 'I trust the coconut and jam slice meets your approval?'

'My hopes are high. Busy in here.'

'Post-hike carbs, I'd say.' She sipped at her herbal tea, tucked her hair behind an ear. 'So, did you feel the lure of the bright lights, or are you happy to be back among the tractor tailbacks and...'

'Coconut and jam slices? Always.' He broke off a

corner and chewed. 'Took some time to adjust, and I had a few sleep problems. But I prevailed. I didn't break down. And it made me focus on the future.'

An elderly Scottish terrier meandered over from another table, and Maggie scratched its muddy beard. 'So, how's that shaping up? The future. Rosy? Uncertain?'

'Who can tell? Hatfield said something that reinforced what we were talking about. Making changes.' He took a long guzzle of coffee, making her wait. 'I can't stay at that cottage any more. It's served me well, but it's just a roof, a few walls...'

'A machine for living in.'

He chewed more cake. 'Who's that? Gaudi?'

'Le Corbusier.' She leaned forward. 'Rent it out. Move to the Roaches.'

'Near to you?'

She gave him a look. '*With* me.'

He nodded. 'That's one way of avoiding any more disruption for Bruce.'

'I'm not talking about *tomorrow*. But soon. You know what I think?'

'Of course I don't.'

She pointed to the cake. 'Apart from your dietary habits, I think you might be maturing. Just a tiny bit. You have shown signs of this before, you know. And you're a lot less messy than when we first met. So long ago now, I barely want to think about it.'

'Mum told me to not go back.'

Maggie squeezed his hand. 'No, Jake. She told you to

not *look* back. I think there's a difference. She wasn't telling you to never revisit or re-evaluate. She was urging you to not let the past define you. And this would be taking a clear step forward to creating that kind of future.' She held his eye. 'A shared future. You can never get a completely clean break from the past. There will always be baggage. But—'

'Is this going to be something about how sharing the weight can lighten the load?'

She sipped her tea. 'If you like. And the dark forces don't always have their way, you know. That bastard, Levi Wilmot. He was killed in prison.'

'Did you tell Mia?'

'Of course. She was refreshingly teenage about it. A shrug and a request for festival spending money.'

Sawyer laughed. He pushed the cake around the plate with a fork. 'Mia will be okay.'

'She's been talking to that other boy. Joshua. The one who was at the house with her. He's not okay. But she's helping.'

'Oh... Is she following in your footsteps? Counselling. Fixing.'

'Well. Good prospects. We'll never be short of broken people.'

He slurped his coffee. 'That's a good point, if a bit gloomy.'

'Says Mr Effervescent.'

'Good one. I'd been thinking of options for changing my name. We can discuss it over this sumptuous dinner you're going to make for me tonight.'

'The deal was, you have to be really good. Remember?'

He held her eye, raised an eyebrow. 'Talking of sparkly personalities, how are things with Austin Fletcher?'

'Jesus. He's like a stone. They want to offer concessions. But that's hard to do while he's not even saying anything, apart from *your* name. He has that horrible oily tobacco smell. I still remember the time he was watching my house.'

'He used to be more of a psycho for hire.'

'So, why is he asking for you?'

Sawyer shrugged. 'We've had a couple of moments. And he's probably read about me. You'd be surprised how wide those articles have spread.'

'But why the hell would he murder three people? One of whom we know was a murderer himself?'

'Fletcher is one of those people who has violence baked into his bones. You know the score. The age-old story with male violence. Somewhere along the journey there'll be humiliation. A score to be settled.'

'Without doubt,' said Maggie. 'The desire to replace shame with self-esteem. Anyway. I have one more interview scheduled this evening. Then he's someone else's problem. Normally, I wouldn't be quite so reactionary, but he just makes my skin crawl.'

They indulged in a moment of people-watching.

A sunburnt man in shorts and hiking boots, trying to balance an open Clive Cussler paperback under his elbow while eating bacon and eggs.

A mother and young daughter sharing a plate of rolled Staffordshire oatcakes with cheese. The daughter squelched out a blob of HP Sauce on the side of her plate and sniggered at the noise.

An elderly couple in matching rain jackets, despite the warm weather. The woman pored over a newspaper crossword while the man sat with his eyes closed, half-smiling as he answered her questions about clues.

'Look, Mags,' said Sawyer, whispering. He nodded to the elderly couple. 'It's us. In twenty years' time.'

She glanced over. '*Twenty* years?'

'Thirty, then. Just remembered... I realised something earlier today. I've never been to the cave with you.'

'Thor's Cave?'

'Yes. When I was in London, I had a memory of being there as a child. Those two have just reminded me. I hit my knee on a rock and a similar couple helped. It was the year after Mum died. She'd taken me up there for the first time the previous spring. In the memory, I was there with Dad and Michael. I'd run off ahead. The woman asked me if my mummy was there, inside the cave somewhere.'

Maggie smiled. 'And that must have stuck with you. The idea would have been soothing. That your mother *was* there, in a way. She had introduced you to the cave originally, and so it's come to represent your place of safety. If I were a Freudian, and I'm not, I might even say that it's a proxy womb. A place of ultimate protection, interchangeable with your mother's nurture. It would have comforted you, and I bet it still does, subconsciously. When you enter, you change. You transform, from the outside version of yourself, the troubled you, into a regressed form. Unsoiled and innocent.'

He stared at her, nodding. 'Sometimes a cave is just a cave, Mags.'

50

Sawyer ran, through the twilight, along the edge of the farm fields at the base of Kinder Scout. He kept his pace down, savouring the rhythm and motion, gorging on the zesty air. His randomised Favourites playlist matched the unhurried mood: The Orb, DJ Shadow, Depeche Mode, and an incongruous blast of Yazoo as he passed a herd of droopy cows on the lower slopes.

At the foot of the Jacob's Ladder stone steps, he diverted towards Edale village and ran through the centre, past a sparse group of pavement drinkers outside The Old Nags Head. He threaded past the hikers on the narrow rambler's road and slowed to a walk as he approached the cottage.

A silver Range Rover sat at the end of the farm trail that ran round the back of the house. As he passed, he looked in through the rear window. The interior looked new, uncluttered. A long black duffel bag lay across the rear seat footwells.

Sawyer crossed the private driveway bridge and unlocked the front door. He switched on the sitting room light and, as he turned to set down his water bottle on the window ledge, he caught movement from the path behind.

His head clunked hard into the door and he was down on his knees, pain flaring at the base of his skull.

He pushed up off the floor, trying to roll onto his back, but his attacker anticipated, and hit him again, with something flat and heavy, on the back of the head.

His arms gave way and he flopped down onto his chest.

Knees on his back. Powerful arms pulling his wrists together, binding them tight with a plastic cable tie.

He dragged his leg free and drove a knee into the floor, arching himself back, snapping his head high but connecting only with air.

'Oh!' A male voice from behind. 'I love it. Backward headbutt.'

Accented. Eastern European. Russian?

Strong hands, securing tape around his ankles.

Sawyer's head throbbed from the impacts, and the room dipped and listed as the attacker hauled him up by his armpits and sat him upright on a kitchen chair.

He squeezed his eyes tightly shut, willing himself to stay conscious. A second chair scraped the floor as his attacker sat close, knee to knee.

Sawyer opened his eyes. The man stared at him through the eyeholes of a black balaclava with red stripes around the eye and mouth holes. He was powerfully built, with biceps straining against a fitted red T-shirt. Black leather gloves, khaki combats. A collapsible baton lay on the floor by his work boots.

He reached an arm across and raised Sawyer's chin, studying his eyes. 'Are we sitting comfortably?'

Sawyer mumbled something and the man leaned in closer.

'What was that?'

'I said I'm just pleased to see you.'

The man smiled. 'I feel like I should ask for your autograph, Mr Sawyer.'

'People usually do that before they tie me up.'

The man scraped his chair forward, pushing his knees into Sawyer's. 'I have only one question. But I will have someone else check the answer while you are here with me. If the answer proves lacking, then I will punish you and ask the question again. We will repeat this process until I am satisfied with the answer.'

'I understand. Just, please. No maths.'

'Maths?'

'So, what's in the bag? *My First Torture Kit*?'

The man sighed. 'You may think your humour is unique, or even brave. But it is not intimidating. And it will not help you when I break your elbows. It will not help you when I take out your teeth or cut off your testicles.' He got up and walked over to the kitchen. 'I like to use the tools at hand, if possible.' He opened a few drawers and held up a rotary pizza cutter. 'One of my favourites.'

'Versatile,' said Sawyer, between deep breaths.

'The best thing, though, is for the person to give me a good answer before I have to bring out any toys. Then I don't have to clean up any mess.'

Sawyer shunted his chair around to face the man. 'Are you Romanian?'

The man balked. 'I had a Romanian girlfriend once.' He mimed a spit. '*Kurwa*.'

'You skipped a day at Sadism School,' said Sawyer. 'You're supposed to give me information up front. Tell me your plans, so that when I get out—'

'You won't get out of this. Life is not a fucking Bond film.' He walked over, sat down on the chair. 'And I'm not a sadist. That's just a convenient label for the people who accept their true nature.'

'But if you're going to torture me... To be ruthless, you have to dehumanise me, right?'

The man regarded Sawyer with a steady gaze, searching him. 'I think it's often the opposite. Cruelty isn't something to be corrected. It's central to who we are. The best torturers understand this. They connect with their victims' humanity to get what they want. Any idiot can—'

'Break someone's elbows?'

The man smiled. 'You are funny, but you shouldn't be so confident. You shouldn't think you're untouchable because you're police. I've disappeared police before. I have a friend in the West Country. He has farm machinery that's good for disposal. Feed the remains to animals.'

Sawyer nodded. 'Environmentally friendly. So much

more responsible than dumping bodies in lakes or woodland.'

The man darkened. 'Where is Curtis Mavers?'

'Last time I saw him, he was running away. Are you the guy who killed Levi Wilmot?'

'I had hoped we could get through this with no mess.' The man got to his feet. 'You *will* tell me where he is. And you will also beg for your life.' He leaned in closer. 'If you beg hard enough, I might let you keep one of those green eyes.' He opened the front door and headed outside. 'Back in a moment.'

Sawyer listened to him walk down the path, open the car door.

He stood up and rolled the cable tie around between his wrists until the locking mechanism rested at its weakest point at the top. Then he raised his wrists high behind his back and drove them down, forcing his elbows out to the side.

The tie snapped.

Sawyer dragged himself to the kitchen drawer and pulled out a pair of scissors. He hacked through the tape binding his ankles.

Boots pounding the floor.

The man fell on him, locking an immovable arm round his neck. Sawyer flailed behind with the scissors, but the man held himself out of reach.

Sawyer pushed his feet off the floor, scrambling backward, slamming into the table. The man forced a palm onto the back of Sawyer's head, tightening the chokehold. Sawyer reached behind and prised his fingers away, jerking his own body forward as he levered the man's arm over his head, palm up.

He flipped himself round to face the man, twisting the arm with force, dislocating the elbow joint.

The man bellowed with pain and snatched up the baton with his other hand, swiping for Sawyer's head. He ducked, but the blow caught him full on the shoulder.

Sawyer reared back as the pain flared through his arm, dropping him to his knees. The man faced him, backing away, clutching his elbow. He stumbled through the front door, retrieving the black duffel bag from the end of the path, then ran for the Range Rover.

Sawyer took up the scissors and ran to the door.

The car skidded out of the farm track and roared away along the road, into the night.

Sawyer took out his phone and tapped on a name in his Contacts list: *GERRY SHERMAN*. The call connected immediately.

'Sawyer?'

'Gerry. Listen. Are you on the Buxton custody desk?'

'Yeah. Graveyard shift. What's up?'

He slumped onto the sofa, holding his shoulder. 'I need an ANPR check.'

51

Jakub Malecki propped his phone into the Range Rover dashboard holster.

'Call Leon.'

'Calling Leon Stokes.'

He tore through the Hayfield crossroads, testing his elbow. Every slight movement sent a spasm of hot pain through the joint.

'Malecki.' Stokes's voice. 'What's going on?'

'I think the fucker broke my arm.'

'What?'

'That police bastard.'

Stokes kept the volume low. 'Did you get anything on Mavers?'

'I'm sorry, Leon. He said the last time he saw him he was running away. And he knew about Wilmot.'

'Do you think he knows where Mavers is?'

'I don't know.'

Stokes exploded. *'Nobody. Fucking. Knows.* Some

lowlife Scouse scally making a mug out of us all.' He paused for breath. 'I've had Doyle on the phone tonight. His man Kinsella turned up off Seaforth Rocks with a bullet in the back of his head. He's raving about payback. This thing is *off the scale* fucked-up now. Mavers mentioned Sawyer's name. I've got info on them working together. My dealers are getting robbed. *I'm* getting robbed. And our competitors are sitting around watching us do fuck-all.'

'I can go back for Sawyer with some help. He won't talk, so I take his tongue.'

'It's not Game of Fucking Thrones, Jakub. We need to send a bigger message than you maiming some mentalist copper. And we need to do it *now*. Something big that shows we can't be fucked with.'

'Peyton,' said Malecki. He rolled over a pothole, jarring his arm. 'Fuck! *Cipa!*'

'Get some ibuprofen, will ya? Peyton's on his way, with friends. Meet him in fifteen. I'll send a location.'

52

Kelvin Sullivan gathered his papers and closed his laptop. 'DC Moran, Ms Spark. I feel we've rather run out of road. Perhaps it's time to call it a night?'

Maggie glanced at Moran, standing by the door. The interview room was windowless, airless, and it had become a full-time job to ignore the sweat patches under Sullivan's armpits.

Moran stepped in and leaned on the table. 'Fletcher. I hope you realise, you have gained no ground here. You've just delayed our victory.'

Austin Fletcher sat with his chair angled away, head lolled to the side, eyes almost closed. He looked like he was dozing.

Moran pulled away and opened the door. '*Stan.*'

A bald, burly man in a short-sleeved black shirt walked in and stood behind Fletcher. 'Come on, Austin. Back to your den. You're making me late for dinner. I'm already in the doghouse. Losing my hair through the stress.'

Fletcher rose to his feet, filling the tiny space with his bulk and breadth. He followed Stan to the door, taking slow, measured steps.

As Sullivan stuffed his laptop and papers into a briefcase, Moran slipped past Fletcher and intercepted him as he emerged into the corridor lined with custody cells and utility rooms. He leaned in to Fletcher's ear and spoke in an angry hiss. 'You're a fucking idiot if you think Sawyer will protect you. He'll be a free man while you rot away in some shithole cell. Last chance.'

Sullivan hurried out of the room. 'DC Moran. *Please*.'

Moran pushed his face close to Fletcher's. 'Are you really willing to spend the rest of your life in prison out of loyalty to some dodgy detective who couldn't give a shit—'

Shouts from out front, beyond the connecting door that led to the station reception and custody desk.

Stan sighed. 'What the bloody hell's going on now?' he shouted. 'You alright out there, Gerry?' No answer. Stan ushered Fletcher into his cell and closed the door.

More shouts. Male voices.

He walked down the corridor and peered through the tiny glass window in the connecting door.

Sullivan followed Stan to the door. 'DC Moran, could you please sign me out? It's been a long day.'

Maggie came out of the interview room and stood beside Moran, checking through a notepad.

Stan unlocked the connecting door and Sullivan pushed his way past, muttering.

A loud gunshot sounded out in the reception area. Sullivan gave a shout and fell forward in front of the custody desk. Sergeant Gerry Sherman shouted something, but was silenced by a second shot, closer and louder. Stan lunged back into the cell corridor, pulling the connecting door shut and locking it.

'Oh, fuck. Jesus fucking—'

He lumbered up the corridor and followed Moran back into the interview room.

Maggie stared at the window in the connecting door. Eyes appeared, peering through. Male. Behind a sky-blue balaclava.

'More fuckin' coppers back here. Go!'

The man disappeared and someone bigger kicked at the door. It clattered against the frame, making Maggie startle, but didn't open.

She ducked into the interview room.

'Okay,' said Moran. 'Stan. What's happening out front?'

Stan tried to settle his breathing. 'Fuck, *fuck.* They shot Gerry. And... Fletcher's brief. I saw the blood on the custody desk and floor. Jesus Christ. This is a *police station.*'

Male voices out in the private car park at the back of the station.

Another crash, as the intruders tried to break through the connecting door again.

'How many people did you see, Stan?' said Maggie.

'Uh... Two. Both wearing balaclavas. One blue, one black and red. The bigger one in the black and red... He shot Gerry. No, no, *no*.'

A crash from the other door at the back.

Stan poked his head out of the room. 'Jesus Christ. Now they're trying to get in through the car park. We've got to get help. I'm calling someone.'

'Dial the emergency number,' said Maggie. 'It'll connect to the nearest station.'

'Tell them we need AFOs, not bobbies,' said Moran.

More crashes, from both doors.

Maggie ran out into the corridor and stood before the locked evidence room door. 'Stan! They're going to get those doors open soon. Is there anything in evidence we could use to help? Barricades? Weapons?'

'*Gun.*'

She turned. Fletcher's pinhole eyes regarded her through the window in his cell door.

Stan exited the interview room. 'Called it in. No idea how long it'll take. Oh, Jesus. *Jesus, fuck.*'

Maggie held his shoulders, got in his face. '*Stan.* Weapons?'

'There's the Glock we took off Fletcher,' said Moran, stepping out.

'Was it loaded?' said Maggie.

'The magazine was removed and stored separately. Shelf locations are in the desk drawer. Stan, open the room up.'

Stan fumbled with his ring of keys and unlocked the evidence room. Moran and Maggie pushed their way in.

Stan dropped his keys and knelt to pick them up, just as the front door crashed open and two men in black balaclavas broke through. One raised a pistol and fired once, missing Stan. He fired again, hitting him in the side of the head.

He slumped over, silent.

Maggie cried out as Moran crouched, grabbed Stan's keys and pulled the evidence room door shut behind them.

Shouts from the two men as they charged down the corridor.

Moran pulled out the shelf location list from the desk drawer. 'Gun is P7. Ammo D3.'

They scanned the markings on the metal cages that lined the shelves. Maggie found the silver magazine, while Moran pulled out the Glock.

Banging on the evidence room door. More crashing from the back door.

Moran took the magazine and checked it. 'Full. Fifteen shots.' He loaded the gun and held it in both hands, aiming the muzzle down at the floor.

A shout from outside the back door. '*Get round the fucking front! Door's open.*'

Moran unlocked the evidence room door.

Maggie grabbed his wrist. 'What are you doing? Stan said he called it in.' Moran wrestled her hand away, but she gripped his wrist again. 'We need to wait.'

Moran pushed his face close to Maggie's. Sweat

streamed down his forehead. '*No*. We don't. We don't know how many are back there. Now they know the front door is open.'

'The two out there are armed, Ross. You're not Jason bloody Statham.'

He shrugged her away. 'Fucking popguns. Converted replicas.' He waved the Glock. 'This is a G17. Semi-auto. *Stay down*.'

Moran threw open the door as one of the men ran past, startling him. He fired, hitting him in the thigh. The shot was a thundercrack in the narrow corridor. The man cried out and fell to the floor.

Maggie ducked away, staying low between the evidence room shelves.

Moran dropped to a knee and aimed again, as the man tried to scramble to his feet. He fired two more shots, hitting the man in the head and back, then turned to the far end of the corridor.

Maggie screamed as Moran's head snapped hard into the door frame, jolted by a bullet that had struck him in the neck. He staggered, tried to raise the gun, but then slumped to the floor as another bullet hit him. He dropped the Glock in the corridor and fell face down into the doorway.

The second man ran past Moran's body, out to the reception area, shouting for help.

Maggie crawled out from between the shelves and checked on Moran. There was too much to process: the wounds, the blood, the terror. She tugged at her ears, trying to clear the ringing from the gunshots.

'*He's dead.*'

She looked up. Fletcher's eyes again, at the cell window.

Shouts from the front. More voices.

Maggie snatched up Stan's keys, searched through the numbered tabs, found the key for Fletcher's cell.

She slotted it into the lock, turned it.

Gunshot from the connecting door. The bullet struck the wall behind Maggie and she ducked back into the evidence room, slamming the door shut as another bullet cracked into the floor behind, splashing her with Moran's blood.

The man with the sky-blue balaclava strode down the corridor, holding a sawed-off single-barrel shotgun at his side. The colleague of the man shot by Moran followed at a cautious distance, pistol raised. Another man with a black-and-red balaclava hung back by the connecting door.

'He's fucked,' shouted the man's colleague. 'There's a woman, as well.'

'She a copper?' said Sky-Blue Balaclava.

'I don't fucking know!'

Sky-Blue Balaclava waved his shotgun. 'I want this place cleaned *the fuck out*. Not a scrap of filth. Billy, check all the rooms. Quick.'

He strolled into the interview room as Black Balaclava—Billy—shuffled from door to door, breathing fast, checking the door windows.

He pushed open the door of Fletcher's cell.

Fletcher's hand shot out and grabbed his wrist. He

slammed the door into Billy's face once, twice, wrenching it from the top hinge. It tilted over and hung into the corridor, clinging to the lower hinge.

Billy fell, dropping his gun. Fletcher grabbed it and stood over him, firing twice, down into the top of his head. Fletcher grimaced and tossed the converted pistol down the corridor. He picked up the Glock and ran across to the evidence room.

The man in the red-and-black balaclava fired, grazing Fletcher's shoulder as he ducked into the evidence room.

Fletcher beckoned to Maggie, and she emerged from behind the desk. He checked the Glock's magazine and held the gun to his chest with one hand, listening at the door.

One of the men called out. '*Who the fuck*?'

Sirens from outside, but distant.

Fletcher pushed the door open, leaned out and fired. Sky-Blue Balaclava slipped back into the interview room as the bullet hit the wall by the connecting door, just missing the man in the black-and-red balaclava, who retreated into the reception area and ran.

Fletcher aimed at him, but he crouched and slipped away, turning into the corridor to the main station doors.

Sky-Blue Balaclava shouted from the interview room. '*Malecki! You fucking shit-out.*' He stepped out of the room, holding the shotgun on the evidence room doorway. 'Eh! Fuckface. We're playing rock, paper, scissors, yeah? You've got the paper and I've got the *fucking* scissors.'

Fletcher glanced at Maggie. '*Lupara*. Shotgun.' He shook his head.

Sky-Blue Balaclava sauntered down the corridor. 'Come on. Poke your head out.'

Movement in the reception area.

Sky-Blue Balaclava laughed, keeping the shotgun trained on the evidence room. 'It'll take a week to scrape your brains off the walls.'

Sawyer slipped in through the connecting door, keeping low. He crept towards Sky-Blue Balaclava.

As he reached the interview room, he called out. 'Hey!'

Sky-Blue Balaclava spun and the shotgun boomed. But Sawyer had ducked into the interview room. He darted back out and rushed the man, ducking as he swung the empty barrel in defence. Sawyer staggered him with a left jab, then floored him with a right haymaker. He picked up the spent shotgun and slid it into the interview room behind.

Fletcher opened the evidence room door and stepped out, Glock down by his side. He stood before Sawyer, eyeballed him, then ran, through the connecting door, down the entrance corridor.

Sawyer turned. 'Mags?'

Sirens, from the streets behind the station.

He walked down the corridor, cautious. As he reached the collapsed door of Fletcher's cell, Maggie burst out of the evidence room and ran for him. She held him in a tight bear-hug, her body convulsing.

Sawyer wrapped a hand around the back of her head,

keeping her close. 'Mags. It's okay. *You're* okay. You're safe. This is bad. But... We're good. We're good.'

She pulled back, gazed up at him, wiping away tears. 'Jake. What *is* this? Did they come for Fletcher?' Maggie turned her head, caught movement over Sawyer's shoulder. '*Jake!*'

Sky-Blue Balaclava had raised himself, almost upright. He lifted his arm above his head and backed away, towards the connecting door.

Sawyer turned and watched him go, side by side with Maggie. He moved forward, then froze, as he saw the grenade in Sky-Blue Balaclava's raised hand.

As the man reached the door, he inched halfway around the frame and into the reception corridor. He pulled the pin, smiled, and rolled the grenade back in the direction he'd come from. It skittered along the corridor floor and clunked off the wall, coming to rest by Billy's body, a few feet from Sawyer and Maggie.

Maggie turned to run but stumbled, slipping in a puddle of blood. She clambered over Billy's body, struggling to get upright again.

Sawyer ran for the half-detached cell door and tore it away from the hinge. He gripped it by the sides and careered across the corridor, calling to Maggie.

'Get down! Cover your ears.'

He slipped in the blood, crunched his knee on wood splinters, almost dropped the door.

Maggie had pushed herself into a small recess by one of the locked cell doors. She was foetal, covering her face.

'Turn away!'

Sawyer corrected himself and lunged for her, holding the door up to shield them both.

Whiteout.

Eruption.

Then silence.

53

ONE WEEK LATER

The dreams came slowly, seeping over his consciousness. At first, the colours ran, the faces warped. But then... voices. Familiar sounds and places. And the voices took form and texture, evolving into patterns, wafting in and out of the light in the room.

There was bliss in the oblivion, but eventually he broke through, and time became more measured and linear.

And then, one morning, he found himself wide awake, and heard himself speak.

'*Maggie.*'

Keating got up from the chair beneath the open window and crouched at his bedside. 'Jake? Are you with us?'

Another face loomed in from the left. *'Jake.'* His brother Michael. Shaven head. Green eyes.

His brother's hand on his.

Time lapse again. Someone else in the room. Darker outside.

'Mr Sawyer?'

Grey moustache. Dark suit. Yellow tie.

'My name is Robert Holsgrove. I'm a consultant neurosurgeon.' Holsgrove sat down by the bed. 'And I'm extremely pleased with your progress. I don't want to lay too much on you at once, but you've been through quite a range of treatments, first at Cavendish in Buxton, and now here at the Manchester Centre for Clinical Neurosciences. I believe you had an exploratory laparotomy at Cavendish, and a haemothorax, which was drained.' He checked his notes. 'Nothing else significant in the primary survey. Generalised abdominal tenderness in the secondary. I would expect that to continue for a week or so. You've suffered mild traumatic brain injury, but I'm confident you won't suffer any lasting—'

'Maggie.' Sawyer hitched himself up on his pillow. He looked over at Keating.

'She's okay. She's here, too. In a different area. Critical care. She suffered a more serious concussion. Brain swelling. They had to put her into an induced coma, Jake. But she's... Signs are good. Justin is with her. And the children.'

Sawyer reached for the bedside table, took a drink of water. 'When can I see her?'

Holsgrove caught Keating's eye, shook his head.

'Not for a while,' said Keating. 'She needs more time to wake up and recover. I think she also had a procedure to repair some organ damage. Liver and spleen.'

Sawyer swallowed the water. Its ice fell through him, but there was no warmth to chill.

He lowered his head.

His heart felt raw in his chest. Exposed, peeled open.

His brittle bones. His rusted joints.

He was too frail to bear this weight. There was too much of it all. Too much to know. Too much to feel. Too much to regret.

The breaths came quickly. Pulsing. Shuddering.

He slumped forward, first weeping, then sobbing.

Holsgrove stepped away to make room for Michael, who reached out for his brother, enfolding him in his arms.

Michael was big and powerful, but he couldn't stifle Sawyer's volcanic agony, as the sobs melded into howls, then screams, muffled by Michael's chest.

Sawyer pulled away, his green eyes strafed by rage. 'I tried to save her. I *had* to save her.'

Keating rested a hand on his shoulder. 'You did, Jake. You did save her.'

54

Dale Strickland sank into the custom leather upholstery and rolled his glass of Glenfiddich, jostling the ice cubes. His driver jerked the Mercedes out of the Piccadilly gridlock and slid onto the Manchester overpass.

The call connected, and Leon Stokes's gravelly tones chafed against the sleek interior.

'Let's not get too cosy, Dale. You should be on a burner.'

'Don't worry. I just wanted to let you know that I'll be away for a while.'

'Away, as in?'

Strickland laughed. 'Not prison. Far, far away.'

'Going anywhere nice?'

Strickland sipped his drink. 'I think it's best that we retain a bit of mystery to our disengagement.'

Stokes paused. 'We got Mavers.'

'When?'

'Picked him up a couple of days ago. He was right where you said he'd be. So... Yeah. Thanks for that.'

Strickland smiled. 'You're not used to deferral are you, Leon? How is he?'

'Wolves, lions. No contest.'

Strickland drained his glass, slotted it into the seat-back holder. 'I'm hearing a lot of fallout from the mess you left at Sawyer's station. If only you'd stuck to what we agreed—'

'Like you say, Dale. I'm not big on deferral. You walk into my place, all confident. Confidence makes me nervous. I wanted to hear Sawyer's take on Mavers first hand.'

'And what about Mavers's take on Sawyer?'

Stokes sniffed, held the moment. 'He says the attacks on me and my boys were nothing to do with Sawyer. It was all your work.'

'Well. He would say that, wouldn't he?'

'He wants a word.'

'With me?'

A door opened at Stokes's end. He moved into another room and lowered his voice. 'He says he's got something you need to know. I'm intrigued. And, if you don't mind, I'm gonna put you on speaker. No secrets.'

The line crackled.

'Hello, Dale.' Mavers sounded flat. Rough. 'I appreciate your time. I know you're a busy man.'

Strickland exchanged a glance in the rear-view mirror with his driver. 'Curtis. How are you?'

Mavers fell into a hacking cough, took a few deep

351

breaths. 'I'm sound. Never been better. These boys are keeping me topped up with fresh blood.'

'Sorry it had to end this way, Curtis. I take no pleasure—'

'Who said anything was ending? I knew I wasn't getting on any plane without insurance, Dale. In the end, I took my chances. Another one for the regrets pile. But I got transport from the gay lad who came to get me up in Birkenhead. So, I had a look at your bird's place in Bakewell. Kept me head down. Watched her coming and going for a couple of days.' He whistled. ''kin ell. Punching well above your weight there, lad.'

Strickland sat up in his seat, blue eyes blazing. 'I'm on my way there now. I swear, if you've done anything—'

Mavers laughed, loud but wheezy. 'Not my style. And you can hardly make my life much worse than it already is right now. Nah. I just thought I'd make meself known to her. Get it in your head that if anything happens to me... You know the score.'

The CALL WAITING alert flashed on Strickland's phone screen. He checked the Caller ID.

Eva.

'But, here's the thing, Dale.' Mavers switched to a mocking whisper. 'I know something you don't know. You seen that Criminal Minds programme? I'm what they would call a significant witness. You are going to want to hear about what I saw. And if you let these manky Mancs have their way, you'll never know.'

Strickland switched to Eva's call. 'Sweetheart?'

Breathing at the other end.

'Eva?'

The breaths grew in volume and frequency.

Strickland exchanged another glance with his driver, steeled himself. 'Who is this?'

'*Creepy Crawley.*'

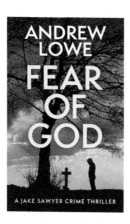

BOOK EIGHT IN THE **JAKE SAWYER** SERIES

JAKE SAWYER is damaged. Haunted by guilt after surviving an attack that left four people dead, he's drawn in to the case of a recently released murderer, tortured to death and dumped at a Peak District beauty spot. Sawyer suspects delayed vigilante justice, but as further victims emerge, he realises the motive runs deeper into the past, and he may be facing an insatiable killer guided by a higher power.

As Sawyer grapples with the case, his self-destructive urges threaten to overwhelm him. And when the love of his life is marked for death, Sawyer's long-suppressed trauma finally breaks out in a devastating explosion of righteous fury.

https://books2read.com/fearofgod

JOIN MY MAILING LIST

I occasionally send an email newsletter with details on forthcoming releases and anything else I think my readers might care about.

Sign up and I'll send you **a Jake Sawyer prequel novella**.

THE LONG DARK is set in the summer before the events of CREEPY CRAWLY. It's FREE and totally exclusive to mailing list subscribers.

Go here to get the book:
http://andrewlowewriter.com/longdark

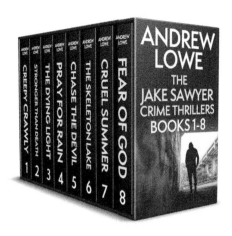

BOOKS 1-8 IN THE **JAKE SAWYER** SERIES

AVAILABLE IN EBOOK and PAPERBACK

READ NOW WITH **KINDLE UNLIMITED**

https://books2read.com/sawyerboxset4

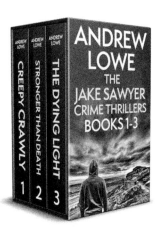

BOOKS 1-3 IN THE **JAKE SAWYER** SERIES

AVAILABLE IN EBOOK and PAPERBACK

READ NOW WITH **KINDLE UNLIMITED**

https://books2read.com/sawyerboxset1

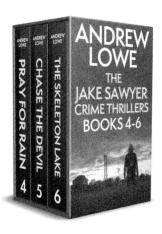

BOOKS 4-6 IN THE **JAKE SAWYER** SERIES

AVAILABLE IN EBOOK and PAPERBACK

READ NOW WITH **KINDLE UNLIMITED**

https://books2read.com/sawyerboxset2

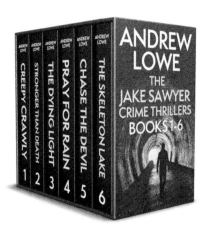

BOOKS 1-6 IN THE **JAKE SAWYER** SERIES

AVAILABLE IN EBOOK and PAPERBACK

READ NOW WITH **KINDLE UNLIMITED**

https://books2read.com/sawyerboxset3

ACKNOWLEDGMENTS

As ever, a thousand thanks to **Detective Constable Ralph King**, for his patient and exhaustive answers to my impatient and exhausting texts and emails.

Thanks to **Dr Sohom Das,** for his insights on forensic psychology and secure units.

Bryony Sutherland did the editing, keeping me honest about post-heart attack health matters and cat whereabouts.

So-So Design did the cover.

Special thanks to **Julia** for listening to me go on about it all.

Andrew Lowe. London, 2022

PLEASE LEAVE A REVIEW

If you enjoyed **CRUEL SUMMER**, please take a moment to leave a review or rating on the book's **Amazon** page.

Honest reviews of my books help bring them to the attention of others, and connecting with readers is the number one thing that keeps me writing.

Go here to leave your review:
https://books2read.com/crlsummer

THE JAKE SAWYER SERIES

THE LONG DARK
CREEPY CRAWLY
STRONGER THAN DEATH
THE DYING LIGHT
PRAY FOR RAIN
CHASE THE DEVIL
THE SKELETON LAKE
CRUEL SUMMER
FEAR OF GOD
TENDER IS THE NORTH
BLOOD NEVER SLEEPS (2025)

BOOKS 1-3 BOX SET
BOOKS 4-6 BOX SET
BOOKS 1-6 BOX SET
BOOKS 1-8 BOX SET

GLOSSARY

ACT – Acceptance and Commitment Therapy. A form of psychotherapy that uses acceptance and mindfulness strategies along with commitment to behaviour change.

AFO – Authorised Firearms Officer. A UK police officer who has received training, and is authorised to carry and use firearms.

ALF – Animal Liberation Front. A political and social resistance movement that promotes non-violent direct action in protest against incidents of animal cruelty.

ANPR – Automatic Number Plate Recognition. A camera technology for automatically reading vehicle number plates.

AWOL – Absent without leave. Acronym.

BSE – Bovine Spongiform Encephalopahy. Colloquially known as 'mad cow disease'. A neurodegenerative condition in cattle.

CCRC – Criminal Cases Review Commission.

Independent body which investigates suspected miscarriages of justice in England, Wales and NI.

CI – Confidential Informant. An individual who passes information to the police on guarantee of anonymity.

CBT – Cognitive Behaviour Therapy. A form of psychotherapy based on principles from behavioural and cognitive psychology.

CID – Criminal Investigation Department. The branch of the UK police whose officers operate in plainclothes and specialise in serious crime.

COD – Cause of Death. Police acronym.

CPS – Crown Prosecution Service. The principle public agency for conducting criminal prosecutions in England and Wales.

CROP – Covert Rural Observation Post. A camouflaged surveillance operation, mostly used to detect or monitor criminal activity in rural areas.

CSI – Crime Scene Investigator. A professional responsible for collecting, cataloguing and preserving physical evidence from crime scenes.

CSO – Community Support Officer. Uniformed but non-warranted member of police staff in England & Wales. The role has limited police powers. Also known as PCSO.

D&D – Drunk & Disorderly. Minor public order offence in the UK (revised to 'Drunk and disorderly in a public place' in 2017).

Dibble – Manchester/Northern English slang. Police.

EMDR – Eye Movement Desensitisation and Reprocessing. An interactive psychotherapy technique used to relieve psychological stress, particularly trauma and post-traumatic stress disorder.

ETD – Estimated Time of Death. Police acronym.

FLO – Family Liaison Officer. A specially trained officer or police employee who provides emotional support to the families of crime victims and gathers evidence and information to assist the police enquiry.

FOA – First Officer Attending. The first officer to arrive at a crime scene.

FSI – Forensic Science Investigator. An employee of the Scientific Services Unit, usually deployed at a crime scene to gather forensic evidence.

GIS – General Intelligence Service (Egypt). Government agency responsible for national security intelligence, both domestically and internationally.

GMCA – Greater Manchester Combined Authority. Local government institution serving the ten metropolitan boroughs of the Greater Manchester area of the UK.

GMP – Greater Manchester Police. Territorial police force responsible for law enforcement within the county of Greater Manchester in North West England.

GPR – Ground Penetrating Radar. A non-intrusive geophysical method of surveying the sub-surface. Often used by police to investigate suspected buried remains.

HOLMES – Home Office Large Major Enquiry System. An IT database system used by UK police forces for the investigation of major incidents.

H&C – Hostage & Crisis Negotiator. Specially trained law enforcement officer or professional skilled in negotiation techniques to resolve high-stress situations such as hostage crises.

IED – Improvised Explosive Device. A bomb constructed and deployed in ways outside of conventional military standards.

IDENT1 – The UK's central national database for holding, searching and comparing biometric information on those who come into contact with the police as detainees after arrest.

IMSI – International Mobile Subscriber Identity. A number sent by a mobile device that uniquely identifies the user of a cellular network.

IOPC – Independent Office for Police Conduct. Oversees the police complaints system in England and Wales.

ISC – Intelligence and Security Committee of Parliament. The committee of the UK Parliament responsible for oversight of the UK Intelligence Community.

MCT – Metacognitive Therapy. A form of psychotherapy focused on modifying beliefs that perpetuate states of worry, rumination and attention fixation.

MIT – Murder/Major Investigation Team. A specialised squad of detectives who investigate cases of murder, manslaughter, and attempted murder.

Misper – missing person. Police slang.

NCA – National Crime Agency. A UK law

enforcement organisation. Sometimes dubbed the 'British FBI', the NCA fights organised crime that spans regional and international borders.

NCB – National Central Bureau. An agency within an INTERPOL member country that links its national law enforcement with similar agencies in other countries.

NDNAD – National DNA Database. Administered by the Home Office in the UK.

NHS – National Health Service. Umbrella term for the three publicly funded healthcare systems of the UK (NHS England, NHS Scotland, NHS Wales).

NHSBT – NHS Blood and Transplant. A division of the UK National Health Service, dedicated to blood, organ and tissue donation.

OCG – Organised Crime Group. A structured group of individuals who work together to engage in illegal activities.

OP – Observation Point. The officer/observer locations in a surveillance operation.

Osman Warning – An alert of a death threat or high risk of murder issued by UK police, usually when there is intelligence of the threat but an arrest can't yet be carried out or justified.

PACE – Police and Criminal Evidence Act. An act of the UK Parliament which instituted a legislative framework for the powers of police officers in England and Wales.

PAVA – Pelargonic Acid Vanillylamide. Key component in an incapacitant spray dispensed from a handheld canister. Causes eye closure and severe pain.

PAYG – Pay As You Go. A mobile phone handset with no contract or commitment. Often referred to as a 'burner' due to its disposable nature.

PM – Post Mortem. Police acronym.

PNC – Police National Computer. A database which allows law enforcement organisations across the UK to share intelligence on criminals.

PPE – Personal Protective Equipment designed to protect users against health or safety risks at work.

Presser – Press conference or media event.

RIPA – Regulation of Investigatory Powers Act. UK Act of Parliament which regulates the powers of public bodies to carry out surveillance and investigation. Introduced to take account of technological change such as the grown of the internet and data encryption.

SAP scale. A five-point scale, devised by the Sentencing Advisory Panel in the UK, to rate the severity of indecent images of children.

SIO – Senior Investigating Officer. The detective who heads an enquiry and is ultimately responsible for personnel management and tactical decisions.

SOCO – Scene of Crime Officer. Specialist forensic investigator who works with law enforcement agencies to collect and analyse evidence from crime scenes.

SSU – Scientific Services Unit. A police support team which collects and examines forensic evidence at the scene of a crime.

Tac-Med – Tactical Medic. Specially trained medical professional who provides advanced medical care and support during high-risk law enforcement operations.

TOD – Time of Death. Police acronym.

TRiM – Trauma Risk Management. Trauma-focused peer support system designed to assess and support employees who have experienced a traumatic, or potentially traumatic, event.

Urbex – urban exploration. Enthusiasts share images of man-made structures, usually abandoned buildings or hidden components of the man-made environment.

VPU – Vulnerable Prisoner Unit. The section of a UK prison which houses inmates who would be at risk of attack if kept in the mainstream prison population.

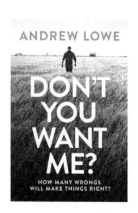

**WHAT IF THE HOLIDAY OF YOUR DREAMS
TURNED INTO YOUR WORST NIGHTMARE?**

Joel Pearce is an average suburban family man looking to shake up his routine. With four close friends, he travels to a remote tropical paradise for a 'desert island survival experience': three weeks of indulgence and self-discovery.

But after their supplies disappear and they lose contact with the mainland, the rookie castaways start to suspect that the island is far from deserted.

https://books2read.com/savages

ABOUT THE AUTHOR

Andrew Lowe was born in the north of England. He has written for *The Guardian* and *Sunday Times*, and contributed to numerous books and magazines on films, music, TV, videogames, sex and shin splints.

He lives in the south of England, where he writes, edits other people's writing, and shepherds his two young sons down the path of righteousness.

His online home is andrewlowewriter.com

Follow him via the social media links below.

Email him at andrew@andrewlowewriter.com

For Andrew's editing and writing coach services, email him at andylowe99@gmail.com

facebook.com/andrewlowewriter

x.com/andylowe99

instagram.com/andylowe99

tiktok.com/@andrewlowewriter

bookbub.com/profile/andrew-lowe

amazon.com/stores/Andrew-Lowe/author/B00UAJGZZU

Printed in Great Britain
by Amazon